THE SISTERS WHO MOURN

KAYLA COSENTINO

Edited by Rose Dinsmore

Cover Art by Yosbe Design

1st edition 2026

Contents

Prologue

Selmana Hormanick had never feared death until she saw it etched across her sister's face. Lewellyn's screams echoed in the bedchamber, raw and piercing, her black hair plastered to her damp neck and face. Midwives frantically flurried around her bedside, skirts rustling like wings as they darted from basin to bed. One fetched boiling water, the steam rising in the room, making it suffocatingly warm, while another placed wet cloths along Lewellyn's fevered brow, trying to keep her calm as her own hands trembled. Voices overlapped in a desperate chorus, sounding more like a prayer than reassurance.

"Breathe, my lady, breathe."

The healer knelt between her legs, concern knitting his graying eyebrows together as he surveyed her. Selmana knew that look. It was the look of defeat.

Selmana watched them with eyes wide, her heart pounding so violently that she thought it would rip through her chest. The chaos of the chamber suddenly blurred all around her, the midwives pacing back and forth, the hissing of the boiling water, the murmured prayers, and all she could focus on was Lewellyn. Her silver eyes locked onto her twin's terrified gaze as her trembling hand searched for Selmana's. She met her sister's grasp, holding it with all she had in her, as if she could keep her on this mortal plane with nothing more than sheer will.

The doors to the chamber opened, the glittering knob catching the candlelight and scattering it into dancing orbs across the room. The glow was mocking, a playful display of gold in a room heavy with the stench of iron and inevitable death. The midwives froze for a moment, their frantic motions stilled by the intrusion. The silence that followed was brief but suffocating, broken only by the wet, ragged hitch of Lewellyn's breath.

In walked King Lionel, his blonde hair cascading in loose waves to his shoulders. His green eyes narrowed in annoyance, as if the cries and chaos in the chamber were an inconvenience rather than a tragedy. He did not rush to his wife's side; he did not even reach for her hand. Instead, he stood at the foot of the bed, inspecting the blood-stained linens with a look of visible disgust. He turned to the healer.

"When will my son be born?" he asked, ignoring both the sisters, even as Lewellyn's agonizing cries filled the room once again.

The healer stood up quickly, his hands crimson, and Selmana sucked in a gasp at the sight. Lewellyn's eyes widened in alarm, terror flashing across her pale face, but Selmana soothingly rubbed her hand, pushing her own fear down as she turned her attention back to the king and healer, the latter speaking in a low hushed voice.

"The baby is not facing the right way," he said, his tone heavy with dread. "All attempts to turn him without harming the mother have failed. If we do not act soon, both will be lost."

The words hung in the air like a death sentence, cold and final, extinguishing even the faintest flicker of hope. Lewellyn's grip tightened around her sister's hand, her nails digging into her skin, as the weight of what had just been spoken settled.

Only then did the king's gaze flicker to the sisters before quickly returning to the healer.

"Do what needs to be done," he said, his voice as cold as the stone floor beneath them. He turned on his heel, not waiting for a response, nor offering a final word of comfort to the woman who had spent hours in agony to preserve his legacy.

The healer nodded, ordering one of the midwives to fetch more cloths and boiling water. The shift in the room was palpable, urgency turning into something colder. Tears slipped down the midwives' faces as they whispered soft prayers to the goddesses. Selmana did not pray. Instead, she pressed her forehead to her sister's. "My strong sister, you can do this. You *have* to do this."

Lewellyn's hand grasped the back of her twin's neck, pushing their heads closer together. "I... love... you," she whispered, voice full of sorrow.

This time, as the healer plunged his hands inside her, Lewellyn did not scream; instead, she let out soft grunts, her body bucking. The silence was even more terrifying than the screaming had been. Selmana pulled away from her sister, horror consuming her.

"Stop! You are killing her!" she screeched, about to push the man when a strong force grabbed her from behind, pulling her back. She kicked and screamed at the soldier who held her back until she fell silent, hopelessness washing over her as her sister's silver eyes went lifeless. No one said her name. No one noticed when she took her last breath, everyone too focused on the thing that was killing her.

A wail pierced the night and the soldier released Selmana. She collapsed to the floor with a dull thud before crawling to her sister's side, whimpering as she felt the cold already seeping into her skin.

The king entered the chambers once again. He did not rush to the bedside to mourn his wife; he did not even spare a glance at the pale, lifeless body of the woman who had died to give him an heir. His gaze slid past her, as if she were nothing more than discarded cloth, fixing instead on the bundle in the midwife's arms.

Disappointment dripped from his voice like acid as he learned of his child's gender.

"A girl?" he spat, the word sounding like a curse.

Sadness quickly turned to rage at his words—a deep, boiling, seething rage that clawed its way up from the hollow pit of her grief. Her body trembled as she stood on shaking legs, pointing one finger at the king. "You will pay."

She crashed through the castle, her footsteps echoing like thunder as she made her way to her chambers to retrieve what she needed. Tears of grief and anger streaked her cheeks as she thrust the door open and lifted the edge of her mattress, decorative pillows toppling to the ground as she threw it aside. Her silver eyes locked onto the worn black leather book she kept so carefully hidden. The anger she felt only heightened when she clutched it to her chest, as if the book itself fed into her rage.

Faint whispers of warning echoed in her mind from her mother and her grandmother as she made her way to the open space of the royal garden. Yet, the warnings only sharpened the hollow ache inside her, reminding her of how utterly alone she was now.

Swiftly, she pulled the dagger she kept strapped against her ankle and opened the book to the page she needed, placing it on the open grass. Her hand shook ever so slightly as she raised the blade, then sliced a horizontal line right below the crease of her left arm. The slice stung, a slight hiss escaping between gritted teeth before she made the same cut on her right arm.

The air crackled with an invisible force as Selmana thrust her arms above her head, blood flowing freely down her arms, as she called to the spirits of the Unknown. She danced around her altar gracefully as she chanted the ancient language of her kind, the Oracles. She knew it was forbidden magic, that there would be consequences, but rage and grief overtook any sense of right or wrong.

"Why do you summon us, child?" a slithering voice whispered.

The sound pebbled her flesh, but she bowed her head to honor the Unknown. "I seek revenge and I beg you for the power to bestow it."

The voice laughed, "It will cost you."

"I have nothing left. They have taken everything from me."

"There is always something worth taking."

Before Selmana could even pause to reconsider, the spirits launched themselves upon her. An ear-splitting screech filled the night air as her knees crashed onto the garden floor, her fingers digging deep into the soil as they fed upon her. She felt her youth being harvested. Once raven black hair turned silver and bones became brittle with an unnatural aging as her life source spilled from her. Right when she believed she would die, the pain dulled as the power she requested began to pulse within her blood.

"It is done," the spirits said in unison. The garden fell into a terrifying, unnatural stillness.

Selmana smiled as she opened her wrinkled eyes. Her breath was slow and steady, no longer ragged with grief but filled with a terrible calm. Shadows rippled from beneath her skin like living ink, bleeding across the grass before they spilled beyond the garden walls and spread over the whole of Linnosa.

CHAPTER 1

Thunder clapped, echoing throughout the cold war room as a storm thrashed outside, rain pounding against the castle wall. Lightning cast unnatural shadows across the maps that covered the walls, and the chandeliers shook ever so slightly, their crystal pendants chiming a nervous melody against the howling wind. Rheanna sat next to her sister, Cyra, the Queen of Linnosa. Power radiated off her, feigning unwavering strength, but only Rheanna, as her younger sister, could see the way she was fraying at the seams. Rheanna's eyes drifted to the two empty spaces that should have been occupied by their sisters, one dead and one on a mission of vengeance. The vacant chairs seemed to mock them, ghosts of absence that screamed louder than any spoken grievance. She swallowed the lump that grew at the back of her throat at the thought of Petra and Aella. Cyra needed her to be present right now.

Rheanna took a slow, deliberate look around the room, her eyes scanning the faces of the council members gathered around the familiar oval table. The wood was dark with age and polish, reflecting the candlelight in a dull gleam. Varying degrees of mistrust and anxiety were apparent on the faces of the council members. The northern representatives, Norton Hansfield and

Marine Glen, were loyal to the crown, their gazes fixed toward the head of the table as they waited for the Queen to officially start the meeting. In contrast, Lola Donovan from the South kept her gaze fixed firmly on her lap as she mindlessly chewed on her fingers until the sides were chapped and bleeding. The Western representatives, Sidney Tapia and Levine Alaverz, were engaged in a quiet conversation, too far on the other side of the table for Rheanna to make out. Jasper Talmadge, one of the members from the East, was staring daggers at Cyra, not easily forgetting the last council meeting where she had almost turned him to ashes. Surprisingly, his counterpart, Bianca Solo, sat on the opposite side of the table from him, closest to Cyra, besides Rheanna. Instead of her usual scowl, her face held an openness Rheanna had never seen before, something that seemed almost foreign on her sharp features.

When Cyra spoke, whoever was not already silent fell quiet, her authority outweighing everything else in the room. "Thank you all for gathering here today," she began, her voice steady. "I know a lot has happened and we have much to discuss. I hope we can do that in a calm and orderly manner." She sent a pointed glance toward both Bianca and Talmadge.

Bianca nodded back, but Talmadge's face morphed into a sneer, his mouth opening. "It seems we were right not to trust you. You have been hiding things from this council. That child is evidence of it," he spat, his voice laced with anger.

"Hold on right there," demanded Norton, his hand slamming flat against the table. "Accusations are not to be thrown at our Queen. Let us hear from her first."

Several heads nodded and turned toward Cyra. Even Lola looked up from her bloodied fingers, the mention of a "child" drawing her attention like a moth to flame. Rheanna turned to her sister and offered a small, encouraging smile. They both knew this was coming and had already prepared what she should say.

Taking a shaking breath, Cyra sat up in her chair, holding her chin high and steadying herself. "Hollin is my daughter."

Gasps sounded around the table, sharp intakes of breath that seemed to suck the air from the room. Marine covered her mouth with her palm, her weathered skin stretching over her cheekbones, while Talmadge smiled in grim satisfaction.

Before anyone could say anything, Cyra continued, "I did not tell you all about her existence in fear. I did not want her to feel the anger and discontent that my sisters and I have been faced with. She is a child of only five years of age. I will not subject her to the scrutiny of you all. Not to mention, we have enemies around every corner who are trying to kill us."

"What of her father?" asked Sidney.

"He's dead," declared Cyra.

A heavy silence fell across the table and Rheanna watched as slow nods of acceptance followed her words, but she knew the truth, or at least as much as her sister would give her. Hollin's father was not dead; he was fae.

This was something both sisters had agreed not to tell the council, but they knew sooner or later it would be revealed. Certain characteristics of hers were tell-tale signs of fae, such as her pointed ears and unnatural beauty. For now, her ears were hidden beneath pretty fabrics and her beauty could be easily explained away, but in time, she would grow tall and strong. Her mannerisms would most likely favor fae, as did most halfling children's, and no one could imagine how her magic might be affected.

Talmadge let out a sigh to bring attention to his discontent, a theatrical exhale to draw eyes. "You claim he's dead, but who was he?"

Cyra's golden gaze narrowed on him, but despite her tumultuous emotions and magic the past few weeks, she controlled herself. "All you need to know about him is that he gave our kingdom an heir that is stronger than any of you could imagine."

"Does she possess magic?" Bianca spoke for the first time, her voice surprisingly gentle.

Rheanna studied her, surprised by her calm disposition. Instead of the cruel beauty she usually held, her grey eyes were soft and her dark blonde eyebrows were relaxed.

"Yes, she has Earth magic," Cyra confirmed, and once again, the room filled with sounds of surprise, a collective murmur that rose like a tide. "Which brings us to another topic for discussion. The return of Earth magic."

Lola spoke hesitantly, her voice barely above a whisper, "My daughter is among the awakened."

Rheanna held her breath for a moment, shocked by this revelation. Despite living in the castle, she rarely saw the Donovan children as their mother kept them sequestered within their chambers.

"She may be useful. How old is she?" asked Talmadge, his eyes gleaming with predatory interest.

Lola's dark eyebrows shot up and her brown eyes danced frantically between her queen and fellow council members. "I... she... she is only two years old... I–" she stammered.

"Your child, nor any child or unwilling participant, will be used in this fight," Cyra stated, shooting another glare that could melt steel at Talmadge.

How Talmadge could even suggest using Lola's child was beyond Rheanna. Her head shook disapprovingly as he huffed in his chair, his ego seemingly more bruised by the Queen's glare than by what he had implied.

"We do need to keep a record of the magic wielders in the kingdom, though," Sidney said, leaning forward with calculated interest.

"That will only lead to the persecution of those with magic," Cyra countered immediately. "We have seen it happen too many times in this kingdom, especially during the Banishment. We can ask for volunteers in this fight, but I will not force anyone."

"Be careful, my Queen," seethed Talmadge. "You almost sound like a fae sympathizer."

The room became deathly still as Cyra's molten gaze returned to Talmadge yet again. Beside her, Rheanna's crystal eyes hardened as she shot daggers at him. They were the only ones in the room who knew of Hollin's true fae heritage, a secret that left them on edge, especially with her sudden appearance at the castle and in the capital.

Cyra leaned forward, palms splayed against the wood of the table. "And what if I was?"

The silence was only broken by the small gasp that escaped Lola's mouth before she clapped a hand over it. Talmadge's expression grew dark before he broke into a triumphant smirk.

"Well, that would be treason, wouldn't it?'

Rheanna's heart hammered in her chest as she glanced around the room. Every member of the council had their eyes trained on their Queen, curious about her answer. She could feel the heat of her sister's magic as she struggled to contain her anger and disgust.

"I would advise against you speaking another word." Rheanna's words snapped the council from the confines of tension and the room spun into a frantic cacophony of voices.

Talmadge continued rambling about his outrage while the Northern and Western council members fought in support of Cyra. Bianca remained quiet, pale eyes studying everyone, while Lola looked on the verge of tears.

Cyra lowered her head into her hands, massaging her temples for a brief moment. Then, she let out a deep breath, her palms slamming against the wood of the table, silencing the council once again.

"Enough." The word came out in barely more than a whisper, but the authority that it was said in was palpable. "I would say accusing your Queen of treason is an act of treason in itself, council member Talmadge," she said, looking him in the eye.

When he did not respond, she continued, "This council is meant to serve Linnosa, to serve *me*. If any of you feel incapable of maintaining that responsibility with dignity and respect, then

I would advise you to pass the duty on to someone who is able. I am sick and tired of us tearing each other apart."

"We all want the same thing," Rheanna added. "To protect Linnosa and its citizens." She reached out her hand to place it on her sister's.

"Why are we focusing on the fae and questions of the Queen's daughter when there are much more pressing matters?" Bianca turned to Talmadge. "If we want to save our kingdom, we have to work together."

Rheanna, surprised at Bianca's response, gave her a small smile, which was returned before Bianca bowed her blonde head.

Norton and Sidney exchanged looks before Norton cleared his throat and said, "Ms. Solo is correct. This is a time to support our Queen instead of disrespecting her." He turned to Cyra and asked, "Where is your betrothed?"

Rheanna's thoughts turned to Atlas Nicola, her sister's future King and the heir to the Hefguard throne. Since their engagement, Cyra had made it a point to include him in all matters, both familial and political. But today, his attention was elsewhere: with his soon-to-be step-daughter. Atlas had mistakenly brought up fishing once to Hollin, and ever since, she had begged him to take her. For Cyra's peace of mind, Ron accompanied them as well.

"He is spending the day with my daughter," Cyra said, a small smile playing on her full lips.

Norton nodded in approval. "It is great for the royal family to be a united front during these times. We do need to discuss the wedding details, though."

Rheanna held in a sigh. They had already discussed the wedding several times and decided they would be married as soon as Atlas's brother, Malcolm, and the Hefguard reinforcements arrived. The extra security during the wedding would be essential, given what had happened during Cyra's coronation. Instead of hosting an event that would bring royals and diplomats from all over the world, this wedding would be small to keep from gathering attention, with only a few from Hefguard and Linnosa in attendance.

"The wedding planning is going well and will take place after Hefguard arrives," Cyra said through gritted teeth.

"We will have another council meeting when they return to discuss where to send the reinforcements. For now, I think we are done. What do you think, Cyra?" Rheanna stated. She knew when her older sister had too much and decided to save her.

Smiling gratefully at her sister, Cyra agreed. "Yes. Come to myself or Rheanna if you need anything in the meantime."

The sisters rose together and walked out, the rest of the council following suit, the chamber emptying in their wake.

Chapter 2

The gentle chirps of birds and the sweet aroma of fresh wildflowers surrounded Cyra and her horse as they made their way down the bumpy stone path to River Solace. The late afternoon air blew the loose crimson curls that fell out of her braid as the humidity frizzed them, creating a wild mane that framed her face. As they drew closer to the alcove, her hand shot out instinctively to pet her horse's black mane. She had not been back to the river since the day of Petra and Luca's send-off. At that time, she had been so weak from her burnout, yet the memories of the funeral were sharp in her mind.

"Mommy!" squealed Hollin, snapping Cyra out of her reverie. A blur of pink and red hues sprinted across the black and brown pebbled beach as Hollin made her way to her mother. Small flowers erupted in her path, sprouting from between the pebbles and blooming quickly. Cyra smoothly dismounted from her horse and squatted down to meet Hollin with open arms. The five-year-old collided into her chest, causing Cyra to rock back on her heels.

A hearty chuckle rose from her throat as she made eye contact with her betrothed. Atlas stood with his hands in his pockets, a grin plastered across his face that sparkled in his green eyes. This was the most casual she had ever seen the Prince of Hefguard dressed; he wore a loose blouse and tan riding pants, both of which were soaked with water. Ron stood at his side, dressed in his royal armor as he often was, though Cyra told him it was unnecessary. He was a part of the family.

"I caught two fishies today, Mommy! I got to hold them, and then Atlas showed me how to put them back," Hollin expressed excitedly. She then leaned in and whispered conspiratorially, as if sharing a secret, "They breathe in water like we breathe in air, so they can't stay out too long."

Cyra smiled, running a hand tenderly down her daughter's long braid and adjusting the pink fabric covering her ears before standing up. "That is wonderful, Holli. Did you behave for Atlas?"

The little girl's cheeks reddened as she looked between her mother and Atlas. "Well..."

"Oh no, what happened?"

"She was great. I haven't had this much fun in a long time," Atlas responded, his smirk widening as he winked at Hollin.

Hollin twirled her fingers before confessing, "I did push him in the water."

Cyra sighed in exasperation. "Hollin, now why would you do that?"

"It was an accident," defended Atlas.

"Not really," the little girl said sheepishly, looking down at her feet.

At that, Atlas erupted in laughter, bending at the torso as he clutched his stomach with his right arm. "Don't worry about it, Cyra, truly. Little Holli and I are getting along fine," he managed to choke out after calming down. Cyra blinked in surprise at the use of her nickname. Her daughter only allowed a select few the privilege of using it.

Ron's lined face filled with joy as he shook his head, saying, "These two'll be the death of me."

Hollin skipped over to Atlas and grabbed hold of his hand. "He is my new friend, and I think it is okay that you two are getting married!"

"I am so glad you approve, Holli," Atlas smiled, patting her strawberry-blonde head affectionately.

As Cyra helped her daughter onto their horse, she surveyed Atlas. He picked up the fishing poles, gently winding the line and securing the sharp hook onto the metal loop. Her mind began to wander as she mounted herself, waiting for Atlas and Ron to pack their own horses and head back to the castle. She had never imagined herself falling in love again or Hollin potentially having a father figure in her life, but Atlas brought a sense of hope. Not only was he kind and attentive, but he had also proved to be trustworthy, something very few were. After Ivan's betrayal, Cyra thought she would find it hard to trust again; Atlas made it anything but.

The mere thought of Ivan quickly turned to images of her baby sister's blood and the unnatural tilt of her neck. Cyra's heart began to pound violently in her chest, sweat gathering along her brow as her breath came out in quick gasps. She saw Petra, still with an open book in her lap, the once-white pages now soaked crimson.

Feeling Cyra's sudden change of emotion, the horse stopped its trot down the path, and Hollin twisted in her seat, emerald eyes staring up at her mother. Another pair of emerald eyes—that stared unseeing—mirrored back in her thoughts. She clutched her head, nausea taking over.

"Mommy?" Hollin asked anxiously.

Cyra snapped back into the moment at the sound of her daughter's voice. She was on a horse. Hollin was in her lap. They were safe.

"Cyra..." Atlas hesitantly called from his horse, one arm outstretched toward them, but he could not reach them as a circle of flames engulfed Cyra, Hollin, and their horse. Immediately, Cyra called it down.

"I..." she started, but stopped, not knowing what to say. Her magic had grown as restless as her spirit.

Ron had already dismounted from his horse, his brown eyes filled with worry as he stood by her side. His aged hand rubbed the small of her back. "Are you okay?" he asked.

Cyra nodded, nudging her horse forward, but three pairs of eyes were still watching her carefully. She sighed, squaring her shoulders. She was not okay, but the Fire Queen would never admit it.

Rheanna heaved, her lungs burning with exertion, as she dodged a fist, spinning to the side and throwing out a punch of her own. She barely grazed her opponent's side before he grabbed her wrist and spun her into his chest, her back pressed firmly against it. Both of his strong arms wrapped around her, holding her tightly in place. She wiggled, trying to get free for just a moment before her core lit up from the movement, a spark of desire igniting low in her belly.

"Oh, don't stop," joked Ripley as he placed both hands on her shoulders and pushed while turning her to face him.

Her pale cheeks reddened as she shook her head. "Don't be gross." She struggled to suppress a small smile, biting the inside of her cheek to keep it at bay. Ripley had quickly turned into someone she trusted and found solace in after Petra's death and Aella's departure. Too much was going on not to find comfort in some form or another.

"I think you like it," he purred, tilting her chin up toward him with a finger he dragged up from her collarbone, leaving a trail of fire on her skin.

She gulped. "And if I do?"

"Then it is only my duty to comply, princess." His head dipped down to meet hers, but instead of a kiss, he took her bottom lip between his teeth, nipping her before stepping back with a triumphant smirk.

She closed her eyes, sighing. "Such a tease."

Still holding her close, he brought his mouth to her ear. "Command it, and I'm yours." His breath tickled her, sending goosebumps across the flesh of her neck and down her arms.

"Do you listen well to orders?" Her question came out breathy and uneven.

"When it's someone as pretty as you giving them," he murmured, his eyes darkening to a stormy hazel.

Rheanna pulled back then and was immediately met with the hunger in Ripley's hazel eyes. It matched the need that pulled at her core. His eyes drifted from her mouth back to her gaze before he leaned forward, the air between them crackling with tension.

"Aunt Rhe!" Hollin's shrill voice filled the open area of the sisters' private training arena, causing Rheanna and Ripley to jump away from each other, scrambling to put a respectable distance between their bodies. They awkwardly shifted from foot to foot, fidgeting as the young girl and her mother came into view.

"Good afternoon, Hollin," Rheanna greeted, toying with her long fingers, suddenly fascinated by the hem of her sleeve to hide her embarrassment.

Cyra's golden gaze danced between the couple, sharp and knowing, amusement lighting up her face as she took in the sight of the two. Rheanna glared at her sister ever so slightly, silently pleading with her not to make a comment.

"I caught two fishes today!" exclaimed Hollin as she spun, her little pink slippers sliding effortlessly along the uneven cobblestones. Small flowers bloomed from in between the cracks, their petals bursting open in a riot of color at her feet. Rheanna's heart clenched at the familiarity of the action within this training yard.

The entire space was full of reminders of their youngest sister. Petra and her power still covered the columns, vines and wildflowers climbing each one, thriving even now, even without her tending to them. They draped over the stone like heavy tapestries, a living memory. The slabs of rock and boulders with blown-out pieces from her training still littered the yard floor, marks of a power that was now gone. Rheanna took a deep breath before responding to Hollin. "That is amazing! Did you have fun?"

"Yes! I went fishing, and now Mommy says I will practice my magic," Hollin said excitedly, clapping her hands. Small rocks around her began to vibrate ever so slightly off the ground.

"I was hoping you would help us with that, Rhe," Cyra said, then turned to Ripley, "And maybe you could teach her some self-defense?"

Ripley's face broke out into a grin. "Help the little future Queen of Linnosa? With pleasure."

With that, the adults brought Hollin to the middle of the yard. Cyra and Rheanna explained to her how they felt their magic and how they were able to use it.

"Alright, Hollin. For today, all I want you to do is try to move around those little rocks." Cyra pointed to a few scattered pebbles that lay near a human-sized boulder. Since Hollin had only ever really shown the blooming part of her earth power, they wanted to see if she was capable of something else if she tried on purpose.

Hollin nodded, her expression turning solemn with determination. "I can do it!" The second the little girl's emerald gaze fell on the rocks, they flew into the air, whipping upward with violent speed, dancing at the highest point of the boulder next to them. She squealed with joy. "I did it! I did it!"

"Yes, you did, Holli. Now–" Cyra was cut off as the boulder exploded into a million shards, the sound like a cannon blast in the enclosed yard. In a blink, Cyra had a wall of fire in place, a roaring curtain of orange and blue flame, shielding everyone from the piercing rocks as she dove for Hollin, covering her with her body. Rheanna flinched, the air getting knocked out of her as she hit the cobbled floor, Ripley shielding her, his weight pressing her into the stone. She peeked from the gap between his arm and the ground. The shards incinerated the second they hit Cyra's fire. It was over almost as soon as it started.

Ripley pulled her face toward his, a hand under her chin, his touch frantic. "Are you alright?" His hazel eyes were full of concern, the earlier playfulness replaced by raw fear.

She pushed up to her elbows, grimacing at the dull ache in her side. "I'm fine, just a little sore from where you tackled me to the ground."

He shook his head as he stood up, offering a hand and pulling her up, hauling her to her feet with effortless strength. They both turned to Cyra and Hollin, who were slowly standing up as well, both their eyes wide and startled.

"I'm sorry, Mommy," Hollin said before she broke out in tears.

Cyra blinked several times, but then knelt down to her daughter, pulling her close. "You did nothing wrong, my bean." She soothingly ran her hand down her daughter's pink waves.

"I hurt you. And Aunt Rhe. And Ripley," she said between tears.

"Oh no, you didn't hurt us at all," Ripley reassured with one of his goofy smiles. He gestured to himself and Rheanna, spreading his arms wide to show his unbroken state. "Look, little queen."

Hollin shifted in her mother's arms to look at the two, her cries turning into soft hiccups, her lashes wet and clumped together.

"You are very strong, and we are all going to help you become stronger," Rheanna said. She knelt in front of her niece, wiping the tears from her freckled cheeks before gathering her up in her arms. "Why don't we all get a nice cup of warm chocolate? That can cheer anyone up."

Hollin nodded her head fiercely, the motion jerky against Rheanna's shoulder. Rheanna walked with the girl in her arms, her mind racing with the sheer force of power she had just displayed and how they would all have to keep her safe.

Chapter 3

Voices carried through the damp crawlspace, echoing through the floorboards above. The lack of light in the small space only accentuated the feeling of insects and rats skittering across the legs of Aella Voelbel and Karif Lin. They lay on their bellies, pressed into the cold, gritty earth, arms touching as they listened intently to the conversation unfolding above them.

"That girl is now queen, and the only hope we had is lost," a gruff voice said. Aella was surprised at the tinge of sadness that filled his words, as if he genuinely mourned the loss of Petra.

"We must continue our mission. Even if that means wiping out the entire royal family," a female voice responded, her tone sharp and unyielding, devoid of any hesitation.

Aella's eyebrows pulled together. She could understand why she was met with so much discontent, but why did these people hate her sisters so much? Rheanna was kind and Cyra was a good leader; they just needed to give them a chance.

"I heard news that the queen has a daughter. One she kept hidden, but who is now in the castle," the man with the gruff voice revealed.

"Are you sure? There are too many rumors."

"Our informant in the castle confirmed it. It is true."

Aella didn't realize she was holding her breath until Karif bumped her with his elbow. She couldn't make out his face in the dark, but she knew there would be comfort and reassurance in his gaze even through the pitch black.

Cyra had a daughter. This was how she found out she had a niece. For a moment, Aella felt betrayed all over again, a fresh wound slashed across old scars. But then, she thought that if she were in Cyra's position, would she want the world to know about her child? Yet, Aella was not the world; she was her sister. The news of an informant was anything but surprising. It was the very reason they were cramped in the crawlspace right now, listening instead of killing: to get information. It had been Karif's idea, of course.

"We could make a move on the child," the woman suggested.

Aella stiffened. Her muscles coiled, ready to spring through the floorboards, regardless of the consequences. No one would touch her family again. But she didn't move.

"I think that would be wise. Use her as bait and get rid of them all." The male voice sounded excited, and heavy footsteps began to pace the room. Aella squinted, trying to make out their faces between the floorboards, but to no avail.

There was a beat of silence. "Or we could raise her to be our Queen. The Cleanser Queen. The Queen of the people. She could inspire others to join our cause and create an opportunity we did not have before."

The man chuckled. "Now that's an idea. We could give the people something to fight for. A true Queen."

The rest of the conversation circled around the idea of kidnapping the child, but no concrete plans were finalized. Once they left the room and were gone for a few minutes, Aella and Karif crawled on their elbows toward the exit, their bodies aching from the prolonged stillness. Pushing the door open, Karif poked his head out first to scan the shadows before nodding down at Aella and hopping out. She quickly followed, dusting the cobwebs and dirt from her leathers, and they walked in silence until they made it to the dark alleyway next to the Boisseau Inn, where they were staying while in Aponte, a Western city that bordered the South. They had followed leads until they had found a Cleanser base here. Karif had made Aella promise she wouldn't kill anyone, though she itched to avenge her sister. Information was more valuable. And it was clearer now than ever that the Cleansers were not the ones who had murdered Petra. Aella vowed to make the true perpetrator suffer when she found them. She took solace in knowing that Ripley was watching over her sisters.

Karif turned toward her once they were tucked in a corner. "You didn't know about the princess?"

Aella shook her head.

"She will be safe. Ripley is there, and her mother has considerable power."

Aella nodded. "I know."

Aella wondered what the girl looked like or how old she was. Her chest squeezed, the ache familiar, but she was not prepared for the deep betrayal that settled within her.

"Don't let this come between you and your sister." Karif could always read her so easily, so she turned her face away from him, looking up at the night sky.

"Now more than ever, we need to protect them." No little girl would come to harm under her care again.

"We will. We will figure this all out." With that, Karif left Aella in the alleyway, disappearing around the corner and into the inn.

Aella took a deep breath, tucking a strand of silver hair behind her ear. She kicked a nearby barrel, sending it smashing against the brown brick of the building, the wood splintering with a satisfying crack. Water poured from the broken pieces. She watched as it soaked into the muddy ground. Taking another breath, she turned from the alley.

Instead of the usual chatter and clanging, this inn had a quiet, unnerving feel. Only a few patrons graced the tables, their faces darkened by hoods as they sat hunched over, conducting their quiet dealings. The few lights in the room added to the eerie atmosphere, casting long, distorted shadows that stretched across the floor like grasping fingers, the dark wood furniture blending into the flooring. Cobwebs hung in each corner, but the rest of the inn was clean and tidy.

Aella paid no mind to the other customers, heading straight for the bar and the pretty woman who tended to it. Leona, all curves and pale skin, with the kind of beauty that demanded attention, was the daughter of the family who owned the inn and the true face of it. The establishment, known as the place for quiet conversations and dealing, had its name due to Leona. She had fostered it to become a safe spot for dangerous conversations with her wit and charm. Everyone who stepped foot into the inn naturally respected her, though she was only twenty-eight years of age. Even as a young girl, Aella remembered admiring the way she could command the space.

Karif already sat at the bar, his chin in his palm, as he flashed Leona a stunning smile. Her returning smirk was anything but shy, only one of her dimples exposed. It turned into a full-on grin as she took in Aella.

"Perfect timing. I need someone to help me humble this man," Leona's raspy voice purred, her large brown eyes narrowing on Karif.

Aella slid into the seat next to her friend as she said, "Let me guess—he is trying to convince you to join him in his bed?" Her eyebrow tilted up as Karif chuckled.

"I don't need to do any convincing for that."

Leona shook her head, turning to fill a jug of ale for Aella. She couldn't help but notice how Karif's gaze followed the woman's backside, hugged by form-fitting khaki pants. Her auburn hair reached the small of her back in loose waves, only pinned back on the sides. She had watched him lust over her for years. Once, years ago, Leona had allowed him in her bed, but never again. Aella believed Karif might even be in love with her—something he would never admit.

Those thoughts of love quickly turned to Natalie, whom she had loved. Her eyes closed for a brief moment as she remembered the way Natalie's skin felt, how her fingers moved effortlessly through her silky hair. Sharp betrayal pierced her heart as she recalled the moment she pulled off the Cleanser mask and it revealed her lover. She might not have killed her sister, but she was complicit in it. If the Cleansers had not invaded, perhaps Aella could have protected Petra.

Shaking her head slightly, she reached out to accept the mug Leona presented her, taking a sip. The deep amber liquid tasted bready with a hint of clove, and she felt the heaviness it added to her gut. When she went for a second gulp, she chugged it, a small bit of it escaping and dribbling down her chin.

"Take it easy. We don't want a repeat of Ross," Karif scolded with a grimace.

Aella broke into a smile, reminiscing on a night three years ago filled with mischief. She had never considered her life easy, but it was easier when all she had to do was kill. Now that she had people worth saving, things had gotten so much more complicated.

"I would like to see the assassin princess let go a bit, actually," Leona whispered, leaning in.

Aella's violet eyes hardened. "That won't be happening. I have too much to do."

Leona brushed off the roughness of her words and shook her head. "You assassins are far too serious for me. I thought maybe now that you were a princess, you would have mellowed out a bit."

"If anything, it has made her worse," Karif said before taking a sip of his ale.

Aella felt her face heat and her hands tightened around the cup in her grasp. "I'm sorry that the murder of my sister and the threat to my family has been an inconvenience to you both."

Leona's face immediately lost all traces of humor, her doe eyes widening as her hand reached out to touch Aella's forearm. "You know that's not what we meant."

Aella jerked her arm away from the beautiful woman, placing the cup of ale down with a loud clatter before spinning on the stool and walking away. She didn't meet Karif or Leona's gaze as she stalked to her room. The beginnings of a panic attack threatened, her body tensing. With every step, she willed it away.

She had no more time to be weak. She never had.

CHAPTER 4

R HEANNA AND CYRA DID not speak as they wound their way down the cold black and gray stone of the staircase. Yellow light from the candles placed on the walls every few feet sent flickering shadows in the hall. The lower they descended, the more the temperature dropped, sending chills racing up Cyra's arms. Their casual day dresses swished, brushing against the stone in waves of beige and lavender. The beige belonged to Cyra, a tight corset of olive green around her waist that accentuated her bust, while Rheanna's dress of light purple emphasized the slight tan she had developed while in the Eastern climate.

They stopped when they reached the bottom, looking at each other for a second, gold eyes meeting blue, before Cyra took a deep breath and stepped toward the opening that led to the dungeons. She hadn't gone back since the day she had tortured Natalie with her powers. Guilt and shame bit deep in her gut, churning the light breakfast of strawberries and toast she had. Natalie may have been a part of the Cleansers, but she was not the reason Petra was dead.

Cyra felt the comforting weight of her sister's hand as they held hands, Rheanna reassuring her and nodding as she pulled her forward. She remembered the anger, the pain she felt the last time she walked past these cells. She used it to center herself, reminding her of who she was and why she could not let that fury control her again.

Stopping in front of Natalie's cell, she observed it. Now, a cot lay where the thin mattress in a mess of hay had once been. A bucket lay in the corner for relieving herself. Natalie sat up as they approached, flinching as she met Cyra's gaze and backing up against the cold stone, a thin gray blanket falling off her in the process. It revealed a waxy brown scarring on her left forearm, the edges puckered and pieces of dead flesh flaking off. Cyra clutched her stomach with one arm, a small gasp escaping her lips. While Natalie was no longer dirty and now, properly clothed, fear radiated off of her, dark circles swallowing half her face. Her dark eyes darted between the sisters with a frantic, prey-like motion.

"I...I'm sorry," Cyra managed to get out. Rheanna squeezed the hand she was still holding, providing a steadying support.

Natalie flinched at the sound of her voice but attempted to scoot from the wall and to the edge of the cot. Agony flickered across her face with the movement, and Cyra tried to imagine the damage her fire had left upon the woman's abdomen and thigh. The thought made her nauseous.

"Did you find who was responsible for Petra?" Natalie's dark eyebrows pulled together.

Cyra nodded. "We did."

Natalie let out a sigh of relief, tears pooling in her almond eyes. "I hope you made them suffer."

Instead of answering, Cyra let go of her sister's hand and stepped forward, pulling the dungeon key from the hidden pocket in her dress. Natalie's eyes widened and she gulped as the queen opened the cell. She sat stiff on the cot as Cyra kneeled in front of her. Her golden gaze burrowed deep into Natalie's brown ones.

"I should have never used my powers on you. It was a moment of weakness and grief. I am a queen and you are my subject. And now, I know you may not want to provide it, but I need your help."

The fear in Natalie's face seemed to lift a bit as wonder filled her gaze, her eyes growing large. "I will do anything. I know what I did was wrong and I want to make it up to you. To Aella."

Cyra shook her head, knowing her younger sister would not approve of what she was about to do. "Do not get it twisted. I do not trust you, but unfortunately, I do need you."

"What can I do?" Natalie asked, eager to please.

"Tell us everything you know about the Cleansers," Rheanna said from behind Cyra, stepping into the small cell.

Natalie looked between the two sisters, fire and water, and without even a second of hesitation, she nodded. She moved closer to the sisters, wincing again from the wounds they could not see, before she began to talk.

"The Cleansers aren't just run by one person, but more of a group of people, and everyone always keeps their faces concealed. I could pass a member and have no clue."

It made sense. Their anonymity was their biggest strength. They were everywhere and nowhere all at once.

"Do you know how many of them are in the castle?" Cyra asked.

Natalie shook her head, her expression serious. "No, but I know there has to be more than me. I know there is a spy within the castle who holds power. I'm not talking about a maid or guard. This is someone who has access to you and information."

Rheanna and Cyra shared a look before their attention went back to their prisoner. Cyra's mind raced as she combed through her thoughts. Almost automatically, her doubts were put upon the Eastern representatives and their disdain for her. Bianca Solo and Jasper Talmadge sat at the top of her "guilty" list. Since the moment she and her sisters had returned, they had whined about their discontent. It would explain Bianca's sudden softness towards them; perhaps she realized she could accomplish more with honey instead of venom.

"You have no idea who it may be?" asked Rheanna, head tilting. Cyra could practically see the thoughts bouncing around her head.

"I know they must be on the council. That must have been how I made it into the castle. You can't just walk into a job for the royal family," Natalie replied.

Cyra thought for a moment. If someone had gotten Natalie into the castle, then there had to be a trail.

Rheanna grasped her sister's upper arm. "I have an idea on how we might get that information without it looking like we are poking around."

Glancing at Natalie, Cyra nodded and said, "We can discuss that in private."

Rheanna agreed before asking, "Why do they hate Cyra so much? What could she have possibly done to make them want her dead?"

"They don't just want her dead." The prisoner gulped. "They want you all dead."

Cyra's golden eyes widened. What did this mean for Hollin? Her sisters weren't safe and neither was her daughter. She might have suspected it, but it was so different *knowing* it. She looked to her younger sister, whose ocean eyes were like saucers, a hand clenched at her stomach.

"But why?" Cyra gasped out.

"Its not like they hate you as individuals," Natalie explained. "They feel as if you do not have Linnosa's best interests at heart. They felt as if Petra, having been born and raised in the capital as a princess, was the rightful heir. But even before that, the rebellion against your parents and the royals in general was brewing due to the monster attacks."

"It doesn't make sense. We were all raised in Linnosa. We are all a part of it. Cyra lived in the castle for nine years," Rheanna insisted, her dark brows pulling together.

Cyra's face scrunched in confusion as well. It didn't make sense. Sure, she could understand why the rebellion could have started due to the monster attacks, but the sisters not being "royal" enough made no sense.

Natalie mirrored their confusion as she spoke, "I... I know that now, but for some reason it felt right back then." She paused, tears welling in her eyes. "I am from a small town in the West that borders the North called Faragon. My mother and father were both killed in a monster attack. We had not heard rumors of the monsters when they came. No one was prepared."

The tears fell down her cheeks freely as she stared blankly ahead. When Rheanna spoke, Natalie jumped, rubbing the wetness on her face. "We are sorry for your loss."

"I barely got out. It was too late for me to save my parents, but I got to my baby cousin. A few of us took horses and ran. At that time, I would have joined anything that I felt would avenge them." Natalie looked up at the two women. "Once I got to know you all and fell in love with Aella, it was too late. They threatened to hurt Garrick when I tried to back out. I just have to pray the people I left him with have protected him."

The shame and guilt Cyra felt before doubled as she took in Natalie's story. She was a girl trying to protect someone she loved, just as they were.

"Where is Garrick now?" questioned Cyra.

"When the Cleansers threatened him, I was able to give notice to the others we escaped with and they promised to move him." Natalie paused. "He is only seven years old and he is all I have. I... I cannot give you any more information about him."

Cyra raised an eyebrow but sighed and nodded. She understood where she was coming from. "We all have those we must protect, but we are not done, Natalie. You will be helping us from now on."

"I know," Natalie responded, a strong resolution to her voice. "Whatever you need from me."

Crya nodded, walking out of the cell and locking it once Rheanna was out. As they walked back to the first floor of the castle, Cyra's guilt hardened into determination.

CHAPTER 5

R HEANNA MOVED SWIFTLY THROUGH the halls, her lavender dress swaying as she searched for two maids in particular. After their talk with Natalie, Rheanna brought up her idea to bring Aella's informants in so that they could poke around in a more inconspicuous manner. Rheanna silently thanked the gods and Ripley for the stamina she had gained as she scoured the halls. The beat of her heart was a constant thrum.

A sigh of relief escaped her as she spotted the familiar brunette and ginger maids dusting a painting that definitely did not need the attention of both. Cora noticed Rheanna first, her eyes going wide as she tapped Laney hard on the shoulder. The redhead turned, her mouth dropping into an "O" shape before quickly shutting her mouth. They exchanged a look before both sets of hazel eyes returned to Rheanna and they bent over, curtseying to the princess.

"I have been looking for you two everywhere," Rheanna said, exasperated.

The girls nervously looked at each other again before Laney giggled and said, "How can we help you, Princess?"

"I know you previously reported to Aella, but the Queen and I need your help while she is away."

Laney began to fidget, biting the nail of her thumb, anxiety clearly coursing through her. Cora spoke for the first time. "We would be delighted to aid Her Majesty." Her words were certain, but she pulled nervously at a dark strand of hair.

Rheanna tilted her head. "Are you sure? Is something wrong?"

Cora bit her lip, glancing at her friend before answering. "We spoke to Princess Aella about this, but there have been threats made to people and their families. Not to either of us directly, but it is frightening."

"I completely understand. If you can't help–"

Laney interrupted her. "No, of course we will!"

Cora hit her arm, eyes wide, but said, "She didn't mean to interrupt you, Princess, but we will do anything for you. We are loyal to Princess Aella."

Rheanna gave them a small smile. "Thank you both, but I will warn you that it could be dangerous."

Instead of answering, the young maids nodded, waiting for Rheanna to go on. "I know we can't talk out here so..." Rheanna paused for a minute, thinking, then added, "I have an idea."

She gestured for the girls to follow her and they made their way down one flight of stairs and twisted down halls until they ended up in front of the heavy wood door of her parents' quarters. She pulled on the doorknob, holding it open for the two younger girls. Rheanna took in the perfumed air of the room and the familiarity while shutting the door. She placed her head against it, closing her eyes. The last time she was in this room,

Petra had died, but staff rarely graced these hallways, and maids came to clean the room only once a week.

Pushing those thoughts aside, she focused on what she needed to do. Opening her eyes, she watched as Laney and Cora walked around the room, lighting the candles as the sun was beginning to set in the bay window. When they were finished, they stood awkwardly in the middle of the opulent room.

"Sit," Rheanna suggested, pointing to the rich brown loveseat with golden trim across from a marble hearth.

They followed her order, sitting straight, as if they were afraid to touch the chair or get comfortable. Rheanna took a seat on an oak box chair across from them, a full cushion covered in a gold fabric sitting on top of it.

Looking them both in the eye, she folded her hands in her lap. "We have gained some information that there is a spy in the council."

Laney gasped and Cora's eyes widened even more than before as she finally slouched back and rested against the chair.

"What can we do to help?" Laney asked, her freckled face contorted in confusion.

Rheanna explained what she and Cyra had learned from Natalie, detailing how she wanted the two girls to snoop around without getting caught or being too obvious. Their jaws dropped when she told them about Natalie and how she was a Cleanser. Cyra had worked hard to keep it quiet, not wanting to cause unease or panic within the castle.

Laney raised one brow. "It does make sense, though, if you think about it. She did arrive out of nowhere and then became close with Princess Aella very quickly."

Cora scoffed, shaking her head. "It's disgusting. She deserves better than to be treated like some pawn. She is our princess."

A small smile graced Rheanna at the sentiment, happy that she and her sisters were not the only ones who got to see the other side of Aella and truly appreciate it.

"And she's stunning. Why couldn't she have picked me?" Laney giggled, then clapped a hand over her mouth. "I'm so sorry, Princess."

Rheanna laughed. "It's okay. I have a feeling we are all going to get a lot closer."

Laney and Cora grinned, the latter saying, "We will do whatever we can to figure out who is trying to hurt all of you."

"Thank you. We appreciate it, and please, if you ever feel unsafe or if anyone threatens you or your families in any way, let us know. Cyra or I or when Aella comes back. We will protect you," Rheanna reassured them.

They both nodded, looking at each other yet again, but this time with a look of determination. As Rheanna and the girls walked out, she had no doubt in her mind that they would do whatever was necessary, especially since it would be helping Aella. But she was afraid of the danger that she might have just led them to.

CHAPTER 6

S TIFLING HEAT FILLED AELLA'S lungs as she trudged through the desert sand. The dry wind picked it up, blowing it into her face. She pulled tightly on her wrap, shielding her eyes from the small particles that threatened to scratch them.

Karif and Aella shuffled into a tavern, sighing as they pulled off their face shields. The reprieve was short-lived, however, as the stifling heat followed them within the large space, packed with travellers of all kinds: men, women, and children of varying shades and walks of life. One woman in particular drew Aella's attention. With skin like polished obsidian and eyes a vibrant cerulean blue, she was the most striking person Aella had ever seen. Her midnight hair fell to her waist in tiny, intricate braids with what looked like seashells woven into them. Aella's awe turned into fury as she took note of the iron shackles wrapped around both her petite wrists and her waist. A chain stretched down her dress and disappeared underneath, presumably around her ankles. Her dress itself was dark blue but covered in debris and torn in several places.

Aella's attention shifted to the man who held her chains like a leash. He was a burly man, standing several inches taller than the already tall prisoner he held. A long beard, stringy and graying, fell across his chest. Just from the sight of him, she knew he was a trafficker. She had seen enough in her line of work to know. His dark eyes met hers, a smirk appearing on his face as he yanked the woman's chains, pulling her down roughly as he sat down in a chair at a table.

Aella started forward, but Karif grabbed her elbow. "Not our place," he hissed in her ear.

She turned to him, ripping her arm from his grasp. "This is my family's kingdom. Like hell it isn't my place."

His gray eyes stirred, glancing at the chained woman before saying, "Fine, but not here. Not yet."

Aella took a deep breath, steeling herself to ignore the trafficker and the woman before making her way to a table with Karif. It took everything in her not to glance back at the woman. Trafficking in Linnosa was strictly prohibited, but of course, it still happened. Aella rarely ran into them, but when she did, she added to her kill count. She would never stand for the imprisonment and selling of people.

Looking around, the tavern was similar to most in the area, with wood walls reinforced with cement to keep out the whipping sand. Several tables made out of some kind of cheap wood filled the room. Almost every table was occupied, and the chatter in the space was overwhelming. Aella was about to speak when a barmaid came up to their table.

"What can I get y'all today?" she said, a fake smile plastered across her chubby cheeks.

Karif flashed a dazzling grin that didn't seem to faze the woman and said, "Just two house specials today, ma'am."

She nodded. "No problem, sir."

Once she had bustled off, Aella leaned toward Karif and whispered, "So, what are we going to do about that woman?"

Karif sighed and rolled his eyes. "One thing at a time. We are here to gain intel for your sisters, for you, remember?"

"I think my sisters would understand if we took a break to free a slave," Aella scoffed, sinking back into her chair.

"We will help the girl," Karif replied, "Just relax. Now is not the time."

Aella tried to calm down, but she felt drawn to the woman. Despite her best efforts, she looked toward her and the trafficker again. This time, the woman met her stare. Her eyes held a firm resolution, as if she was declaring, "I will not break." She held her chin up high, dirt clinging to the curves of her face. A yank on her chains had her turning toward the trafficker. Aella turned away then and surveyed the crowd. She knew there was no point in trying to point out any Cleansers. From hunting them the last few weeks, she had learned how different they all were. There were no tells; they blended in and could be anybody.

The barmaid returned with two bowls of steaming stew, pieces of bread, and cups of ale on a tray. She placed them in front of Karif and Aella, told them to enjoy, and left them to eat. Aella took a spoonful of soup and grimaced. The meat was chewy, the broth under-spiced, and the vegetables undercooked. Karif coughed, a little bit of the soup spilling down his chin.

"God damn, that is awful," he said under his breath.

Aella laughed. "You should dine at the castle, then you'd really be horrified." Her humor was short-lived, though, because her eyes, of their own accord, strayed back to the woman. She was staring blankly ahead as the trafficker ran a grimy finger down her sharp cheekbone. His other hand clenched her thigh. Aella's anger rose.

"Karif," she hissed.

He looked up, following her gaze, and muttered, "We will get to her," before returning to his tasteless meal.

"We cannot wait," Aella demanded.

Karif heaved a breath. "When they go to their rooms, we will follow. No need to make a scene in this fine dining establishment."

Aella deadpanned him and shook her head, but ripped a piece of the dry, stiff bread and stuffed it in her mouth. She would not forget about the woman, and she knew, in her heart, neither would Karif. He was just being smart; she was being impulsive.

When the man finally rose, jerking the chain and dragging the woman toward the stairs, Aella's muscles coiled like a bowstring. She slipped from her chair, Karif following close behind. They kept to the shadows, a few steps behind, the noise of the tavern masking their pursuit.

At the end of the hall, a door creaked shut. Karif gave Aella a look, one finger pressed to his lips. She only tilted her head, a smirk tugging at her mouth with the silent confidence of someone who had ended far worse men.

They got to the door and Karif eased the latch. Aella darted in first, low and fast. The trafficker turned, startled, just as she slid beneath his outstretched arm. Her twin daggers flashed, slicing the chain at the woman's ankles and then raking a shallow cut across the back of his leg. He roared, stumbling.

Before he could recover, Aella pivoted, driving the heel of her palm into his nose with a sickening crack. The man reeled back against the wall. Sword at the ready, Karif barreled in then. The trafficker swung a meaty fist, but Aella was already behind him, swift as a shadow. She leapt, planting a foot against the wall for leverage, and locked an arm tight around his throat from behind, bringing him to the ground.

"Stay down," she hissed in his ear, one of her blades pressed against the tender spot just beneath his jaw.

He thrashed, his size making the room shake, but Aella's grip only tightened. He tried to throw her off, but she was small and impossible to dislodge. Karif stepped in, slamming his sword pommel into the trafficker's temple. The man went slack with a groan and Aella let his head fall to the floor with a thump.

She stood and, with a flick of her wrist, cut the irons from the woman's wrists, the shackles hitting the ground with a dull clang. The woman stood even taller, rubbing her raw, free skin.

"Can you walk?" Aella asked evenly, despite the rush of adrenaline.

The woman's chin lifted. "I can do more than that."

Karif chuckled. "Then move. We've just kicked a hornets' nest."

Boots thundered down the hall. Aella grabbed the trafficker's chain, looped it around the door handle, and pulled it taut to bar it shut. The wood groaned as fists pounded from the other side.

"Window!" she ordered, already yanking the dusty shutters open. Hot desert wind roared in, carrying sand with it. She glanced at the woman, then at Karif. She grinned, sharp and wild. "Time to run."

CHAPTER 7

T HE SMALL, PINK-HAIRED GIRL sat in a bed of various wildflowers in the royal garden, calling to the earth around her as it responded. A twist of her fingers sent a vine crawling up her forearm, tickling her and resulting in a fit of giggles. Her mother gazed on, perched on a shining marble bench, watching in amazement at the way the greenery responded to her daughter. Even though Cyra had seen Petra use her powers numerous times, it felt different with Hollin, as if the flowers were truly alive and responding to her. She swore the flowers, vines, and even the earth itself shifted to remain closer to her daughter as she walked and played.

The garden had been fully developed by Cyra's late sister, Petra. Walls of shrubs and various plant trees, such as peach, apple, and pear, graced the courtyard. Instead of polished cobblestone, beds of wildflowers grew between and over the rocks. Dragonflies, honey bees, and butterflies flitted around, collecting pollen and nectar from the bushes of rose, lavender, hydrangea, and honeysuckle. Birds of all shapes and sizes splashed in the birdbath and dined in the feed, though Cyra's personal favorite were the hummingbirds, beautiful and lethal.

She admired how they defended what was theirs, not allowing anyone to endanger their nests.

Rheanna slid onto the bench beside her, her cool hand resting on her older sister's. Ripley stood at the entrance of the garden, a soft smile on his lips as he watched the young princess with amusement.

"I spoke to Laney and Cora. They'll help us, but I am afraid it will lead them into harm's way," Rheanna spoke softly.

Cyra breathed deeply through her nose, her gaze still fixed on her daughter. "We must all make sacrifices."

Rheanna stiffened beside her. "They are just girls."

Cyra's head snapped to Rheanna, molten lava meeting glacial ice. "Petra was just a girl. Hollin is a girl. Goddess be damned, Aella and you are just girls, whether you guys want to admit it or not. We cannot and will not lose one of our girls again." Her eyes trailed back to her daughter, Ripley now kneeling beside her, covered in small white flowers.

"You think I don't know that? But Laney and Cora are our girls as well. Just because they are not royal does not make them any less worthy of protection."

Cyra looked at her sister once again, her cheeks turning red with a mix of shame and frustration. Rheanna's eyes narrowed.

"I didn't mean it like that. I just... I meant our family," Cyra struggled to find the words, but guilt began to churn in her gut.

"I want to protect our family as well, but our people deserve that same protection. You are Queen, Cyra. You can't be selfish," Rheanna reasoned.

Again, Cyra looked from her sister and up at the sky, sighing. She wished she could be selfish. She wanted to take her sisters and her daughter and run far away from here. There was not only the danger of the Cleansers, the monsters, the Oracle, but also the danger of Hollin's heritage. She could only hide the truth for so long, especially in the capital. Once someone spotted her pointed ears, it was over; there would be no more hiding.

"There is just so much at stake with Hollin. Rhe, I need to keep her safe." She felt a tear trail down her cheek and quickly wiped it away.

Rheanna rubbed her sister's forearm as her voice softened, "I know, and we will. You are not alone."

Cyra knew she was not alone. She had Rheanna and Aella, even if the latter was not physically there.

Her thoughts turned to Hollin. When she couldn't be with her, either Atlas or Ron stayed by her side. She had waived Ron of any guard duty, but he still insisted on sleeping in the rooms next to Hollin and Cyra, who shared the same room. Many people watched out for Hollin, but it was not enough. It would never be enough.

Instead of voicing all of that, the Queen simply said, "I know."

Silence stretched between them, filled only by Hollin's laughter and the buzz of wings among the flowers. For a moment, it felt like peace.

"You don't have to carry this burden alone, you know," Rheanna murmured, her eyes on the patch of sky above them. "You will break yourself if you try to hold it all at once."

Cyra tilted her head, studying her sister's profile. Rheanna's words were gentle, but beneath lay a truth that stung.

"And if I let go? Who will catch her?" Cyra whispered, her voice brittle. *Who will catch me?* she thought.

Rheanna turned, her blue eyes steady, unflinching. "I will."

The two sisters held each other's gaze until Hollin's squeal broke the tension. Ripley had woven a crown of daisies for her and she placed it proudly on top of his auburn hair, declaring him her knight. The sight pulled a small laugh from both sisters, the sound mingling, brief and fleeting like birds scattering into the air.

Suddenly, a deep horn bellowed in the distance, low and resonant, rolling across the courtyard like thunder. The garden stilled and Ripley instinctively scooped Hollin into his arms. Even the hummingbirds froze midair before darting off in a flurry. A second blast followed, sharper and closer, answered by the faint but unmistakable rhythm of marching feet echoing through the streets of Reddel.

Rheanna's hand tightened on Cyra's forearm. "What is that?"

Cyra rose from the bench, her skirts whispering through the wildflowers as her golden eyes flicked to the garden gates. "The Hefguard," she breathed, the words tasting both sweet and sharp on her tongue.

Relief uncoiled in her chest. At last, reinforcements. The weight of the kingdom would no longer rest solely on her shoulders. Atlas's family had come which meant the whispers of a wedding could finally become reality, their vows binding the two kingdoms.

And yet, the relief was laced with unease.

Their arrival also meant there would be no turning back. The horns were a summons, the rhythm of marching feet an unyielding reminder that the time for stillness was gone.

Ripley shifted Hollin higher into his arms, his expression unreadable as he glanced toward the sound. The crown of daisies slid askew on his head. Hollin's tiny hands clutched his tunic as her wide eyes sought her mother's. Cyra forced a smile for her daughter's sake, though her heart hammered in her chest.

"It's all right, Holli," she murmured.

The third horn blast echoed through the stone corridors of Reddel, and it seemed as if the whole kingdom held its breath.

Hefguard had come.

Chapter 8

T HE AIR IN THE castle had shifted. Every breath held a weight, as though the stones themselves braced for the company soon to arrive. Rheanna moved in silence beside her sister, their steps echoing down the long corridor of pale stone. Hollin's little hand brushed her skirts, skipping ahead, then darting back again as if she too felt the charge in the air. Ripley followed close at their heels, his hand never straying far from the hilt at his side, his eyes sharp, scanning every shadow that flickered in the alcoves.

They passed under the arch into the receiving hall. Golden doors soared high, their carvings gleaming beneath the light of the teal chandelier. The council stood already assembled in a long line. Norton, Marine, Lola, Sidney, Levine, and Jasper, leaning faintly on his cane, with Bianca poised beside him. Not one spoke, frowned, or whispered complaints. They had chosen silence and the mask of unity. Whether or not it was the truth, the foreign kingdom would see them as one.

Atlas stood at the center of it all, waiting. He was dressed in emerald and black, Hefguard's colors, his shoulders straight beneath polished armor. The crest of the mountain and crystal glinted silver at his chest, catching the chandelier's light. He inclined his head to Cyra and though his eyes softened at the sight of her, his posture remained every inch the prince of Hefguard.

Hollin darted forward before anyone could stop her. "Atlas!" she cried, voice carrying through the cavernous chamber. He bent swiftly, scooping her into his arms. She looped her arms around his neck, crown of daisies tilting as she buried her face against him.

"Holli," he murmured. He kissed her strawberry-blonde hair once before setting her back on her feet. The little girl ran back to her aunt, half hiding behind Rheanna's skirts. She caught the faintest tug at Cyra's lips, but she quickly straightened her shoulders, golden eyes fixed on the chamber doors that led beyond.

"Ready?" Atlas asked.

Cyra nodded. "Let them in."

The horn sounded again, reverberating against the stones. The chamber doors opened, revealing the massive brass gates that had begun to rise, the chains rattling loud enough to shake the receiving hall. Warm air swept in, carrying with it the dust of travel and the sharp tang of steel. Rheanna's heart thudded as light reflected over the emerald banners trimmed in black.

The crest of Hefguard snapped high in the wind, a dark mountain peak carved bold against green, a silver crystal gleaming at its center. Soldiers poured through in disciplined lines, boots striking the stone in unison. Their armor was dark, the mountain and crystal painted bright upon breastplates and shields. Yet even at a glance, Rheanna knew this was not their full strength; too few filled the square. The rest had already gone to the Black Lake, to the borders where monsters terrorized the towns.

Two riders pushed through the soldiers, the lines breaking. Cyra and Atlas moved out into the afternoon air, their own party following behind.

Queen Elspeth Nicola moved with quiet authority as she dismounted. The green cloak that swept behind her bore Hefguard's crest in silver thread. Her dark hair was streaked with white and tied into an intricate braid atop her head. Prince Malcolm followed at her side. His black hair curled at the ends, damp from the march, his satchel bouncing lightly against his hip.

Atlas stepped forward with Cyra, both rulers side by side. He inclined his head. "Mother. Malcolm." His voice carried across the courtyard.

Elspeth's chocolate gaze swept the council, then the crowd gathered beyond the walls. Her voice was soft, yet reached even the farthest soldier. "Hefguard stands with Linnosa."

Together, Cyra and Atlas bowed their heads. "You are welcome in Reddel," Cyra said, voice steady. "Your presence honors us."

Elsepth nodded once, her dark eyes sliding to Hollin, still half hidden behind Rheanna's skirts. For a heartbeat too long, her gaze lingered. Rheanna smoothed a hand over Hollin's waves, guiding the girl's attention to her as vines twitched faintly against her boots.

Malcolm cleared his throat, stepping forward with casual ease. "For those counting heads, yes, only part of our force is here." His mouth curved faintly, as if he were already laughing at some unseen jest. He continued, waving a hand toward the horizon. "The rest are already making themselves useful against the lake, which, I'm told, is not a lake at all but some unholy cauldron that brews monsters. Spiders the size of barns, wolves with... scales. Charming place, really."

The corner of Cyra's lips twitched despite herself which only served to widen Malcom's grin. "But don't worry, we left plenty of men to defend your city. Hundreds of soldiers who start sulking if they don't swing a sword every morning."

A ripple of easy laughter threaded through the first few lines of Hefguard soldiers. Even the council seemed to ease, a small shifting of weight like people waking from a too-long vigil.

Cyra folded her arms across her chest, her posture guarded despite the softening of the crowd. "We are grateful, but our kingdom faces monsters you couldn't dream of."

"No," Malcolm agreed easily. "What you face is a nightmare. But nightmares can be endured with the right poultice and a few good friends." He offered her a look of genuine respect. "And perhaps, if we're lucky, a stronger queen than most kingdoms deserve."

The words, though lightly spoken, carried weight. Cyra's chin lifted a fraction.

The Queen of Hefguard had not moved, but when she spoke, her voice spread through the courtyard, gentle, steady, and kind. "They will look to you and see more than crowns and banners," she said, her eyes softening as they swept the gathered soldiers and citizens. "They will see the promise Linnosa endures. That even in grief, you have not faltered. That is what will give them hope."

Rheanna's chest loosened. *Hope.* It was a word she had not dared let herself think these past days, but hearing it spoken aloud settled into her bones like warmth.

Two figures slipped into the edge of the crowd; Laney, her red hair bound tight and freckles flushed against her cheeks. Beside her, Cora fidgeted with her sleeves, eyes darting nervously toward the Hefguard lines. They should not have been this close, but they were, and the tilt of Cyra's head gave Rheanna permission to leave. She held Hollin's small hand and followed the girls into a distant corridor where the cheers of the courtyard became a muffled roar before stopping.

"Rheanna," Laney whispered, her gaze fixed on the cobblestones. "The Cleansers moved again last night. Red paint in the town square. *The Beloved.* They wrote it with candles burning beneath until dawn."

Cora swallowed. "People are talking," she added, "Petra's name keeps their grief alive and the Cleansers are feeding it."

Rheanna gripped Hollin's shoulder, pulling her closer. She forced her face to remain serene, but inside, her stomach churned with nausea. Petra's corpse had barely been laid to rest, yet the Cleansers wielded her name like a weapon.

She thanked the girls and fell back into her spot with Hollin just as the last horn echoed, long and low, sealing the procession. Atlas offered his arm to Cyra. Elspeth moved behind them, Malcolm at her side, and the council fell into step as the entire party turned inward, back toward the castle's golden doors.

The crowd outside erupted in a final, thunderous cheer, but as the brass gates began to shut, all Rheanna could hear were the whispers of rebellion and doubt, the restless undercurrent that no alliance could silence. She lingered on the threshold, Hollin pressed close to her side, Ripley a steady wall at her back. Ahead of her, Cyra and Atlas walked in unison, a mountain and a flame, unbreakable.

CHAPTER 9

T HE NIGHT SWALLOWED AELLA, Karif, and the woman as they slipped free of the traffickers' grip. Aella's blade had found its mark, quick and silent, but the outcry of another slaver shattered the moment.

"Run," she hissed, already dragging the woman by the wrist.

She stumbled at first, skirts dragging in the sand, but there was a startling strength in her grip when she steadied herself on Aella's forearm. Karif took the lead, weaving them into the maze of narrow streets. The air reeked of smoke and sweat, the din of the marketplace long gone silent, leaving the howl of the wind magnified.

A shout rang through the night and torches flared in the distance. Aella's instincts surged. She shoved the woman against the wall of a mud-brick house, holding her breath as shadows darted across the alley's mouth. Karif leaned close, whispering, "Two of them. Maybe three."

Aella smirked, though her pulse pounded. They darted across the street, feet sinking into the sand and slowing them down. Karif vaulted a low wall with ease, Aella on his heels. She turned to help the woman over, but she was already following, surprisingly graceful and landing lighter than Aella expected. Not quite the helpless damsel, then.

Still, she lagged as they pushed deeper into the town. The streets thinned, opening into the edge of the desert. Aella caught sight of the dunes rippling pale beneath the stars as her eyes scanned the area for cover.

"There," Karif whispered, nodding to the dark outline of stables set apart from the town's border.

They sprinted the last stretch, the sounds of pursuit fading behind them. The horses stirred at their arrival, hooves shifting in straw. Aella shoved the door shut and barred it with a beam of wood. Only then did she let herself sag against the wall. They kept quiet until they no longer heard their pursuers, sitting in an empty stall. It may have smelled like horse crap and hay pricked and itched at Aella's legs, but at least they were sheltered from the whipping wind.

"What is your name?" asked Karif, looking over at the striking girl.

She lifted her chin. "Kaelith Selora Ocevaris." Her voice was clear and deliberate, each syllable precise.

If anyone else had presented their full name in such a way, Aella would scoff and roll her eyes, but something about this girl demanded respect.

"A pleasure to meet you, Kaelith," she said with ease, offering her hand. Kaelith tilted her head, staring at her outstretched hand before Aella awkwardly let it fall back into her lap.

"You may call me Kae," the woman said. "Thank you for helping me." Aella took note of how she used the word "helping" instead of "saving." She was not the type of woman who needed saving often.

"Where are you from?" Karif spoke, his dark hair sticking up at odd ends from their journey into the desert.

Kaelith looked between Karif and Aella, calculating and debating. "My home is the sea."

Aella and Karif looked at each other, eyebrows furrowed and confusion clear on their faces. It seemed she did not deem them worthy of knowing the truth, but instead of pushing, Aella let it go. "What were you doing when you got caught by the traffickers?"

Kaelith did not answer the question. "I have to get a warning to the Queen of Linnosa," she stated instead, her face serious.

Aella's heart pounded. "What do you know of the Queen?"

Kaelith's face remained calm and empty. "I know that I must give this message to her. To protect the child."

She had to be speaking about Hollin, but what were the odds that they just so happened upon a woman who was making her way to her sisters, to her niece? What could this woman possibly know?

"I am the Princess. The Queen is my sister," Aella said, wondering if Kaelith would stick to her story.

Her face brightened for the first time at this, her cerulean eyes growing large, and she clapped her petite hands. "Perfect," she said, her voice lighter than before. "I shall accompany you back to Reddel."

"We aren't going to-" Karif began before Aella put her hand up to stop him. Her brain started spinning. If there was even a sliver of a chance that this woman knew anything that could protect her niece and her sisters, she had to follow it, and if this woman set out to do harm to them, Aella would make sure she was there to protect them.

"We will take you there."

Karif's jaw slackened. "We?"

Aella shook her head at him. "Well, at least I will."

"Don't we have some other matters to attend to?" His brow rose, staring intently at Aella.

"Matters that involve my sisters," she enunciated each word slowly. "I need to get back to them anyway and you can continue to investigate for me?" she shrugged.

"Oh, sure, I have nothing better to do, I suppose." Karif scoffed, his voice full of sarcasm. Aella rolled her eyes. She knew he had left his duties at the Guild as the Dispatcher to help her for too long, but she also knew he hated playing that role. He was not the same man his father, Creaton, was. Whenever he walked into that space, he had to pretend to be heartless and push down the kindness and empathy only a select few had ever seen. She wanted Karif to leave behind that life entirely, but he felt he kept people safe by controlling the Guild.

For a while, none of them spoke. The only sounds were of the horses moving in their stalls, tails flicking at flies, the air thick with manure and dust. The building groaned as the outside wind pressed against the stable walls. Aella sat cross-legged in the hay, her back against the rough wood. Kaelith's presence pressed on her like a tide—silent, constant, and impossible to ignore. The seashells in her braids caught the overhead lantern light, glinting with each small tilt of her head.

"You're too calm," Aella finally said, her voice low. "Most people, after being kidnapped, almost sold, running for their lives, would be shaking."

Kaelith met her gaze evenly. "I don't believe in wasting energy."

"And here I thought you were mysterious." Karif let out a dry laugh. "Turns out you're just insufferable."

Aella caught a flicker of amusement ghost across Kaelith's lips before it vanished, her expression turning peaceful once again.

"What did you mean when you said the sea is your home?" Aella pressed, leaning forward slightly, placing her elbows on her knees.

Kaelith drew a finger through the hay, tracing a pattern that looked almost like waves. "The sea does not belong to me, nor I to it. We are... intertwined. It speaks to me and I listen. A name. A warning." Her cerulean eyes lifted, pinning Aella. "Hollin."

The sound of her niece's name, spoken so calmly, made Aella's throat tighten. She had never even met the girl, but the need to protect her was primal. She masked her feelings with a glare. "You want me to believe you heard my niece's name in the ocean?"

"Believe what you want. The tide is indifferent to doubt." Kaelith tilted her head, unruffled.

Karif groaned, rubbing his temples. "Fantastic. We've picked up a prophet who speaks in riddles."

"But we know Hollin is in danger. We can't ignore it," Aella snapped.

Kaelith smiled faintly as if Aella had passed some unspoken test. She tucked her knees to her chest, closing her eyes and resting her head against the stall wall.

Despite the quiet and the fact that Karif agreed to keep watch while she rested, Aella couldn't bring herself to sleep. Her violet gaze kept drifting back to the mysterious and serene Kaelith. The woman sat still, her breaths even with sleep. Aella could not believe how peacefully she slept after everything she had been through, but then, she didn't understand the woman at all. There was an unworldly presence about her. Aella wondered if bringing her back to Reddel was the right thing to do. A deep feeling in her gut told her she had to, her instincts screamed that she was safe, so it had to be right.

"You're staring," Karif spoke into the quiet night, causing Aella to flinch ever so slightly.

She glared at him. "I'm just watching her."

"Same thing," he said with a yawn. "Just try not to fall in love with another mystery. We are already drowning in them."

She shot him another glare and looked away. His words needled at her more than she'd like to admit.

CHAPTER 10

G RATEFUL THAT THE TRUE formalities were over, Cyra dressed for an intimate dinner with Atlas, his family, Rheanna, and Hollin. The previous night, the Hefguard had arrived and they had their formal dinner with the council and Hefguard dignitaries who arrived. Everything had gone well, filled with pleasantries, small talk, and a grand meal honoring their allies.

Cyra dressed herself in a gown of light pink, the sleeves falling off her shoulders and exposing her collarbones. It fell in dollops of fabric to her feet, exposing a creamy lace fabric underneath with matching pink slippers. She moved on to aiding Hollin, who sat on their grand bed playing with dolls, her pointed ears exposed with her hair tucked behind them.

"Alright, Holli-bean. Time for you to get dressed for our dinner with Atlas's family," Cyra said.

Hollin jumped up and down on the bed, screeching with delight, before she bounced off it and headed to the bureau that held her gowns. The little girl had been in a sour mood after Cyra told her she couldn't join them for dinner last night. Instead, she had been left with Ron, to her great dismay.

She pulled on the hem of a magenta dress, shouting, "Mommy! I want to match you!"

Cyra laughed, petting her daughter on the head and retrieving the dress from the closet. The magenta dress had embroidered vines and flowers running down its skirts, the sleeves in a similar fashion as her mother's. She helped Hollin into it, untying the strap of matching fabric wrapped around the top of the hanger she would use to hide Hollin's ears.

"How would you like your hair today?" Cyra asked, booping the tip of her daughter's nose.

"I want it down!" Hollin declared so Cyra moved to tie the headband in place, but Hollin put her hands up. "No, Mommy. I want my ears out."

Cyra blinked several times, arms still out, the ribbon dangling. Her mouth opened and shut several times before saying, "Holli, you know we have to cover them to protect you."

Hollin stomped her foot, spider web cracks ricocheting from where it hit the ground. Her mother placed her hands on each of her shoulders. "You need to stay calm."

"I don't want to hide anymore. I am a princess." Hollin's words were accompanied by a twirl, small white flowers erupting around her.

"I know, my darling girl, but this is to keep you safe. I don't want to hide you either," Cyra said when the little girl stopped spinning.

Hollin's lower lip popped out, tears filling her emerald eyes. The flowers that had erupted only moments ago began to wilt, disappearing into dust as her emotions rose. Cyra's heart beat hard against her chest. She suddenly felt desperate to make her daughter understand. It wasn't as if she wanted to hide Hollin's true identity from the world. This was not a choice, but a necessity. Since the Banishment, the fae and all other species who looked different or survived on magic had been hated. Stories of traffickers selling and murdering those who were caught here had circulated for years. The rumors may have died down, but Cyra would not take that risk.

"Come here," she reached out for Hollin, and her daughter collapsed into her chest, sobs shaking her tiny frame. "I love you, Hollin, and I need to do what I can to protect you."

Instead of responding, Hollin only cried harder. Her tears fell onto Cyra's bare chest that her dress left exposed. Cyra rubbed soothing circles into her daughter's small back. After a few moments, Hollin's cries began to let up, only small hiccups escaping her. Her freckled cheeks were red and covered with wetness, her eyes bloodshot. Cyra smoothed the strawberry-blonde hair out of her face and tucked it behind her ears, rubbing her fingers over the points while doing so.

"You are beautiful. Your ears are beautiful. No part of me wishes to hide any part of you, bean. But..." she paused, trying to find the words to explain it all to a five-year-old. "There are people who want to hurt our family and people who would want to hurt you just because of your ears."

"But why, Mommy? What have I done?" Hollin sniffled, rubbing her nose.

Cyra sighed, shifting to lift her daughter and placing her on the edge of their gold and orange futon. She kneeled in front of her, making sure to be careful of her dress, and placed both hands on the little girl's lap.

"You have done nothing, my perfect, sweet girl. People are just afraid of what they do not understand. You are powerful, and not only do you have magic from me, but also the magic from the fae due to your father." Cyra flinched at the last part. They had never talked about the fae or her father, but Hollin was intuitive, and she knew she was different.

"What is fae? And who is my father?" Hollin's head tilted, her little face scrunching in confusion.

Cyra looked up at the ceiling, sighing. "Listen, bean. Aunt Rhe and I will teach you everything tomorrow, but right now, we need to get to this dinner. Don't you want to see Atlas and his family?"

Hollin gave her mother a glare before pushing off the couch and nodding her head. "Okay, put my headband on."

Cyra wrapped and tied the fabric around her head, bending over to kiss the top of it. "Thank you."

Hollin turned with sass and folded her arms over her chest, stomping to the door. Just at that moment, a knock sounded at the door, and Hollin skipped to it, her mood immediately improving. She flung it open to reveal Atlas, standing with his hands in his pants pockets. He wore an all-black outfit with intricate green embroidery along the hems of the blouse. It opened ever so slightly in a V-cut, exposing a bit of his chest.

"Atlas!" screeched Hollin as she threw herself against his legs. He lifted her up with ease, hugging her before placing her back on her feet.

"Are you ready to meet my mother and brother?" he asked, a smile gracing his lips.

She nodded eagerly. "Yes! A real queen and prince!"

Cyra laughed and Atlas said with a chuckle, "You are in the presence of a queen and prince right now."

Hollin shook her head, looking between them both. "No, it is different. They are special," she said, her eyes twinkling.

"Whatever you say, little one," he said fondly before looking up at her mother. "You look stunning." His eyes ran over her body, slowing upon her exposed chest as he gulped.

"Thank you." Cyra smiled and winked at him, walking toward the door.

The three of them made their way down the gilded halls, the flickering of lanterns casting shadows along the many portraits of long-gone ancestors. One day, a portrait of Cyra, Atlas, and Hollin would grace these halls, probably not long after the wedding. Then it would be updated if their marriage produced more heirs. Cyra had never thought of having any other children, but what if Atlas wanted more? She looked at him, biting her lip. He met her gaze, a dark eyebrow raising in question. She snapped her head away. These were not thoughts she needed to have just before dinner with his family.

They reached the small dining chamber, a room Cyra had chosen because it felt more like an embrace instead of the proclamation the formal dining hall declared. The vaulted ceiling arched lower here than in the grand hall. Hand-painted beams showed wheat stalks and late-summer swallows, faded by time and polish. Cream tapestries softened the stone, stitched with scenes from the valleys. The hearth had been lit early, logs crackling with that rich scent that always always reminded Cyra of the royal garden in autumn. Beeswax candles in brass cups dotted the oval table. She had told the servants no towering arrangements tonight, just low vessels of rosemary and rose cuttings from the garden, their scent clean and familiar.

Atlas walked beside Cyra, their arms brushing occasionally while Hollin skipped at her mother's other side, her magenta skirts bouncing with each step. The trio cut a picture Cyra knew the servants would whisper about later: queen, consort-to-be, and little princess. For a moment, she let herself savor it.

Rheanna was already waiting in the dining chamber, her gown a sleek sea-silk blue that caught the candlelight like river water. She rose gracefully from her chair as soon as the doors opened and Hollin barreled toward her with a squeal. "Aunt Rhe!"

Rheanna bent low, arms opening to catch her niece, and Hollin crashed against her with such a force that she stumbled back, laughing. "Careful, bean. You'll knock me into the fire."

"You look like the river tonight," Hollin stated, pulling back to examine her. "Shiny and pretty."

Rheanna's cheeks pinked as she smoothed Hollin's hair. "And you look like a flower plucked straight from the garden." Her eyes flickered to Cyra, softening further. "You both look wonderful."

Cyra smiled as she moved closer, pressing her hand briefly over Rheanna's. "Thank you for being here."

"Anything for family," Rheanna said simply.

Her gaze brushed toward Atlas and she offered him a polite nod. Atlas inclined his head in return, and Cyra felt the brush of his hand against hers, steadying her before the night truly began. The doors opened again and the Hefguard royals entered. Queen Elspeth was in a deep, evergreen velvet, pearls catching the candlelight at her ears, and Malcolm trailed beside her with an easy grin already in place.

"Cyra," Elspeth said, "Your home is truly beautiful."

"Thank you," Cyra said, stepping forward. "Please, come in and let us eat."

She stepped into the room and Malcolm bypassed them all. He had Atlas's height and long-fingered hands. Cyra noticed ink smudges on his thumb as if he had been writing only moments ago. The faintest tell of herbs clung to him as if he had been in a garden. He swept a comically low bow at Hollin rather than Cyra, his grin widening as the little girl giggled.

"Is this the famous Hollin," he said, eyes lighting, "or a decoy the Queen employs to distract her guests from stealing the best bread rolls?"

Hollin gasped loudly. "You steal bread?"

"Only to test it for poison." Malcolm placed a palm on his chest. "If I perish, you will know your kitchen is unsafe."

Atlas made a sound that was between a sigh and a laugh. "I warned you earlier not to start with death jokes."

"But I am a healer witch," Malcolm returned, entirely unbothered. "It's only responsible of me."

"Very responsible," Hollin agreed, eyes huge. "What's a decoy?"

Rheanna choked on a laugh and transformed it into a polite cough as Elspeth's gaze slipped to her with the mildest glimmer of amusement.

"Come," Cyra said. "Let's sit."

Cyra took the place at the head of the long, polished oak table with Atlas to her right and Rheanna to her left. Elspeth sat opposite Cyra, where conversation could cross the table comfortably. Malcolm slid between his mother and Atlas as if he had always belonged there. Hollin was sandwiched between Rheanna and Elspeth, which made Cyra's muscles tense before the feeling passed. Elspeth smiled down at Hollin like she had been waiting all day to hear what the child had to say.

Servants moved quietly around them, pouring red wine from the South into their goblets. Trays of charred leeks with lemon were carried in alongside roasted root vegetables lacquered with honey and thyme, the scent wafting through the hall, mingling with the scent of roses from the table's centerpiece. A lamb shoulder was placed at the center, so tender that it fell apart at the nudge of a spoon. Seeded bread arrived still warm from the ovens. A simple custard cooled on the sideboard while they ate.

"Your tapestries," Elspeth said, soft as always, after the first pass of dishes. "They favor the fields over the battles."

Cyra followed the Queen's gaze to a stitched ladder leaning against an apple tree, tiny figures up in the leaves, skirts and trousers dangling. "My mother chose them. She said anyone who sat long enough at our table should leave having seen some fruit."

"Fruit is a kind of hope," Elspeth muttered.

Hollin reached for a roll and Atlas, without looking away from Elspeth, moved the butter closer to the young girl. These small movements, the quiet choreography that people built long before vows, warmed Cyra more than the fire.

"What do you do?" Hollin asked Malcolm, roll in one small fist, butter knife in the other like a tiny soldier with a sword. "Atlas holds big swords and does important walking.

Mommy holds fire. Aunt Rhe reads to me and she sometimes sings and sometimes cries–" She froze once she saw the look on her mother's face. The knife slipped from her hand and landed on her plate with a metallic clink. "I mean..." she stammered quickly, "she is very nice."

Rheanna, blushing, pressed a finger to Hollin's nose. "Traitor," she whispered, smiling.

Malcolm pretended to deliberate. "Well, sometimes I hold very tiny swords, called needles." He leaned forward, lowering his voice. "I am a healer. A witch, if you like old words. I brew very smelly things that taste like sadness but make you better anyway. And I talk to plants until they give up and grow."

Hollin went still with awe. "You talk to them? I can make plants grow too."

"I have learned that they are quite stubborn," Malcolm confided. "Like Atlas."

Atlas smiled. "I am not stubborn."

"He says stubbornly," Malcolm said.

Rheanna laughed and Elspeth's eyes softened to caramel. Cyra cut a piece of lamb and slid it onto Atlas's plate without looking, and he nudged his knee against hers under the table. The motion tightened her airway for a heartbeat. She had imagined this type of family. Only Petra and Aella were missing.

"Are witches scary?" Hollin asked, watching the steam curl above her plate.

"Some are," Malcolm said cheerfully. "But that's usually because they haven't eaten yet. Bread helps." He popped a piece of bread in his mouth for emphasis.

"That's also true for soldiers," Atlas muttered.

"And queens," Rheanna added softly, sending a smirk toward her sister. Cyra rolled her eyes as she forked a piece of lamb into her mouth, the meat melting over her tongue.

"Do you know the most important food of any royal feast?" Malcolm asked, leaning across the table with a conspiratorial look at Hollin.

"The meat?" she guessed, crumbs clinging to her lips.

"The bread," Malcolm declared.

Cyra laughed. "You and this damned bread."

"It tells you everything you need to know about a kingdom. If it's good, the people are happy. If it's bad, the rulers should be thrown into the moat."

Hollin gasped, eyes wide. "Into the moat?"

"Malcolm–" Atlas groaned, hand over his face.

"Quiet, brother," Malcolm demanded, waving him off. He tore a roll in half with great ceremony and slid a piece onto Hollin's plate. "Now, as the official Bread Inspector of Linnosa, you must give the verdict. Is your mother's kitchen safe?"

Hollin puffed up, clearly delighted with the responsibility. She bit into the bread with exaggerated care, chewed, then tapped her chin with one finger. "It is..." she paused, "safe, very safe. But the butter is not salty enough."

"Ah," Malcolm said gravely, pointing at Atlas. "You heard her. Arrest him at once."

"Why me?" Atlas asked.

"Because you look guilty," Malcolm shrugged, replying without hesitation.

Hollin dissolved into giggles, clutching her roll as if she were holding a royal decree, crumbs scattering across her plate.

Elspeth had eaten very little. She watched the scene unfold, her eyes moving from face to face, a small smile tugging at her lips. Her gaze lingered on Hollin's laughter, on Cyra's watchful composure, on Malcolm's easy charm, committing it to memory so she could later ponder it all. When she finally spoke again, it was to Rheanna.

"You move like water," she said with a gentle familiarity. "Even when you are still. I can see the river in your form."

Rheanna blinked, caught off guard. "I suppose that makes sense given my affinity for the element. I have always felt the most myself while near water."

"It shows. My husband told me once that Hefguard steel is strongest when tempered in the river, not the forge. I sense you have that same strength. The kind that cools and shapes without breaking."

Rheanna's cheeks flushed faintly. She ducked her head, murmuring a polite thank you. Cyra, watching her sister, felt something twist in her chest. Pride and a touch of sorrow that it had taken a foreign queen to make Rheanna hear such words spoken aloud.

"Tell us a story," Hollin said to Malcolm, her tiny fists hitting the edge of the table in demand.

"A story," he mused, pretending to pet a nonexistent beard. "Very well. A story about the time Atlas tried to ride a goat."

Atlas set down his wine, his head falling back. "No."

"Yes," Malcolm said, his eyes dancing with wicked delight. "Picture it: a young prince with a sword too big for him and a heart even bigger, determined to make a heroic entrance into the village festivities–"

"I was eight," Atlas interjected, rolling his eyes.

"–only to realize the horse he'd been promised was, in fact, the Queen's very favorite prize goat."

Hollin and Cyra hunched over in laughter. Elspeth covered her mouth with two delicate fingers while Rheanna's shoulders shook. The prince in the story had his face in his goblet, chugging the red wine like it was water.

"And this brave child said, 'A goat can be a steed if it has a determined enough rider,' climbed aboard, and within two seconds was headbutted off said steed and into a barrel of spiced cider. He smelled like apples for three days."

Atlas spread his hands, his face flushed. "And yet he leaves out that he was pushed in by the same goat immediately after me and cried."

"I cried because I had skinned my knee," Malcolm said flatly. "You cried because you had lost the goat."

"I did not cry."

Elspeth's dainty voice entered the conversation. "He did not cry."

Malcolm paused, hands over his heart as if pierced. "Maternal betrayal."

Cyra's laughter snuck up on her. It wasn't the polite kind she had practiced at countless gatherings, but the kind that made her slide a little in her chair and press a hand to her ribs. It felt illicit and necessary, like taking boots off after a long day. Atlas's shoulder touched hers, warm, and she let it rest there.

The merriment and food went on. Between buttering bread and telling goat stories, Malcolm taught Hollin how to measure spices with her eyes, describing them as "sparrow steps" and "mouse tails," a secret language of measurements he promised to write down for her later. No one talked about the council. No one spoke about Cleansers or monsters or prophecy. The absence of them was not a denial; it was a choice to let the night breathe.

When the dessert was served, a simple custard poured into little cups and topped with sliced pears, the servants left them completely alone. Hollin tasted hers and made a face of pure bliss.

"Can I stay up with you?" she asked in the next breath, which Cyra had already seen coming. "Pleeease?" She stretched the word thin.

"You have already stayed up," Cyra said gently. "Tomorrow is a new day with much to do and you will be a grumpy bean if you don't sleep."

Hollin shook her head, indignant. "I am never grumpy." She huffed, crossing her arms in front of her chest and narrowing her eyes at the betrayal. She then sighed dramatically, tugging at her headband as if she had forgotten it was there. The thoughtless motion caused fear to jump up Cyra's throat. Rheanna was quick, her hand sliding to Hollin's wrist, the lightest touch, and stilled it.

"We can finish dessert in your room," Rheanna said, calm as a lake at dusk. "I will tell you any kind of story you want."

Hollin considered this, then slid from her chair. She turned to Elspeth. "Thank you for eating with me."

"Thank you for having me."

Hollin lifted her arms and Elspeth hesitated only a fraction of a second before she bent and hugged her. The little girl moved to hug Atlas fiercely, then her mother next, and nodded at Malcolm like a general dismissing a soldier. "You are funny," she decreed. "Tomorrow you will teach me how to make sadness medicine taste good."

"I will bring honey," Malcolm promised.

Rheanna collected Hollin with ease, the little girl wrapping her arms around her aunt's neck. Hollin looked back once at her mother, hopeful, and Cyra mouthed, "To the stars."

Hollin's face erupted with a smile. "To the stars," she echoed back, then disappeared into the corridor with Rheanna. The room exhaled with her departure. Candles hissed softly as one of the logs shifted in the hearth.

Elspeth rose after a few more minutes of gentle talk and pressed Cyra's hands in hers. "We will not keep you. You have had many great responsibilities laid upon you recently." Her eyes slid to Atlas for a breath, a mother measuring her son's place in a room that did not belong to him and finding that he fit anyway. "Sleep, if you can."

Malcolm stood and bowed again, this time properly and to the Queen. He then ruined it by whispering to Atlas, just loud enough for Cyra to hear, "Don't steal any goats."

Atlas pinched the bridge of his nose. "Leave."

"I'm going, I'm going," Malcolm said, holding his hands up. He grinned at Cyra, the devil and a healer both. His laugh followed his mother out like a ribbon.

For a long moment, they didn't speak. Not for lack of words, but for the luxury of not needing them. Atlas's fingers flexed against the table as if resisting the urge to reach for her in the presence of witnesses that were no longer there.

Cyra watched him with a half-amused and half-aroused feeling sparking in her.

"You survived the goat tale," she said at last.

"I will never be free," he replied, and the corner of his mouth tipped. He studied her, gaze moving over the pink gown's off-shoulder line, the curve of her collarbones, the throat she kept bare because necklaces felt like leashes. His voice dropped a shade. "You look like a sin I intend to confess."

Heat crawled up her neck despite the hundreds of times men had said pretty things—dirty, practiced things. This wasn't practiced. It belonged to the small room, the empty chairs, and the hush after laughter. It belonged to the way he was looking at her, like he was starving even though they had just feasted.

"I am the queen," she said, playful, standing and gathering the edge of her skirts. "You cannot confess to me."

"Then I'll be damned." He stood.

She lifted her chin, daring. "Prove it."

They left the dining chamber, Cyra walking fast with Atlas's hand at the small of her back, not urging, just present and hot through the silk. The castle at night was a patchwork of sound: guards' boots like distant thunder in the halls, the hush of the inner courtyard fountain, a single laugh bursting somewhere before it was quickly stifled.

At last, they reached the guest corridor reserved for the Hefguard delegation. Guards posted at the mouth of the hall nodded and looked forward as Cyra and Atlas passed. Someone had banked the lamps to a low flame. The carpets complemented the stone here instead of swallowing it. Atlas's rooms sat near the end, a courtesy to give him quiet, even among his own. He opened his door and let her cross the threshold first. His chamber was lit by a single lamp and the embers of a dying fire in the small hearth. A travel trunk sat open with a meticulous slice of order inside. Folded shirts, a leather-bound book, a pair of gloves placed on top. His large bed sat against the far wall.

Atlas turned to her. "We don't have to–"

She stepped in. "We never have to." She breathed out and closed the small distance between them because she could, because she wanted to, because she had spent the evening watching him pass bread to her daughter and share jokes with his brother, and because in the last few weeks, he had shown patience toward a castle that might have swallowed him whole if he had let it.

He tasted like red wine and something sweet leftover from the custard. His hands didn't rush her body like a man claiming a prize. They found her face first, thumbs brushing along her jaw and then sliding down her shoulders with a gentle patience that made her toes curl inside her slippers. When his mouth parted, she made a sound she would deny in the daylight and tugged his shirt from the waist of his trousers, her hands exploring his waist.

The mattress welcomed them, the room shrinking to breath and fabric and the slide of his palm along her skin. The off-shoulder sleeves gave up easily. He made a quiet sound of pleasure at the sight of her bare chest in the amber light that she would keep in her mind for later, private and wicked.

"Cyra," he murmured like a prayer.

She answered with her mouth and then with her hands. He wasn't elegant in this space. He was earnest, warm, careful, and then not so careful when she arched and begged him not to be. When he paused, she pulled him down again, fingernails marking his shoulder blades.

CHAPTER 11

AELLA GROANED AS THEY approached the brass gates of the castle. It was now just her and Kaelith who finished the rest of the journey through the South and halfway into the East to Reddel, as Karif had to return to the Guild. He promised he would keep a lookout for any news of the Cleansers. Aella steeled herself, rolling her shoulders back. The guards on the gate straightened the instant they saw her, a mix of recognition and relief in their eyes. A ripple of whispers spread through the wind as soon as the brass gate groaned with effort as it lifted. The guards' eyes snagged on Kaelith as the stranger passed under the arch.

"I do not enjoy being stared at," Kaelith said under her breath, her cerulean gaze tracking the sweep of the courtyard. Her shoulders stiffened and she held her chin up as she continued to march past the gates.

"You should be used to it," Aella said plainly, gesturing to the woman's clear beauty.

Kaelith's lips tightened, a flicker of irritation crossing her face.

They crossed the inner ward and cut through the columned hall that led to the war room, passing servants who ducked into side passages too quickly. Word had run ahead of them already.

The door to the war room was already open when they reached it. Maps of Linnosa and their neighbors adorned the walls, pins like stars prickling the paper over the South where the monster reports had multiplied in the last month. The oval table at the center held more maps, a scatter of sealed wax notes, and a tray with an untouched teapot gone cold. The smell of parchment, smoke, and lilies from a small vase filled the room.

Cyra looked up first. She wore no crown, but the weight of leadership had set a line into her shoulders that hadn't been there before Aella had left and Petra had died. Her hair burned in the lamplight as if the two braids plaited along her scalp themselves could smolder. Rheanna stood half a step behind, tall and composed, hands folded loosely as if she had just said a prayer. Aella didn't realize she had been holding her breath until she saw both of them and released it.

"You're back," Cyra said, her voice cracking.

"Try not to sound thrilled," Aella shot back, tossing her cloak onto a chair and ignoring the ache in her calves. The scars on her cheek itched in the warm air. She jerked her chin toward Kaelith. "This is Kaelith Selora Ocevaris. She's the reason I am still not down South, searching for answers."

Kaelith dipped her head. "Your Majesty. Princess."

Instead of answering her address, the two older sisters finally rushed to Aella, capturing her in a sandwiched hug. Tears flowed freely down both of their cheeks, Rheanna's hands trembling as she placed them on either side of Aella's face.

"We have missed you so much."

Aella smiled sadly, grief and love seizing her heart, but she struggled not to let them through. "I missed you both as well."

They stepped away from her, but their eyes trailed her for a minute before Cyra's took Kaelith in. "Thank you for bringing her back to us. Sit. Tell me about your journey."

Aella dropped into the chair nearest the corner of the map of the Southern market routes. "The Cleansers are much more than a whisper now. They're moving like they have found a spine. Enough coin in the wrong hands to make smart men stupid."

Rheanna's fingers tightened into a fist. "Where?"

"Everywhere," Aella said, disgust flattening the word. "Reddel. Calder. Villages that barely have names. They are weaving sermons with supply lines. It is not just torches and pitchforks anymore. They have a plan."

Cyra's eyes narrowed. "Say it."

"They mean to raise a queen," Aella replied, looking into Cyra's burning gaze. "They speak of purity and power, but what they want is leverage." She paused. "They wanted Petra once." A shadow crossed her features. "Now they speak of another child. A symbol they can shape."

Rheanna sucked in a breath that skimmed the edge of a sob and smoothed it into silence. The lilies on the sill trembled. Cyra was frozen in place, her hands hovering uselessly at her sides. She shot Rheanna a look, knowing full well who their sister was talking about.

Aella leaned forward, palms braced on the table, words coming like blades thrown. "They're looking for *your* blood,

Cyra. They whisper about a girl. Not because of magic. They want a puppet with a crown. They want our mother's smile on a child who will speak their orders."

Cyra didn't move. Not an inch. "And where did you hear a story like that?" she asked calmly.

"In a cellar under a market where children are made brave with lies," Aella snapped. "In a bustling tavern. In a village where a man told me he would carry the 'chosen girl' on his shoulders into the capital after they had finished cleansing the filth." She bared her teeth. "I cut his hand off for pointing in the capital's direction."

Rheanna closed her eyes, hand going to her forehead.

Cyra set her hands flat on the table to keep them from shaking. "You heard this and you came home." It should not have sounded like a question.

"I came home," Aella said, the words both heavy and thin all at once, "because I have grown to love my family and will not lose anyone else. Known or not."

Kaelith's gaze slid to the door as if she knew something was coming, but Aella's mouth tightened, and she shifted her focus back on Cyra with that same measured look.

"There is more."

"More?" Rheanna asked, exasperated.

Kaelith's eyes, almost too bright under the lamplight, shifted toward the corridor again. A footstep. Light. Running. The door shuddered as it flung open.

"Mommy!"

Hollin tumbled in like a thrown pebble skittering across a lake. With her strawberry-blonde hair, an olive skirt wrinkled and crooked since she had dressed herself, and freckles a constellation across her face, she barreled toward Cyra but saw Aella and Kaelith and came to a startled stop.

Aella didn't breathe. Her brain tried to make sense of the little girl. The familiar green of her eyes, the tilt of her chin, the way her mouth was already prepping a hundred questions. She had a thousand words ready for Cyra that were edged and hot, but all of them burned away in the face of a little girl who looked like someone she had loved and lost. Petra.

Cyra moved faster than anyone, scooping Hollin to her hip and turning her halfway from the table as if her body could be a door. "Holli-bean," she managed, a smile too bright to be real. "You're supposed to be in bed."

"I was," Hollin said. "Ron told me a story about a rooster who thinks he is a dragon and then–" She squinted past Cyra's shoulder, curiosity eclipsing everything else. "Hi."

Aella had been carved hollow. It was a relief to feel her voice come from somewhere. "Hi."

Hollin blinked at her, then her head spun to Kaelith, and she just stared. Not rudely. Not bravely. More like a bird seeing the ocean for the first time. Kaelith, meanwhile, had gone still in a different way. Not predator still or prey still. Listening still. It was so quiet that Aella could hear the hiss of the candle wick and the faint pat of rain against the windows above. Kaelith took one step forward, slow enough that no one flinched, and then another, until she was close enough to see the pale fuzz of baby hair at Hollin's temples where Cyra had smoothed it.

"Don't," Cyra commanded, her hand tightening around Hollin's shoulder.

Kaelith did not touch Hollin. She simply froze as she observed the little girl. Her voice, when it finally came, was a lullaby. "Little one," she said, "you hum."

Hollin tilted her head. "Like a bee?"

"Like a river," Kaelith said, and something inside Aella's chest pulled taut. Her fingers dug crescent moons into her palm.

Kaelith's eyes lifted to Cyra, apology and inevitability mixed there. "She is... other," she whispered. "It is not why the Cleansers want her. But it is why something else does."

The room contracted. Cyra turned Hollin closer toward the door. "That's enough."

"What kind of other?" Aella asked. She wasn't aware she had stood until her chair scraped and Rheanna's head jerked to her. "Say it plainly."

Kaelith's throat moved. She looked at Aella, then back to Cyra. "Fae," she finally said. "She is fae."

Rheanna made a sound, small and breaking. Cyra's arms tightened around Hollin, whose brows furrowed in confusion, sensing the shift without understanding the reason.

Aella's world narrowed. Her scars buzzed. It wasn't anger. It was a kind of grief that cut crooked.

"Cyra," she said. "You have a child."

"Yes, I have a child," she replied hoarsely.

"And she is fa–" Aella stopped herself, jaw locking. She looked at Hollin and swallowed the word along with the fear. "She is *different*."

Hollin's eyes swung between them. "Aunt Rhe," she said, grasping for normalcy. "Did I do something wrong?"

"No, bean," Rheanna answered, moving to the side of Cyra and Hollin. She straightened the ribbon at Hollin's hairline with hands that did not shake until they were out of Hollin's sight.

Aella wanted to put her fist through a wall. She wished she could sit on the floor and laugh with her niece about roosters who thought they were dragons. She wished Cyra to be the sister who told her things before the world did.

"How long?" Aella asked, her words a rasp. "How long were you planning on hiding her?"

"For as long as it took for her to be safe," Cyra said, eyes on Hollin, voice steadying as if the confession had finally found a place to stand. "I kept her hidden at the Eye of the Storm Inn, but when she manifested powers, Ron brought her here. I was going to tell you when you got back. I had to hide her because people steal children like her, Aella. I could not risk the Cleansers finding her." Her chin tipped up. "Because I am her mother."

"And I am her aunt," Aella returned, pain sharpening on the last word. "I am your sister. You let me walk the length of this rotten kingdom thinking we were looking for answers while you were hiding the only thing that mattered."

Cyra flinched. Rheanna's eyes shone, but she said nothing to interrupt.

Kaelith drew a breath as if the air had edges. "I did not mean to speak it. It came to me the way the tide does, whether I want it or not."

Cyra's gaze cut to her. "How did you know?"

"She hums with it, and if I can hear it, others can as well. That is why I am here. Her name has been whispered among ancient things." She blinked. "Not just the Cleansers. This is older and it wants her."

Hollin thumbed the edge of Cyra's collarbone. "Who wants me?"

"No one," Cyra said, too fast. "No one will get you."

"Will they try?" Hollin pressed.

"Yes," Aella said before she could stop herself.

"Aella," Rheanna warned.

"I will not lie to her," Aella snapped. "She deserves the truth. All of it. Even the parts her mother decides we don't need to know," she seethed.

Cyra's eyes lifted from her daughter to her sister. "You think I did this to punish you?" Heat shivered in the air around her. "I hid her because the world is cruel. Our last name kills. The Oracle cursed Petra's cradle and our crowns. I hid her because of what could happen to her just like it happened to Petra."

The room staggered at the weight of Petra's name and then stilled. Hollin tucked herself more tightly into Cyra's arms as if she could press through skin to bone.

Aella rubbed a hand over her mouth. She had been angry at Cyra, at everyone, since she had learned to make fists. This was not the same kind of anger.

"You should have told me," she whispered. "I was hunting shadows and whispers while a child–*your* child–was being promised crowns by men who think queens are dolls."

Cyra closed her eyes. "I didn't know how to tell you, and by the time I felt I could... it was too late. I didn't know how to make you forgive me for surviving."

Aella's laugh cracked. "You think I want you dead?"

"I think you want me to have bled the same way you have," Cyra said. "And I didn't. I bled... differently." She pressed her mouth to Hollin's hair, eyes closed. "Every day I couldn't see her, my heart broke." She opened her eyes and they were fierce and wet.

The words stirred something in Aella. She looked at Hollin, at the way the child watched them with innocent curiosity and a note of fear.

"They will come for her," Kaelith repeated.

Rheanna finally spoke to Kaelith directly, voice low and calm. "What would you have us do?"

"Choose carefully who you allow in her circle. Keep her close, but not caged, not naïve. Teach her to fight and even run when necessary."

Cyra swallowed. "I have been."

"And I will," Aella added. She met Cyra's gaze and did not look away. "I will protect her. If I am Head of the Guard, I guard her first."

Cyra's jaw worked. She nodded once, grateful and terrified at the same time.

"Now we make a plan," Aella said, the relief of action clearing her voice.

Cyra shifted Hollin to the floor. "Go with Aunt Rhe and go to bed. To the stars."

"To the stars," she returned and allowed Rheanna to take her hand. At the door, she looked back at Aella. "Are you my aunt too?"

"Yes," she said roughly. "I am."

Hollin nodded, a grin gracing her face before she disappeared with Rheanna into the corridor, soft footfalls fading. Rain tapped the stone in rhythmic beats.

Aella dragged both her hands through her silver hair and let out a breath that had been lodged in her chest since she passed the brass gates. "I'm still angry."

Cyra did not apologize, but instead accepted it. "I know."

"I don't want to be," Aella added. "Not with you."

"Then be angry *beside* me. Not *at* me," Cyra said, sounding both old and young all at once.

CHAPTER 12

R HEANNA HAD GOTTEN HER niece to sleep after a warm cup of chocolate and a few stories from both herself and Ron. After, she found herself sitting upon her favorite balcony, unpinning her flowing black hair, only leaving one small braid to frame her face. This balcony was where she and Petra had spent countless hours when Cyra and Aella had been on their mission to the Black Lake. She leaned back on the cushioned bench and looked up at the night sky, a dark blue sheet with twinkling beads.

Meeting Aella and Kaelith kept replaying in her head. Their sister should not have found out about their niece the way she did, but Rheanna could understand why Cyra had kept her a secret. Aella had looked so betrayed with the knowledge of Hollin, but she still brought Kaelith to warn them about others wanting her. They had always known that there was an air of danger around the little girl due to simply being their blood and part fae, but this seemed even greater. It didn't help that now Hollin would be asking questions. She already started the second Rheanna hauled her out of the war room. She rubbed her temples gingerly just thinking about the discourse that would inevitably follow.

The faint patter of feet against stone alerted her to Ripley's entrance, which she knew he only made on purpose so he would not scare her. The light pressure he applied to her throat and chin to lift her face to look up at him brought a smile to her lips. He stood behind her, bent over. She took her own hand and placed it at the back of his neck, only bringing their faces closer. Ripley's eyes danced with hues of green and gold in the moonlight, his smirk causing her core to heat. She did not know what exactly they were, but she quite enjoyed this dance.

"What is such a fine Princess doing out here all alone?" he asked, voice gruff.

Rheanna scoffed. "Isn't it perfect that you are joining me then?"

"Am I?" His eyebrow quirked up.

Rheanna released her hold on his neck and patted the cushion next to her. He chuckled lightly, sitting next to her, close enough for them to brush each other's thighs.

"I heard Silver Death is back," he stated.

Sighing, she nodded her head. "Thankfully, but she brought news of so much trouble."

"It is better for you all to know than not. Is there anything I can help with?"

She looked at him, expecting him to have a suggestive look on his face, but instead, his expression was serious and open. She placed a delicate hand on his bicep and shook her head. "You have done plenty already for my family. Just continue to help us train, especially little Hollin."

He nodded, placing his own large hand over hers and squeezing. "She is a powerful little thing."

"It makes her a target."

"It does. We will protect her, though." He said the words with such conviction that she had no choice but to believe him. Her ocean eyes stared into his and her pulse began to quicken. The effect his mere presence had on her was evident on her face and between her thighs.

She moved closer to him, to the point where their faces were only inches away, and whispered, "Thank you."

He moved closer, his lips brushing hers. "My pleasure." Instead of kissing her lips, his mouth hesitantly made its way to her jawline, then slowly down her neck to her collarbone, stopping just above the top of the dress which cupped her breasts. Rheanna released a shaky sigh and she felt goosebumps rise across Ripley's flesh at the sound.

He pulled the fabric of her dress down with his teeth, kissing softly at the bud of flesh. Another breathy moan escaped her, filling the night. Her fingers wrapped into his auburn hair, torn between pulling him closer and pushing him away.

"Ripley," she gasped his name like a plea.

He stilled at once, his lips brushing her skin but not pressing further, waiting for her to decide. That patience, the restraint of it, only unraveled her further. She tilted her chin, offering him the smallest nod. The growl that rumbled in his chest vibrated against her as his mouth claimed hers at last, no longer tentative. His hand slid from her jaw to the curve of her waist, gripping firmly as they leaned into one another.

Her pulse hammered wildly. Every kiss was rougher than the last until she felt herself pressed back against the cushions, his weight braced above her. Her dress bunched at her thighs where his fingers traced the line of her leg, teasing higher, never quite reaching where she ached and burned the most.

Rheanna gasped against his lips as he neared her center, body aching. He pulled back just enough to look at her, lips swollen, eyes burning with something raw and unguarded.

"You're dangerous, Princess," he murmured, though his thumb stroked the sensitive skin of her inner thigh like he had no intention of stopping.

Her answering smile was wicked and pure all at once. "Then perhaps you should run."

"Not a chance."

He went back to exploring her body with his mouth, kisses trailing lower, leaving fire in their wake. Each brush of his lips made Rheanna's breath hitch. When he eased down her stomach, she let out a nervous laugh.

"Ripley..." she whispered again, her voice trembling but not from fear.

He glanced up at her then, hazel eyes gleaming, a silent question in his expression. When she didn't push him away, when instead her hips lifted ever so slightly toward him, his smile curved.

"You even taste of danger," he murmured, kissing the inside of her thigh slowly as though savoring every second before daring to go deeper.

Her laughter turned into a breathless sigh as his mouth finally found her core, his pace unhurried, almost teasing. She covered her mouth with the back of her hand, stifling the sounds that wanted to escape, her other hand clutching at the cushions beneath her. The world tilted, narrowed down to the soft press of his lips, the coaxing rhythm of his tongue, the unbearable heat building inside her. He seemed delighted in the way she writhed, her legs trembling around his shoulders.

Pulling back just enough to catch her gaze again, his smirk was boyish and smug. "Princess, you're shaking."

"Shut up," she managed, breathless, her cheeks flushed deeper than the night sky above them.

He chuckled low, dipping his head again, drawing another gasp from her lips. This time, Rheanna didn't try to hide it. She let the sounds escape, soft and unrestrained, carried off into the night and to the stars.

When she finally stilled, her chest rising and falling in uneven waves, Ripley returned to her side, gathering her against him as though she was fragile. Her fingers brushed his jaw, tracing the light stubble there, and she laughed softly, still dazed.

"You're impossible," she whispered.

"So are you," he said, pressing his forehead to hers.

CHAPTER 13

THE FEELING OF A little finger digging into her shoulder woke Cyra up before the sun could. It rose in the windows, casting a pink haze across the orange and gold bedroom. She rolled over, placing a pillow over her face and groaning, turning away from her daughter.

"Mommy! Wake up now!" Hollin demanded.

When Cyra didn't answer, the girl began to jump up and down on the bed until she fell, kneeing Cyra in the side.

"Hollin! Goddess damned!" she cursed.

Hollin fell backward on the bed, a giggle escaping her as her mother shot out of bed.

"You are a demon!" Cyra cried and began to tickle the little girl. She squealed, attempting to escape her mother's tickling wrath to no avail. By the time they were finished in their war, they were both gasping for air and heaving, big smiles on their faces.

"Mommy! I want to see my other aunt, Aunt Aella," Hollin whined.

"Okay, okay," Cyra agreed. "Just let me get out of bed for goddess sake."

Hollin bounced around happily as Cyra readied herself and then the little girl. Once they were ready, they made their way to Aella's rooms just down the hall. After their reunion last night, they had decided Kaelith would stay on the couch in her room until they truly knew where her intentions lay. Cyra had a strange inclination to trust the woman, but she could never be too safe when Hollin was involved.

With only one knock, the door was already opening to reveal an up and ready Aella, a stern look on her face until she noticed Hollin.

"Oh, good morning," she said.

"Hi, Aunt Aella! I want to spend the day with you. Also Mommy is going to..." Hollin paused and looked both ways before whispering, "teach me about fae."

Aella raised her eyebrows and looked at Cyra. "Is that right?"

Cyra shrugged her shoulders. "She needs to know and she won't stop asking."

Aella smiled. "My kind of girl."

The three of them started walking toward their private training arena, waving goodbye to a still-sleeping Kaelith before leaving. They were almost there when Hollin could no longer keep her questions in.

"Where did you get that boo-boo on your face?"

The assassin sighed and Cyra went to scold Hollin for asking such a question, but Aella was already answering. "A bad man did this to me." She brushed her fingers along the scars, as if she was reliving the memory, and then shook her head.

"Why?" Hollin asked, head tilting even as they walked.

"Bad men do not always need a reason. Sometimes they just hurt people," Aella shrugged.

Hollin took a moment to consider and Cyra wondered what was going through her tiny brain. The girl may have been young, but she picked up on so much beyond her years. It made Cyra want to preserve her innocence and childhood even more. She hoped the cost of this crown would not be Hollin's cross to bear. She vowed she would do everything in her power to keep it from doing so.

"I will beat bad men up. With you and Mommy and Aunt Rhe," Hollin said defiantly, chin up in the air as they walked into the arena.

Cyra laughed, terrified that one day she might have to, but also proud of the tiny fierce thing she had created.

Aella patted Hollin's head. "We will have you a warrior in no time."

Hollin beamed and began to spin as she made her way to the center of the arena. "Just wait until you see my magic!" She squealed and clapped her hands, small white flowers erupting from them and floating to the ground.

Aella froze and Cyra could read every motion that flitted across her face. Shock, anger, sadness, grief. And then a small half-smile graced her lips.

"Another thing I should have told you," Cyra said.

Aella shook her head in response and muttered, "I see Petra in her. I should have known." Her eyes began to tear and Cyra placed a hand on her forearm, offering quiet comfort.

Hollin looked between them, confusion clear on her face, but instead of asking questions, she spun again and vines sped up from the cracks, twisting around her. That was Hollin, always bringing happiness and joy wherever she went. The vines coiled in playful spirals as they brushed against her arms. She shrieked in delight, twirling faster, until they loosened and fell away in a rain of green leaves.

"See? I'm strong!" she cried, chest puffed out.

Cyra grinned, though her heart clenched. Every new flicker of Hollin's power reminded her that no matter how carefully she tried to hide her daughter from the world, it was impossible. The world would still find a way to demand something of her.

Aella crouched low so she was eye to eye with the five-year-old. "Yes, very strong."

"Will you teach me how to fight, Aunt Aella?" Hollin asked eagerly. "So I can be strong like you?"

Aella blinked several times, her violet eyes flicking from Hollin to Cyra, asking for permission.

"Not too much," Cyra warned. "I still want her to be a child."

"Well, sis, even children need to know how to defend themselves," Aella said. "But... we'll start small."

Hollin clapped, bouncing on her toes. "Yay! Teach me!"

"First lesson," Aella said as she pulled one of her daggers out of its home at her thigh and flipped it easily in her palm. The girl's eyes widened, but Aella only held it out flat, simply showing her the weapons. "Respect your weapon and never play with it or use it lightly. Never forget what it can do."

Hollin nodded solemnly as though she was swearing a sacred promise.

"Good girl," Aella said, patting Hollin on the head.

The little girl plopped onto the floor of the arena then, legs crossed, her curls bouncing as she leaned back on her hands. "Okay. Now, I want to know about the fae."

Aella's brows shut up and Cyra sighed, already bracing herself. She knew this was coming ever since their conversation two days ago. Her daughter deserved to know where she came from; she had just hoped that she could delay this conversation for at least a few years longer.

"What do you want to know?" Cyra asked carefully.

"Everything." Hollin tapped her finger on her chin for a moment, then asked a series of questions. "What are they? Are they like us? And why am I like them?"

Aella shifted, looking between niece and sister, silent but curious since she did not truly know all of the answers either. Cyra knew this part was her job to teach Hollin and hers alone.

"The fae look like us, but also don't," Cyra began as she crouched to sit beside her daughter. "They are more beautiful, older, and stronger. Some say they're closer to the goddesses than they are humans. They have magic bound into their blood, just like you."

Hollin's emerald eyes sparkled with wonder. Cyra brushed a stray curl from her daughter's face, tucking it behind a pointed ear, covered by a strip of fabric.

"Do they look like me?" Hollin tilted her head.

"Some do," Cyra admitted. "Their eyes are bright and they have pointed ears just like you. They're beautiful in ways that can be dangerous. And not everyone trusts them. Not everyone loves them the way we love you."

"Why not?"

"Because people fear what they do not understand," Aella cut in. "And the fae... were powerful, but when magic disappeared from Linnosa, so did they."

Hollin's lips parted, confusion knitting her brow. "But I am here."

Cyra pulled her into her lap and pressed her lips to the crown of her head. "Yes, you are. But because of this mistrust, we keep your magic and heritage quiet to protect you, bean. Not because it is wrong, but because you are precious. Do you understand?"

The little girl chewed her lip, clearly mulling over far more than her five years should hold. "I'll keep it secret for now. But when will I get to meet other fae?"

For the first time, Cyra couldn't find an answer. She glanced at Aella, who only shook her head, not knowing either.

"Someday. But until then, you have us and you now have the truth. Your father was fae and part of him lives in you."

Hollin touched her chest, right above her heart, as though she could feel the truth thrumming there already. Cyra lifted her own hand, placing it over her daughter's. It was scary placing this weight on Hollin's shoulders. She prayed she would not have to carry any more secrets.

Chapter 14

Seeing her family as one again lifted Rheanna's spirits tremendously. Aella being back not only made her feel safer, but it also reunited her family and brought a sort of peace to her. Rheanna watched as Cyra and Aella sparred. This time, Aella agreed to start using her powers, but only on a small scale, like a brush of air to knock Cyra off her balance or push her back a little. Nothing that could do any real damage. Rheanna could see the slight twitch of her mouth every time she conjured her powers, the anxiety that vibrated through her for a moment before. They had all agreed it was pertinent for them to all master their magic, even Hollin, though the young girl had been sent away to study with Ron while the sisters caught up and trained.

"No fair," Cyra grunted just as Aella used an air bubble to encapsulate and put out a tiny ball of fire she launched.

Aella smirked. "Very fair. You just aren't used to my magic."

Cyra huffed and sent a shot of flames at her younger sister, which Aella blew air at. They all froze in shock as the flames grew higher, feeding off the oxygen and coming back towards Cyra. She closed her fist, the fire disappearing entirely.

Rheanna clapped her hands. "Well, that was a neat trick."

"We know to be careful with our powers combining now," Cyra said, laughing dryly.

"I'm going to say that's enough for today." Aella's arms crossed over her chest, eyebrows drawn together, still staring at the space where the magic connected.

"You shouldn't be afraid." The sound of the unfamiliar voice made Rheanna jump. All three sisters turned to the source of the voice, tension coiling in their bodies. Kaelith, in all her beauty, stepped onto the raised platform of the arena. Rheanna could not help but stare at her. The contrast between her dark skin and bright blue eyes was so different that she almost felt otherworldly. She wore a simple black outfit, pants and a shirt, probably Aella's that looked so out of place on her that Rheanna almost laughed.

"I'm not afraid," Aella defended, eyes narrowing.

"Could have fooled me," Rheanna muttered, which turned Aella's narrowed gaze onto her.

Cyra stepped in, eyes rolling. "No arguing. We are going to have Aella confident in her powers in no time."

Kaelith smiled, showing a perfect row of white teeth, as if she could not get any more stunning. Rheanna watched how the woman stared at Aella, waiting for her every move. She could already see something building there, which was good. She deserved someone to love her.

"I would like to aid you," Kaelith stated. She looked each sister in the eye before continuing. "I have many skills that may be useful. I have this knowing sense."

"I hate to admit it, but she does," Aella said, though her eyes were still narrowed.

Rheanna could see Cyra's contemplation, her indecision, just as she felt her own. There was too much at stake to just blindly trust anyone.

Kaelith must have seen it on their faces because she said, "The ocean whispers the secrets of the world. The prophecy, the child, the truth. The other queen in our midst can help with the answers you seek."

With those words, she turned, the trinkets and hoops in her braids clinking. She left them with her words and their thoughts.

"Does she mean Queen Elspeth?" asked Rheanna, her blue eyes widening. Could the queen help them with the prophecy? With protecting themselves and Hollin?

"Perhaps. We don't know what her powers are. Nobody does," Aella added.

"You should ask Atlas," Rheanna suggested.

Cyra shook her head. "I won't dig into Elspeth through Atlas. I will just speak to her, queen to queen."

Rheanna shrugged her shoulders. The thought of going to Elspeth directly terrified her, but she supposed that was why Cyra was queen. She could and would do the hard things.

Night was falling on Linnosa when Rheanna decided to make her way to Aella's chambers. She balanced the stack of folded dresses in her arms as she made her way down the hall. Earlier, she had noticed that Kaelith was swimming in Aella's clothes.

She figured that she and Kaelith had similar figures and that her style better suited the stunning woman.

When she knocked, the door opened slowly to reveal Kaelith, barefoot and in nothing but a large blouse.

"I thought you might be more comfortable in these," Rheanna said, her smile gentle as she held out the bundle. "There are even a few nightgowns in there. If you need anything else, let me know."

Kaelith's cerulean eyes flicked with surprise before softening. She reached out carefully, folding the soft fabrics into her own grasp. "You are kind," she murmured.

Rheanna's lips quirked. "It's not kindness, just comfort. Everyone deserves to feel comfortable, and if you are staying in our castle, it is our responsibility."

Studying her, Kaelith tilted her head, but before she could say anything, Aella flew past them and into the rooms. The air around her was sharp and stifling.

"She's alive," Aella spat, voice raw in fury. "She's still alive."

Rheanna's dark eyebrows pulled together until her face registered with recognition. "Aella–"

"Don't you dare. I am tired of you and Cyra leaving me out. Natalie is breathing and within these walls at that, and no one thought to tell me?"

Kaelith looked between the two sisters, eyes assessing, clutching the clothes to her chest, wary but silent. Rheanna paced the floor, her anxiety climbing.

"So much happened while you were gone. We needed her. We didn't have you," Rheanna struggled to explain, her voice wavering.

Aella's laugh was sharp and bitter. She turned on Rheanna fully, anger radiating from every tense line of her body. "Petra is dead. Natalie may not have killed her, but she might as well have killed her! How many more secrets are there?"

Rheanna stepped closer, lifting her chin even though her heart threatened to give out. "We weren't trying to deceive you, Aella. We were only trying to survive without you and Petra."

The words felt like a confession of weakness. Silence hung heavy between them, broken only by the faint rustle of fabric as Kaelith shifted her grip.

When Aella did not respond, Rheanna's throat ached, words clawing to get out. "You're my sister. There will never be a time I don't choose you."

Aella stared at her, breathing hard, her jaw tight. "Get out."

"Aella–"

"Go. I need space right now."

Rheanna spun out of the room, cheeks red and eyes puffy with tears. Her vision was blurry and she smacked clean into the familiar warmth of Ripley. He said nothing. He simply ran his hand through her hair and hugged her close to his body. His embrace was a solid anchor against the storm of her sister's rejection, his scent and warmth grounding her as her world tilted off its axis. She buried her face in his chest as the weight of it all—the secrets, the fear for Hollin's safety, and Aella's cutting words—undid her.

CHAPTER 15

THE QUIET OF THE night air brushed away the stress of the day as Cyra stepped into the royal garden. The air carried a scent of sweetness from the late blooms that brought a sense of peace and reminiscing to Cyra. She hoped that wherever her baby sister was, she had a garden even larger and more beautiful than the one she had created here. The leaves rustled along the hem of her nightgown as she stepped onto the lantern-lit cobblestone pathway. Shadows danced at her feet, flickering with each step.

Beneath a willow, Elspeth sat with a half-circle of candles flickering at her feet. Her hands were folded loosely in her lap, as if the world beyond the walls could not touch her. Cyra slowed her steps so as not to frighten the witch-queen before easing down onto the stone bench beside her. The night was filled with the hum of crickets and the occasional toad, the garden alive with its own quiet chorus.

"Good evening, Cyra," Elspeth said, her eyes finally flickering open, gleaming faintly in the candlelight. "What brings you out here tonight?"

"The air feels lighter here than it does in the hall," Cyra responded, a heavy truth in her answer. Her voice was tired, carrying the fatigue of the day.

Elspeth's mouth curved faintly. "Stone holds grief. Gardens inspire growth. One weighs you down while the other lets you grow."

Cyra studied her for a long moment while they sat in silence, her golden eyes reflecting the candlelight. This queen and her had similarities that she had never considered before. Both had come from nothing before they were thrust upon a kingdom, expected to reign. It might be a bit different, but she had noticed the calluses in Elspeth's palms and in between her fingers the moment she had met her. It was the evidence left behind by a hard life. Cyra had to make a choice: to trust or not to trust. Kaelith's words echoed in her mind. *The other queen in our midst can help with the answers you seek.*

Cyra drew in a slow breath, steadying herself. "There was a prophecy given to my family when my youngest sister, Petra, was born. Four shall emerge, but only one will rise. And now Petra is gone." Her voice broke, but she kept going. "I don't know what it means, but I don't want to lose any more of my sisters."

"I do not know of prophecies." Elspeth's gaze was steady. "But I can share other truths that might help you in unraveling it."

Cyra was intrigued by Elspeth's words. "Then tell me. Tell me about yourself. Your powers," she asked eagerly.

"Before that, you must be ready to hear of the goddesses, as my power and yours alike only exist because of their blessings."

Cyra nodded and leaned forward on the bench.

"There are hundreds of goddesses," Elspeth began. "They are threads woven into the fabric of this world. Each with her own domain, but bound to one another to create an intricate tapestry. They are balance."

"And Linnosa has lost its connections with them," Cyra thought aloud.

"In a way, yes," Elspeth agreed. "When magic fell here, your people lost their place in that tapestry, in the balance. The threads were cut and the connection with the goddesses' went with them."

The words pressed against Cyra's chest like a stone. "And are your powers gifts from the goddesses?"

Elspeth's gaze did not waver. "Not exactly. Witches are descendants of the goddesses or, well, one goddess in particular. Seradelle, the weaver of worlds. She had children with mortal men centuries ago, before all the goddesses returned to the heavens, and we are their descendants. Her magic runs through our veins in the truest sense," Elspeth explained, running a finger along the veins at her wrist.

"So what exactly are your gifts?" asked Cyra. "I know Malcolm is a healer witch and Atlas is an earth witch."

"I am a witch of the veil. I walk between the worlds of life and death, somewhere in between. I can call upon spirits and converse with them."

Cyra's throat tightened. She thought of Petra again, how sudden it was and how they didn't get to say goodbye. "You speak with the dead?" she asked, gulping against the lump in her throat.

Elspeth nodded. "Yes, but it is not for the faint of heart. Death pulls on everyone; it is only a matter of time until you succumb."

Goosebumps erupted across Cyra's flesh at her words. The night air seemed to grow even colder and the branches of the willows above danced around like whispers.

"I hate to ask, but would you help us?" Despite her warning, Cyra knew they needed to find answers; otherwise, they could not protect each other and the rest of the kingdom.

Elspeth looked at her, gaze calm and critical. "I will help you, but the results may not be the ones you expect, and I must prepare all three of you for the journey before we make the walk."

"We will do whatever is required of us," Cyra reassured. She knew her sisters would not disagree.

Elspeth nodded her head and Cyra took it as her cue to leave. She walked back into the castle, the halls quiet with most of the occupants in bed. Hollin was already tucked into their bed and Cyra was eager to join her. When she turned the hall, she heard Aella's voice raised in anger and the sound of Rheanna's cries.

She tiptoed past a sobbing Rheanna, her head buried in Ripley's chest. He gave Cyra a subtle nod, urging her on and to Aella's door, before guiding the crying Rheanna down the hall.

Cyra did not knock or wait for an invitation to be let into the room; she simply walked in. Aella turned, face furious. "Not right now, Cyra."

"Yes, right now," she demanded. She turned to Kaelith, who was sitting awkwardly on the edge of the couch. "Could you give us a few moments, please?"

Kaelith nodded and swiftly made her way out of the room, closing the door gently behind her.

Aella sat angrily on her bed, arms crossed. "What? Here to feed me more lies? Like not tell me about the fact that Natalie is sitting alive and well in our dungeons?"

Cyra walked up to her sister. "I have never lied to you, and if I'm honest, I forgot about Natalie. We have bigger things to worry about than her."

"What could be more important than the reason our sister is dead? Than the person who betrayed me?"

"Ivan killed Petra!" Cyra snapped. "And I killed him. You are not the only one who has been betrayed!" Tears spilled down her cheeks. She had not spoken about killing him since it happened. She had killed a man who loved her, or so he claimed. The scar on her soul, regardless of what he had done, would mark her for the rest of her being.

Aella stared dumbfounded at her older sister. "What?" was all she could manage.

"Yes. While you ran away, we had to continue dealing with what happened and heal from Petra's death. You. Ran. Away. We could not."

She had not realized the bitterness she felt until this proclamation. Aella ran away from them when it got hard, while Cyra and Rheanna suffered together. None of them had it easy.

"I just don't understand why Natalie is still alive," Aella muttered, her eyes downcast and unable to meet her sister's.

"She almost wasn't. I tortured her, with my fire, for a crime she did not commit."

Aella's eyes snapped up to hers then, widening in disbelief. Her mouth opened and closed several times, but she was unable to find the words.

"We were only surviving here, Aella," Cyra sighed. She slumped onto the bed next to her sister, staring ahead at the roaring fire in the hearth.

"Fine, but," Aella hesitated, then continued. "Is there anything else you need to tell me?"

"Let's see." Cyra thought for a moment before rolling her eyes and looking at Aella. "Okay, so fae child, Natalie's alive, and Ivan is a murderer and now dead, so... I think that covers it all."

Aella's violet gaze pinned Cyra. "No more secrets."

"No more secrets," Cyra echoed, wrapping Aella in a hug that she didn't return, but also didn't fight. For Cyra, that was enough.

CHAPTER 16

T HE WAR ROOM PRESSED in like a coffin, its stone walls
heavy with secrets. Aella hated this room. Too many
voices. Too much cowardice. She would rather be outside, blade
in hand, solving things the way she knew best. She leaned back
in her chair, arms crossed tight and violet eyes cutting across
the oval table. She assessed each member of the council, now
knowing there was a traitor in their midst. One way or another,
the rat would be chased out.

Cyra sat at the head, a circlet gleaming upon her brow,
looking every bit the queen. Her posture was regal, but Aella
could see the tension in her jaw. Rheanna was poised beside
Cyra as if she could smooth the tension out of the room just by
keeping her spine straight and face calm. Aella did not bother
pretending. She wanted this done with, the traitor dragged out
by their throat.

"We gained information with Aella's return," Cyra said,
voice carrying across the chamber. "Someone within these walls
is feeding the Cleansers information."

Murmurs spread across the table. Norton slammed an aged
fist against the wood, causing the candles to flicker. "Goddess
help us. We are bleeding ourselves from the inside out."

Marine, hands clasped as if in prayer, shook her head. "If not for Hefguard, the North would already be lost. Their wards have held against the worst of the monsters. Entire villages have been spared due to their crystals and protection."

"And their healers," Sidney added, smoothing the front of her dark tunic. "Our own physicians were drowning. Hefguard sent reinforcements when we needed them most. Citizens see it, Majesty. They know who stands with them."

"Still, their aid cannot blind us." Levine leaned forward, voice sharp, and continued, "The monsters are not completely under control, and we hear whispers of the Oracle in the West."

The table went still. Even Cyra faltered, fingers tightening against the polished wood. Aella's own fingers drummed against her knife hilt. The Oracle had been forgotten in the chaos of everything else.

Bianca straightened in her chair, and for once, she wasn't smirking. "If that's true, then we must be ready. We cannot be divided if we intend to root out the traitor."

Aella laughed, sharp and humorless. "Oh, does the little viper want to switch sides now? A bit suspicious, don't you think? You spat venom at my sisters and I the last time I saw you."

Bianca's cheeks flushed, but she didn't look away. "I have already chosen my side." Her gaze flicked to Cyra, not in challenge, but out of respect.

"Interesting that you say that now that there is proof of a traitor." Aella's eyes cut daggers into Bianca, her tone dripping with accusation.

Bianca's face grew red, embarrassment clear across her features. Before she could say anything, Cyra's voice cut in, sharp and warning. "Aella."

Aella ignored her. Better her sister give her a glare than risk being charmed by a snake.

Talmadge cleared his throat, no doubt about to say some ignorant comment, when Norton stopped him with his own words. "The girl isn't wrong. Division will finish us faster than the monsters."

"Division is already here," Aella snapped. "There is a traitor sitting at this very table and you all would rather preach unity than drag them out."

The council stirred, voices rising and overlapping until Cyra slammed her palm flat against the table. Fire sparked faintly at her fingertips, threat and warning.

"Enough!" she commanded. "We will not tear each other apart before our enemies can. Sidney and Levine, please keep your ears open in the West. If there are any more whispers of the Oracle, let me know immediately. As for the traitor–" Her gaze swept the table. "They will reveal themselves, and when they do, there will be no mercy."

At least on that, she and her sister agreed. No mercy. The rest of the council felt Cyra's words as they settled over them like a noose. One by one, they rose from their seats, leaving the chamber in silence. No murmurs. No protests. Aella left with them, disappearing into the hall. Part of her wanted to go after Bianca, to corner her and get the truth out of her, but she had to play it smart and keep her cool. Instead, she searched for two girls who were always together.

Finally, she found the pair laughing and gossiping in the garden, a basket of ginger and cinnamon cookies in their laps. Laney's laugh carried through the night air, while Cora's mouth was stuffed to the brim, crumbs dusting her chin. They both froze when they saw Aella approaching, quickly hiding the cookies, though Cora's mouth was still full.

"Princess! You're back," she managed to get out around the cookie.

"You two are thick as thieves," Aella teased. Her tone softened. "Steal those cookies from the kitchen?"

The two shared a guilty look before Laney shrugged, standing up and curtsying. "How can we help you, Princess?"

Aella waved at her, dismissing the formality, and the girl sat back down. "I told you, call me Aella. No more of this princess or formal bullshit. I'm just here to catch up with you."

Cora swallowed the cookie. "Where did you go?"

The assassin shook her head. "That's not important, but I need to know if you have any information for me?"

"Well, we have been helping your sisters in your absence, providing Rheanna with information. We hope that is alright?" Laney said nervously.

Aella shook her head, crossing her arms. "Of course that is fine. I expect nothing less from my little informants. Have you both been safe?"

They looked at each other, and then both shook their heads. Cora said, "Yes, as safe as we can be, but we have been digging into who the spy could be in the council by following the lead of who hired Natalie in the kitchens." She lifted the cookies now as if they were proof of her words. "We haven't found anything concrete, though we think they are either from the West or North."

Aella began pacing in front of the girls, arms folded, with one of her hands on her chin. Her mind ticked through the names: Sidney, Levine, Norton, or Marine. Yet when she thought of a mole in the council, her mind automatically went to Talmadge or Bianca.

"Are you sure? Nothing about the East?" Aella inquired, thinking deeply, her mind turning over possibilities.

"No, not at all," Cora confirmed.

Huffing, Aella paused. "Well, keep an eye out for Bianca Solo and Jasper Talmadge regardless. If you notice anything, report it to me immediately."

"We will, and we will let you know if we find anything new out," Laney said.

Aella grinned. "I knew I could count on you girls."

With that, she turned on her heels, happy with how their conversation had gone. Again, she debated on what to do. Should she go confront Natalie, her ex lover that betrayed her and put her family in danger? She knew she couldn't control herself enough yet to see the woman. She might simply kill her on sight, so instead she returned to her rooms, deciding to see what Kaelith might be up to.

Kaelith had made herself comfortable in the castle in the last two days, but Aella thought she might spend some time with her to try and figure out her true intentions, especially if she was to be around her niece and sisters.

To Aella's dismay, Kaelith was not in her rooms. Instead, she found her in one of the smaller sitting rooms overlooking the gardens. Pale stone walls were softened by faded tapestries of hunting scenes, their colors worn from years of light from the floor to ceiling windows covering the wall. A low table sat at the center, stacked with scrolls and a half-empty goblet of wine. Two armchairs were angled toward the wide windows. Kaelith was in one of them, a book in her lap and the sunlight turning her obsidian skin into polished stone. The woman didn't look like she belonged in the castle at all, but instead in some legend carved into ancient temple walls. She was much too otherworldly to sit with her long legs tucked casually beneath her.

Kaelith looked up from the book as if she had been waiting. "You didn't look for me yesterday."

Aella leaned against the doorframe, crossing her arms. "Wasn't aware I had to."

The ethereal woman shut the book slowly. "You didn't have to, but I wanted you to."

Aella wondered if Kaelith was aware of what she was doing, attempting to start this cat-and-mouse game with her. Aella had given herself once to someone too willingly and she would not make that mistake again.

Still, despite herself, Aella stepped deeper into the room. "I've had bigger concerns than afternoon company."

"And yet here you are." Kaelith's lips curled and she gestured around the room. "Drawn to me."

The words made Aella's chest tighten, made her want to retreat, but she stood there in place for a reason she could not pinpoint.

Kaelith rose gracefully, closing the gap between them with a confidence that most wouldn't dare. "You carry your suspicion like a blade. Pointed at everyone, even yourself."

Aella bristled, heat flaring beneath her skin, but refused to let Kaelith see how much her words affected her. "And you carry riddles like you think they'll keep you alive."

Instead of giving up, Kaelith tilted her head, those impossible eyes catching the light. "I'd rather you try to understand me."

Aella froze. She managed a hard exhale through her nose before she responded. "You don't even know me."

"Then let me get to know you." Kaelith stepped even closer still until the air between them was as taut as a drawn bowstring.

Aella's hand twitched toward her dagger, though she knew she wouldn't use it. This mysterious, beautiful woman would be her undoing if she allowed it.

But she wouldn't.

CHAPTER 17

THE SUNLIGHT BEAT DOWN on Rheanna's dark head, warming her from the inside out as she trailed her fingers over the heads of lavender and foxglove as she walked. Her pale skirts brushed across the dew-damp grass, each step leading her deeper into memory. She came to the royal gardens when she missed Petra. Rheanna saw her in the vines that carpeted the cobblestone and climbed up the lanterns. She smelled her in the wildflowers and rose blooms. She felt her in the sun and heard her in the buzzing of the bees. Proof of Petra covered the gardens and Rheanna felt solace in it.

"Aunt Rhe!" Hollin's voice rang out like a silver bell.

She turned in time to see the child barreling toward hair, hair nearly glinting gold in the light, a stick clutched in her small hands and held out like a blade. "There you are, Aunt Rhe! You better watch out! The monster is on the loose!"

"Monster?" Rheanna crouched to Hollin's height. "Should I be afraid?"

Hollin's emerald eyes widened. "Very. She is big and scary and has teeth this long." She stretched her arms out dramatically.

Before Rheanna could answer, a familiar voice carried over the hedges. "What's all this noise about a monster?"

Aella appeared between two rows of climbing rows, arms crossed and silver hair shining sharp as steel. Hollin squealed with delight.

"You are the monster!" Hollin declared and pointed her stick-sword, immediately on the defensive.

Tipping her head back, Aella groaned. "Goddess above. I came here for some peace and quiet."

"Too late." Cyra slipped out from behind her young sister, a half-eaten apple in hand. "Hollin's already recruited you."

"I don't play games," Aella muttered.

"You kill people for coin," Cyra said with a grin. "This requires less effort."

Rheanna hid her laughter behind her palm, but Hollin had no patience. She marched right up to Aella and pressed the stick to her stomach. "If you don't play, you will make me very sad forever. Do you want that?"

Aella looked down at her niece, whose eyes were large and lip puckered out in a pout. The little girl's eyes were shimmering, fixed on her aunt with innocent intensity.

Aella sighed dramatically. "Fine. I'll be your monster, but don't expect me to go easy."

Shrieking in triumph, Hollin darted back to Rheanna's side. "Ride your sword! We have to fight together."

"I don't have a sword, but I do have my magic." Rheanna spread her hands, a glimmer of blue sparking at her fingertips. With a sweep of her wrist, water shimmered up from the nearby fountain, swirling into a thin stream that wrapped around her.

Aella crouched, hunching her shoulders and making claws out of her hands. She roared as she slowly stalked forward. "I smell tiny princesses who need to be eaten for supper."

She chased Rheanna and Hollin around the courtyard, Cyra laughing as she watched. Suddenly, Hollin ordered, "Charge!"

She rushed forward, Rheanna at her heels. Using her magic, Rheanna flicked the water into a spray that splashed across Aella's face.

Aella growled, staggering. "It burns!"

Hollin rushed in, smacking Aella in the thigh repeatedly with the stick. Rheanna added another jet of water, splashing her leathers until she toppled backward into the grass. Groaning, Aella said, "You got me! Tell my loved ones I died bravely."

The child climbed right onto her chest and crowned her with a circlet of daisies. "You're now a nice monster. You have to promise not to eat people anymore."

Aella lay flat, letting her niece straddle her. "Fine, but only if you pay me in cookies."

Hollin giggled, tipping sideways onto the grass. Cyra plopped down beside them, still eating her apple, and ruffled Hollin's hair. "Lucky for you, Hollin has a connection in the kitchen. Don't you?" she met her eyes and winked.

"Oh, yes. The cooks love me and told me they would give me all kinds of cookies whenever I wanted."

Rheanna sank down in the grass beside her sisters and niece. She couldn't remember the last time they had laughed like this. A weight she had not known she carried eased, if only for a heartbeat.

"Again!" Hollin jumped up and demanded. "The monster comes back to life!"

"You're relentless," Aella said as she rose, swiping grass off her leathers.

"You're slow," Hollin taunted.

That lit a spark in Aella's eyes, dangerous and playful. She lunged and Hollin screamed in delight and terror as she bolted toward the rose maze. Cyra chased after them both, her laughter trailing.

Rheanna stood as she watched her family vanish into sunlight and blossoms. She lifted her hand, calling the water from the fountain once more. It sparkled in the air like a satin ribbon. Hollin squealed when she returned, running back to Rheanna. She let the water fall harmlessly around them, the girl trying to catch the droplets on her tongue.

"Looks like you're under attack," a voice drawled.

She turned, pulse stumbling as she took in the man. Ripley leaned against the stone archway, his red hair mussed as if he had just come from training. His crooked smile and hazel eyes watched her far too closely.

Hollin spotted him and gasped in delight. "Sir Ripley! You're late. The monster is already awake." She ran straight for him and tugged on his hand. "You have to be my knight."

Ripley let the little girl drag him and chuckled under his breath. "Seems like you already have one." His gaze flicked toward Rheanna.

Heat bloomed in her cheeks and she busied herself with weaving water into her hands. The droplets shimmered like jewels, giving her something to focus on besides his lingering gaze. "The kingdom requires more than one knight."

Ripley grinned and picked up a stick from the ground nearby, saluting Hollin. "Then I shall fight by your side, Lady Hollin."

The child pointed her sword at him and began chasing after him.

"I thought I was your knight!" he pleaded, feigning betrayal.

Hollin ignored him, swiping her stick against his leg. Rheanna arched her water across them, sending droplets falling all over them like tiny gems. Ripley swiped dramatically at the air, then turned toward the girl. His stick clashed against hers.

"Help me!" he called as he tumbled over, falling into the grass.

Hollin twirled toward Rheanna. "You have to drown him fast!"

Rheanna raised a brow, but her lips betrayed her with a smile. She lifted her hand and water appeared above Ripley's head like a glistening serpent before it came raining down on him.

Cyra whooped from where she and Aella sat on a bench. "Looks like Ripley's finally been bested."

"I admit defeat. Lady Hollin, you have saved your realm." He gave an exaggerated bow.

And then Ripley's hand brushed Rheanna's as he passed the stick back to Hollin. She glanced up, catching the flicker of mischief in his eyes. He leaned in close.

"Come with me."

Rheanna let him lead her toward the edge of the garden, the laughter of her family softening behind her. They slipped beneath a willow tree, its long branches shielding them like a veil.

The hush beneath the willow was intimate, secretive. Sunlight filtered through the curtain leaves in fractured beams, painting Ripley's face in shifting patterns of light and shadow.

"It was nice to see you smile like that," he said softly.

Her throat tightened. She wanted to answer, but the words stuck. Ripley didn't press. He reached out, his fingers grazing her temple, as he tucked a loose, wet strand of hair behind her ear.

He leaned in. "I missed you," he whispered against the shell of her ear.

Before she could say anything, he kissed her, gentle at first, then firmer. The world around them hushed, the only sound the distant hoots of Hollin's laughter threading through the garden. It was a reminder of innocence, even as Rheanna's heart stumbled into dangerous territory.

CHAPTER 18

After her talk with Elspeth, Cyra felt a sort of lightness, knowing a witch with her powers would be aiding them with the prophecy as well as becoming her mother-in-law. But with the wedding approaching, she wanted to foster that relationship, so she planned an intimate lunch with just herself and Elspeth in her chambers. Hollin was off with Atlas fishing, as that was her new favorite thing to do, which left Cyra able to get ready alone. The olive green gown she slipped on slid across her skin like a velvet kiss as she moved to answer the sudden knock at the door. The open door revealed Elspeth, her hair braided and woven into a low bun. She bowed her head in greeting.

Cyra did the same, then gestured for her to come inside. "Welcome."

A linen cloth was draped across the low table, the fabric wrinkling in lazy folds. Steam curled from a small porcelain teapot, carrying the faint scent of lavender and honey. Beside it sat delicate plates of food. Warm bread sliced into pieces, a shallow bowl of berry preserves glinting, and slices of pale cheese resting in a neat little fan. There were grapes, still clinging to their stems, and thin curls of apple sprinkled with cinnamon. A single dish of roasted chicken, fragrant with herbs, sat beneath a golden cover, its warmth humming through the metal.

Elspeth took a seat, and though Cyra was a queen, she poured the red wine into her golden goblet, taking the moment to acknowledge how they were equals and soon to be family. She had not wished for servants and extravagance today.

"This is very nice. Thank you for inviting me today," Elspeth said before taking a sip of her wine. "I was thinking we would all get together soon to begin preparing you all for the journey into the veil."

Cyra nodded, beginning to scoop a bit of food onto her plate. "While I appreciate your help with those matters, today I want this to be about getting to know each other and our family."

"I am eager to invite you and yours into our lives," the older queen said, also filling her own plate.

"Me too. And I know my daughter is very excited as well. She has not stopped talking about Malcolm since our dinner."

Elspeth released a polite chuckle. "He has that effect on people. Malcolm is the jester while Atlas is the soldier. I fear for them both."

Cyra tilted her head, understanding the feeling, but wanting to know more. "What do you mean?"

Sighing, Elspeth popped a grape into her mouth before responding. "Malcolm is always using humor and is nearly incapable of being serious, while Atlas is far too serious." Pausing, she looked at Cyra. "But, with you and your daughter, I have seen this change. Already, he seems softer. Now, I just need someone for my Malcolm."

Cyra had never thought Atlas too serious. She wondered what he was like in his own kingdom. She thought of her own transformation, how she had gone from a simple barmaid to now the Queen of Linnosa and then betrothed to the next in line for Hefguard. There was a real possibility that at some point, she and Atlas would rule both countries. How would that look? Where would they reside? Would they have to be separated? The questions pressed against her mind like heavy stones, but she swallowed them down with a swig of wine, tempering her anxiety and pushing it to the back of her mind. She had too much to worry about in the present to dwell on future issues.

"I'm pleased we are able to bring that side of him out. He is truly great with Hollin," Cyra said.

"Well, hopefully that means you two might have a few more then?" Elspeth framed it as a question, but Cyra heard the demand behind it. Hefguard needed heirs.

Cyra paused, weighing her answer as her thoughts once again drifted to the future she was just beginning to imagine. "I'll be honest, I never gave it much thought before Atlas, but I am not opposed to the idea."

Elspeth nodded. "I know my husband and I would be happy to have some grandkids, and of course, we will consider Hollin as our own as well."

Warmth filled Cyra at the sentiment. Tears began to prick her eyes as she thought about her own parents, how they would never have a relationship with Hollin. That Hollin would never get to know them. These thoughts quickly circled back to Petra. Her emerald eyes, open and unseeing. She swallowed a piece of chicken. It scraped the sides of her throat despite the moisture and glaze, the sudden lump in her throat making even the simple act of eating feel like a chore.

Elspeth must have noticed because she said then, "You will be our daughter as well. I know your parents' passing must have been difficult, and I am not saying we can replace them, but know that we are here for you." She reached out a pale hand, resting it lightly on top of Cyra's for a second.

The fire queen could not hold it in any longer as silent tears trailed down her golden, freckled cheeks. She went to wipe them away quickly and dipped her head, forcing out a laugh. "I'm sorry. I can be a tad emotional."

"Never apologize for crying. It is a strength to feel your emotions," Elspeth said calmly, chewing on a piece of meat.

Instead of responding, Cyra continued to let the tears trickle down her face as she ate, both queens content in the silence of each other's company.

CHAPTER 19

A ELLA FOLLOWED CLOSELY BEHIND Laney and Cora as they led her toward her sister's resting place. She had never been to River Solace before, but she was aware that was where Petra was sent off. While her sisters were mourning the youngest's death, Aella had hunted for vengeance, a shame she carried low in her gut. Her insides twisted as they ventured closer to the body of water, wildflowers and tall grasses bordering the uneven path. Laney and Cora remained silent, the usual chattiness smothered by the impact of this moment.

Aella thought about her conversation with Cyra a few days ago, where her older sister claimed she had run away. At that moment, she wanted to deny it. She did not allow herself to see the truth, which was that she was incapable of facing Petra's death, of allowing herself to truly mourn. Her memories of Petra training and laughing echoed through her mind. She deserved to live. Aella did not.

As they grew closer to the alcove, laughter reached them, the sound of pure and innocent joy. Two figures came into view, one small and one large, sitting at the river's edge on a bench made of a fallen tree, fishing poles in each of their hands. The skittering of pebbles underneath feet caused the two to turn, the man instinctively going to pull the little girl closer to him, but he loosened his grip when he saw Aella and her company.

"Aunt Aella!" Hollin yelped, her voice bright as sunlight, as she slid off the log and skipped toward their group. Atlas caught the young one's pole before it hit the ground, placing them both against a tree.

Aella froze for a fraction of a second before bending down and letting Hollin fall into her arms. Breathlessly, the child said, "We are fishing! Atlas taught me how. Will you all join us?"

Laney and Cora lingered behind, their eyes darting between Aella and Atlas.

Before Aella could get out an answer, Hollin was already out of her arms and standing in front of Laney and Cora. "Have you ever fished before?" she asked with a tilt of her head and earnest curiosity.

Both of the girls bowed deeply as Laney responded, "No, Princess. We have not."

Hollin grabbed each of the girls' hands in her little ones and began to pull them closer to the water. They looked over at Aella, amusement clear on their faces, but she just shook her head and joined them at the water's edge, her boots crunching softly against the pebbled bank.

Atlas smiled politely at the young women as Hollin declared, "Now, teach them!"

He raised his eyebrows, a faint smile tugging at his lips. "I have taught you everything I know. It is time you teach someone!"

The little girl pushed out her lower lip, but then took her fishing pole from where it leaned against the tree.

"Okay," she said, her voice solemn, as if she were about to impart sacred wisdom.

Her face was serious as she stood in front of the women. She looked at each one of them, assessing their attention before continuing. "So, do this."

Instead of describing what she did, Hollin demonstrated her technique. Holding the rod with both hands, she bent her elbow, the sharp hook narrowly missing the top of her strawberry blonde hair, causing Aella to flinch. Without pause, the little girl threw her arms straight, flicking the fishing line through the air and landing in the glistening water of the river.

She smiled triumphantly, her emerald eyes shining like morning grass in the afternoon sun. Aella's heart clenched, seeing Petra yet again in the child, the effect even more devastating in this place. She knew that letting Hollin in would be another weakness gained, but as she looked into those eyes, she knew she had no choice.

A single tear escaped down Aella's cheek, but she quickly wiped it away. Hollin had handed the rod to Laney, who was now attempting to copy the maneuvers. She flicked the rod too hard, her grip slipping, and the pole spun wildly before landing in the water a few feet away.

Hollin's hands balled at her waist, an eyebrow arching. "You scared all the fish!"

Laney waved apologetically toward the water and said, "I'm sorry, fish."

At that, Cora bent over in laughter, her brunette hair falling into her face as she clutched her stomach. Aella rolled her eyes. "With all that racket, I will be shocked if they ever come back."

The laughing maid straightened herself as her redheaded friend hit her on the back. Laney knelt down to eye level with Hollin, taking each of her small hands in hers. "I am very sorry we scared away your fish."

"You should be!" the child said seriously before giggling and spinning away from Laney. Small wildflowers split from beneath the pebbles, which themselves began to buzz with Hollin's magic.

"She's amazing," whispered Cora as she watched in awe.

Though Aella did not say anything, she had to agree. The child's natural affinity for magic was something no one could deny. The fact that she resembled Petra so much only added to the love that soared in Aella's cold heart. She thought that perhaps mourning her little sister did not have to be such a sad or scary thing. Perhaps seeing the beauty in the world, even in dark times, could be powerful. Petra was good at that, at finding light even in the dark.

Atlas lifted the spinning Hollin off the ground; she naturally held on to him, the bond they had created already evident. Aella watched, craving that same closeness, wishing her niece would reach for her with the same trust.

"I guess that will be it for fishing today," he announced, sending a dazzling smile toward the women.

He handed Hollin to Aella while he began to pack up their rods and attach everything to his black mare. Aella and Hollin walked to the river while Laney and Cora stayed behind to aid Atlas, giving Aella privacy with Hollin. The niece and aunt stood staring at each other for a few moments, green meeting silver. Gingerly, Hollin raised a small palm, tracing the scars along

Aella's face. She almost flinched at the touch, but froze, letting the child feel the broken skin.

"Does it hurt?" Hollin asked, worry flickering in her young eyes.

Aella shook her head. "Not anymore. Now, they remind me to be strong."

"Will I have to be hurt to be strong?"

Again, Aella shook her head, but this time vigorously. "No one will ever hurt you. You are already strong, little one. The Earth answers your call, and you have your Aunt Petra protecting you."

Tilting her head, she asked, "Can you tell me about Aunt Petra? Mommy and Aunt Rhe cry too much."

Aella's heart skipped a beat at how such a young child could acknowledge her sisters' grief when she herself pushed it away. Her eyelids fluttered, recalling her strong, beautiful, and kind sister. How could she explain all of Petra in a way that justified who she was?

"Petra was..." Aella paused for a moment, walking absentmindedly back to the water, adjusting Hollin in her arms. "She was like you. Beautiful and stubborn. She had eyes like emeralds sparkling in the sun and freckles that ran across her nose. Speaking about her nose, it was always in a book, craving knowledge and far away lands."

When Aella looked down at Hollin, her eyes were large with wonder. "I wish I got to meet her."

Aella squeezed her tightly, her voice breaking with quiet honesty as she said, "So do I, little one. So do I."

Chapter 20

THE SOLAR SMELLED FAINTLY of sage and melted wax when Cyra stepped inside. The chamber stretched wide, its vaulted ceiling arched with carved beams that caught the lantern light in warm gold. Rich rugs of red and orange softened the stone floor, their woven patterns faded from years of footsteps. Heavy gold velvet curtains framed the tall window, a sliver of moonlight bleeding through the edges. The walls bore shelves of old tomes, scrolls, and tapestries embroidered with winding trees and sigils. The hearth burned low but steady, casting a ripple of shadows across the space. Candles clustered on gold-plated iron stands filled the air with honeyed smoke.

Aella was already there, leaning back in her chair with her boots kicked onto the low table. Rheanna sat opposite her, hands folded neatly in her lap with her posture as careful as ever. Cyra knew the way her sister's foot tapped was a betrayal of her nerves. Elspeth stood at the center, her presence commanding without effort. Atlas lingered near the hearth, his arms crossed and attention flicking between his mother and the sisters. His gaze landed on Cyra the moment she entered and though he didn't move toward her, she felt the weight of his presence.

"Sit," Elspeth said. "Tonight, we begin."

Cyra and Atlas obeyed, sliding onto a bench next to each other. His shoulder grazed hers, barely noticeable, but enough that warmth spread beneath her skin. She wanted to catch his hand, but instead tangled her fingers into the folds of her gown.

"That walk between life and death is not a thing you can rush into," Elspeth said. "It requires preparation. If you go unready, you will not return. Do you understand?" She looked at everyone around as she said that, her gaze lingering on each of them until the gravity of her words had fully settled in the quiet room.

Rheanna nodded at once. Aella only smirked and said nothing. Cyra forced herself to meet Elspeth's gaze and give a single, firm nod.

"Good," Elspeth continued. She reached into the folds of her robe and pulled out a vial of clear water, pouring it into a bowl on the table beside her. "Balance is the first lesson."

Aella leaned forward, resting her chin on her hand and snickering.

Elspeth only tilted her head. "I suppose you will be the one who struggles the most with this."

The assassin's smile thinned into a sharp line, but she did not argue.

"Rheanna. Come," Elspeth beckoned toward the bowl of water.

Rheanna rose gracefully, the hem of her gown brushing the edge of a patterned rug as she crossed the room.

"Still it," Elspeth instructed.

She drew in a breath and lifted her hand. The water obeyed her instantly, swirling into a small spiral before smoothing flat, but only a second later, a ripple shuddered across its surface. She bit her lip. She tried again, harder this time, forcing the water into submission. For a heartbeat, it stilled. Then it surged, slopping over the rim and spilling across the stone floor.

Her cheeks flushed. "I can't–"

"You can, but right now you are forcing it," Elspeth interrupted. "So it rebels. You must guide it, not command it. Try again."

Rheanna glanced over her shoulder at her sisters. Cyra met her gaze and offered her a nod and a small smile. This time, Rheanna exhaled slowly, lowering her shoulders before lifting her hand again. The water smoothed gradually. The ripples faded until the surface reflected her face without distortion. She held it.

"Well done," Elspeth said and Rheanna went back to her seat, sagging back into her chair. Relief and exhaustion mingled on her features.

The witch-queen turned her gaze to Aella. "Now you."

Aella gave an exaggerated sigh, but rose anyway. "What, you want me to stare into water too?"

Elspeth's expression remained unshaken. "No. Snuff this flame without shattering the wick." She gestured to a nearby candle perched in a wrought-iron holder.

"That's child's play." She lifted her hand, a sharp gesture, and the flame vanished in an instant, but so did the candle. It cracked in two, wax splattering across the table and dripping onto the rug.

Rheanna winced. Cyra pressed her lips together.

Elspeth arched a brow. "Mercy, Aella. Not violence."

"Mercy doesn't keep you alive."

"No," Elspeth agreed. "It keeps you human."

The words hung in the air, heavier than the smoke curling from the ruined candle. For a fraction of a second, something flickered across Aella's face, her mask of indifference slipping just enough to reveal something raw beneath. Fear, perhaps. Memory? But just as quickly as it had appeared, it disappeared, buried beneath the usual defiance.

Cyra noticed it, but it was gone before she could decipher it. Aella tried again, jaw clenched. This time, she drew her power with painstaking restraint. The flame wavered, sputtered, and then finally went out, leaving the wick and candle intact.

Her shoulders dropped, as though the task had required more effort than she cared to admit.

Aella exhaled sharply. "There. Happy?"

Elspeth nodded, her eyes on Cyra now. "And you. Fire can burn, but also provide warmth. Show me."

Cyra rose, aware of Atlas's gaze following her every moment. Her throat was dry, but she knew how to do this. She had done it countless times. She reached for her magic, that familiar heat sparking to life in her veins. The flame curled obediently to life in her palm, golden and bright and never burning her. Fire had always been hers to command, as natural as her breath. Still, she let the moment linger.

She thought of Hollin. Her daughter's laughter when she tucked her close by the hearth. The way her child burrowed into her warmth on cold nights. The flame shifted as her thoughts softened, glowing steady, its light spilling across the table like a hearth in the death of winter.

Elspeth's eyes glimmered. "Your flame is not only a weapon. It is a shield and a hearth."

Cyra's knees felt weak as she returned to her seat. Atlas leaned toward her, voice low enough only she could hear. "That was beautiful."

Her flame had nothing to do with the heat that rose to her cheeks. The fire snapped in the hearth, shadows crawling across the walls.

"Two moons from now, when the in-between is at its strongest, we will walk," Elspeth declared. "Until then, be kind to one another. Practice holding balance in your life."

Cyra swallowed hard, her mind already racing. This could be the answer they had been looking for all along.

CHAPTER 21

Aella's boot struck hard against the stones, each step a promise. She told herself she was only here for closure. Nothing more. The stench of mildew and old blood clung to the dungeons, a heavy, metallic rot that seemed to seep into her very pores, but she had been around much worse.

The corridor narrowed as she descended, the light from the lamp flickering against rusted bars and chains that dangled like broken bones.

Natalie sat huddled against the back wall of the cell, knees to her chest, her black hair a tangled curtain across her face. When she looked up, her almond eyes were rimmed red, raw from hours of silent weeping, but they still held a softness that made Aella's stomach twist. She hated herself for noticing.

"You," Aella said, forcing her voice to be flat. Her hand gripped the bars so tightly that her knuckles went white and the iron groaned under her strength. "You were one of them."

Natalie rushed forward, wrapping her hands around the bars so that their fingers nearly touched. "Aella, please–"

"Don't." The word stung like a blade. "Do not say my name. You lost the right to speak it a long time ago."

Natalie flinched as if she'd been struck, but didn't let go of the bars. "I never wanted Petra to die. I never wanted any of this. I–"

Aella leaned closer, her eyes narrowing into predatory slits. "Don't you dare say her name either. You were lying to us. To *me*."

Natalie's lips trembled, a single tear falling, trailing down the grime on her cheek. "I wasn't lying about how I felt for you. I love you. I always did. Even when I was doing what I was told–"

"Do you hear yourself? Doing as you were told as in getting close to me, kissing me, fucking me." Aella laughed, low and bitter.

Natalie's tears spilled freely now, dripping down her chin. "It wasn't like that. You don't understand. My cousin... they we–"

"Stop." Aella's voice dropped to a dangerous whisper. "Don't make excuses. We all have choices. You chose them."

"I chose you, every moment I could. I thought I could protect you and your sisters," Natalie cried, her voice cracking.

"You failed." Aella's chest heaved with the words. She wanted to carve them into Natalie's skin so she would never forget. "Because Petra is dead, and no matter how many tears you shed, no matter how much you beg for forgiveness, you cannot bring her back."

Natalie's shoulder shook as her sobs echoed off the walls. "I swear to you, I never wanted this. If I could trade my life for hers, I would."

Aella's throat ached. Goddess, she hated this. She hated the part of her that wanted to believe her former lover, the part that wanted to reach out and pull her close. She wished she could reach through the bars and console her, but she could not. That weakness burned through her like acid. She slammed her fist against the iron instead, rattling the bars between them with a deafening clang. Natalie flinched but didn't move back.

"You don't get to beg me to understand. You shattered my trust," Aella hissed. Her voice broke despite herself.

Natalie's gaze fell to the floor and she whispered, "What about us?"

For a moment, Aella saw it all again. The flour fights in the kitchens, the warmth of Natalie's skin against hers, the way she had felt safe for the first time in years. This would cut deeper than any blade.

She swallowed it all down, forcing her face to stone. "There is no us." Aella stepped back from the bars, chest hollow and hands shaking with fury. "I will never love you again," she said, though the words tasted like ash on her tongue.

Then she turned, boots striking hard against the stones as she left Natalie behind.

When Aella returned to her rooms, she slammed the door behind her. The sound cracked down the corridor and into her chest like a physical blow. Natalie's voice followed her like a ghost. *What about us?* She wanted to turn her mind off and escape it. She wanted to burn the memory out of her brain.

Kaelith sat curled on the divan by the window, her dress pulled up where her legs bent beneath her, exposing the smooth curve of her thigh. She didn't look startled at Aella's arrival; instead, she studied her with eyes that saw too much.

"You're shaking," Kaelith said, her voice low.

"Shut up," Aella snapped, kicking off her boots, sending them skittering across the floor. She paced the length of the room. Her pulse hammered so hard she could taste blood in her mouth.

"You need to release that energy," Kaelith murmured, rising from her perch with an otherworldly grace.

Aella spun, fury sharpening. "You know nothing about me. Don't pretend you can read my mind."

Kaelith came closer, every step deliberate as if testing her. She stopped just short of touching her, so near that Aella could feel the heat of her skin and smell the faint trace of salt and jasmine.

"I know what it feels like when your own body is a cage. I know the itch of wanting to crawl out of your own skin," she said softly.

Aella's fists clenched. She fought the urge to shove her away, to spit and snarl in her face. Kaelith's eyes held her in place, seeing right through the armor she wore, to the raw mess underneath that she kept hidden from the world.

"You want to feel something else," Kaelith whispered, her breath warm against Aella's cheek. "Even if it's only for a moment."

Aella tipped her head back, closing her eyes. Goddess help her, she hated how true it was. Kaelith's knuckles brushed along her jaw and Aella snapped.

She grabbed her hard, dragging her mouth to hers with a hunger that shocked even her. It wasn't a kiss of passion; it was a collision. Kaelith gasped against her lips, but didn't pull away. She answered, pressing it in, her hunger just as deep. They stumbled back into the divan, Aella straddling her. Her hands fisted Kaelith's breasts, nipping through the sheer fabric of her nightgown. She ripped at the gown, tearing it violently and exposing the other woman's upper body. Aella licked and kissed her nipples, heat building in her core at the sounds of Kaelith's breathy moans.

Kaelith's hands pulled at her pants, and Aella helped her get them off with frantic movements. She coaxed her core, licking her finger, putting it inside Aella, then added another. Aella's silver head toppled back as she rode Kaelith's hand, her spine arching like a bow.

Suddenly, the hand was gone and Aella watched as Kaelith put those same fingers into her mouth, tasting her with a dark, hooded gaze. Aella knocked the hand out of her way, kissing her with new fervor. She pressed down, her whole body alight. Their hands roamed, exploring each other with a bruising effect. Everywhere Kaelith touched, Aella burned hotter, the feeling a welcome distraction from the hole in her heart. She hated how much she needed it.

There was no room for words. Only the scrape of teeth and pull of breath. It wasn't love, but it was raw and consuming. It was a release she had been clawing for, something to numb the wound Natalie had left behind.

CHAPTER 22

R HEANNA PAUSED IN THE doorway of the grand ballroom, letting the motion pull past her like a current. The air was thick with the scent of beeswax, expensive oils, and crushed herbs. Servants moved in swift, practiced lines as they prepared for the royal wedding, their arms threaded with folded silks the color of cream and gold. Ladders creaked as two boys climbed with garlands trailing down their backs, evergreen and ivy with wisteria hanging. The vines draped from one stone arch to the next, softening the harsh lines of the castle's walls, making the hall seem almost dreamlike.

The long tables had been pulled from storage and rubbed down to a deep, mirror-like brown shine, their surfaces reflecting the flicker of candlelight as though they held a second, hidden fire. A woman with a cloth walked the length of one, breathing on the gold to fog it and then buffing until each candlestick glistened like the sun, blindingly bright.

The high windows were open to the late afternoon, lace curtains shivering with every breath of the wind. Beyond them, the sky was a pale rose and silver, indicating evening's descent. Above, the banners of Linnosa and Hefguard unfurled along the rafters, the stitched crests catching light, the two kingdoms bound together in silk and ceremony.

The hum of voices rose and fell like waves, punctuated by the scrape of chairs and the clatter of silver trays. The ballroom seemed alive, breathing with anticipation.

"Princess Rheanna, would you look at this placement?" a young steward asked, breathless. He held a sketch of the ballroom, rectangles marked for tables and circles where the musicians would set up. "We thought to keep the musicians along the Western wall."

Rheanna stepped forward, her skirts whispering against the polished floor. She studied the sketch, her eyes flickering from the parchment to the hall itself.

"Shift them there," she said, tapping the eastern alcove where the ceiling dipped lower. "They won't fight the rafters there, and the sound will carry down the tables."

"Yes, Princess." He bowed so quickly that his hair flopped into his eyes.

She stepped closer to the long tables, her hands clasped neatly at her waist. The roses were set in gold vases, lilies draped soft white from the edges. Ivy curled like handwriting around every edge, and in the chandeliers above, mirrored disks turned and scattered light into bright fragments across the stone floor.

It was beautiful. It should have been enough to simply call it that.

Then she saw them.

White wildflowers, tucked among the gold and green, their stems still damp with soil.

The sight pierced her chest before she could brace against it. Petra's flowers. The stubborn little blooms she had always gathered with dirty hands, tucking them behind her ears or weaving them into uneven crowns. How often had Rheanna found her younger sister conjuring blooms of these exact flowers?

She felt for one fragile second as though Petra would come bounding into the hall, barefoot and laughing, scattering petals in her wake. The vision was so clear it made Rheanna's throat ache.

"Where did these come from?" she asked a florist arranging the nearest bouquet.

The woman turned around, startled, her apron streaked with green and brown from the sap and soil. Her brown eyes held both fatigue and quite pride as she straightened. "The steward asked for them, Princess. To honor the late Princess Petra."

Her chest tightened further, but she forced herself to nod. "They're perfect. Thank you." Her voice was softer than she intended.

The woman smiled faintly, relief loosening her face. "They look well with the gold."

She lingered by the bouquet, fingertips brushing one fragile petal as though it might dissolve beneath her touch. The hall around her seemed to fade, the bustle of servants and the clatter of trays dimming to a distant hum. For a heartbeat, it was only her and the flowers, a memory resurrected in white. She drew in a steady breath, forcing herself back into the present, back into the role expected of her. The wedding would go on, the garlands would hang, the candles would burn, but Petra's absence would always be stitched into the beauty, a shadow among the gold.

Rheanna turned away before her composure cracked. She needed quiet. Needed air that wasn't heavy with rosewater and beeswax and memory.

She slipped through a side passage, the noise of the hall falling behind her like a door shutting on a storm. The corridor beyond was cool, lined with portraits of long since dead ancestors. Her footsteps echoed faintly on the faded rugs. The stone smelled of dust and history, carrying none of the sweetness of the hall. Here, with only her own breath for company, the thoughts she had tried to hold back came flooding.

Petra should have been here. Petra would have filled the hall with laughter, dragging servants into her chaos until they forgot their chores and indulged her. She would have insisted that the bouquets looked wrong until she could cram in another handful of wild stems. Better yet, she would have created her own floral arrangements, possibly with Hollin's help. She would have sat in the musicians' alcove, clapping along cheerfully off-beat, demanding a song for the occasion. The silence felt like a physical weight, a reminder that the most vibrant soul of Linnosa was no longer there to break it.

Rheanna pressed her hand against the wall as she walked, grounding herself in the chill of the stone.

Her thoughts shifted to Ivan. The memory of his betrayal was a wound that had not yet scabbed, still raw beneath her skin. She had once thought him kind and steady, someone who saw her for who she was and not only as Cyra's sister. That secret softness she had held for him felt like a knife in her own ribs now. It had been Petra who paid the ultimate price.

And then, beyond Ivan, the coronation. The chaos. The screaming. The smell of smoke and blood when joy was supposed to reign. The memory was a ghost that refused to be laid to rest.

Tomorrow was meant for joy too. A wedding and a new beginning for both Linnosa and Hefguard. Rheanna couldn't shake the gnawing fear that joy was fragile, that it would always split beneath the weight of shadow. The Oracle and the Cleansers still lurked out there. She did not know which was more of a threat.

Her steps slowed as she approached Cyra's chambers. The guards, Mikah and another she did not recognize, flanked the door, their spears gleaming in the lamplight. There were more of them now than before the coronation. Even in celebration, the castle did not forget danger. Neither did Rheanna.

Mikah dipped his head in a silent, respectful salute. "She's alone."

Rheanna nodded, pressing her lips together in a wordless gesture of thanks before the door was opened.

The chamber within was quieter than the bustling hall, softer in every way. Thick rugs muted her steps, and the hearth burned with a steady flame that cast long shadows against the stone. The windows were thrown open to the gardens, letting in the whisper of leaves and the scent of night blossoms. It smelled of smoke and soap and the faint, lingering sweetness of the silk ribbon and petals scattered across the desk.

Cyra stood at the window, her hair unbound, her golden eyes reflecting the garden's darkness. She didn't turn immediately when Rheanna entered, but her voice carried across the room. "Rhe."

The sound of her name, softened in her sister's mouth, broke something loose in Rheanna's chest. She crossed the room, touching Cyra's shoulder lightly.

"Are you ready?" she asked.

Cyra's mouth curved into a faint smile, but it didn't reach her eyes. "No one ever is, but I am thankful it is Atlas."

Rheanna sank into the velvet-cushioned chair beside her, watching the garden sway. "I came from the hall. It's beautiful."

"Good." Cyra's gaze stayed fixed outside, but her hand brushed absently against the cold, polished window frame, her fingers tracing the grain of wood.

"They used Petra's flowers," Rheanna whispered, the words feeling like glass in her throat. "The little white wild ones."

Cyra's breath hitched, just faintly. Her eyes closed, her long lashes shadowing her cheeks. "I asked them to," she confessed.

The silence between them stretched, heavy with everything unsaid. Rheanna pictured Petra's hands weaving uneven crowns that never sat straight, her laugh echoing in corridors that were now hauntingly quiet. She wanted to speak, to put words to the raw ache of Petra's absence, but her throat tightened until she could only breathe.

Cyra reached for her hand instead, threading their fingers together in a grip that almost seemed desperate. The calluses in Cyra's palm rubbed against her skin, a grounding weight that anchored Rheanna to the present.

Rheanna forced a breath past the knot in her chest. "I keep thinking about your coronation," she admitted softly. "About how quickly joy turned to fear. I'm afraid tomorrow will be the same."

Cyra turned to her, her golden eyes steady despite the tremor beneath. "I think about it too. Every waking hour. But this time..." She squeezed Rheanna's hand. "We are ready. That's the difference."

Rheanna let the words settle, slow as heavy stones sinking into deep water. They were not enough to wash her fear away entirely, but enough for a bit of comfort.

She met her sister's gaze. "We will face it together."

Cyra's lips curved, the smile more genuine this time. "Together," she echoed, still holding her sister's hand, the word sounding like a vow.

And in that quiet chamber, with the bittersweet scent of wildflowers still clinging to her thoughts, Rheanna believed it.

Chapter 23

A ella sat on the floor, knees tucked beneath her like a coiled spring simply because Hollin had ordered her to. The little girl proceeded to climb into her lap with all the authority of someone who had never once questioned whether the world would make room for her.

"Again," Hollin demanded, her small hands gripping Aella's shoulders as if they were reins on a warhorse. "Higher this time."

Aella sighed, though she didn't move her hands away. "You're going to fall," she muttered, bracing herself anyway.

"I won't," Hollin said confidently, her chin lifting. "You won't let me."

Aella tightened her grip and stood anyway, raising Hollin effortlessly above her head until her laughter filled the room. Hollin kicked her feet, her strawberry-blonde curls bouncing wildly.

Aella felt that familiar, uncomfortable pull in her chest, the part of her that wanted to retreat before it rooted too deeply. Yet she knew it was already too late.

"You're reckless," Aella accused, her violet gaze narrowing playfully at her niece.

Hollin beamed down at her, undeterred. "You're strong."

Aella lowered her back to the rug, setting her down with a gentleness no one else experienced from her. Hollin collapsed dramatically onto her back, arms flung wide.

"I survived," she announced.

Aella snorted. "Oh, what a feat that must have been."

Hollin giggled and popped back up, then bolted for the door. "I'm gonna tell Ron you didn't drop me!"

Hollin disappeared down the hall, high-pitched laughter trailing behind her. Aella leaned back on her hands, legs stretched out, staring at the ceiling as silence consumed her once again.

She had almost forgotten Cyra was there, watching only as a mother could. Her sister sat on the bench by the window, watching with that knowing expression she wore too often lately. The one that said she knew exactly the weight Aella felt.

"You're good with her," Cyra said eventually, her voice breaking the quiet.

Aella scoffed, brushing a stray hair from her face. "She's easy."

"She's not," Cyra replied softly, a shadow of a smile on her lips. "She just feels safe with you."

Aella didn't answer. She never knew what to do with that observation. Hollin didn't know who Aella was. Not really. She didn't know the blood or the blades or the bitter years spent learning how to disappear.

Cyra shifted, her movement deliberate. Aella felt it immediately.

"I would like to speak more with Kaelith. I can tell you two have grown close, but... she seems to know things, and there are so many things I need to know. The Oracle and the Cleansers. Everything is too up in the air."

Aella's fingers curled against the floor. The Oracle's name sent a chill down her spine. The old woman had been quiet, but that did not mean she was not out there, plotting.

"I don't own her. She is free to talk to you if she pleases."

Cyra studied her. "You know that's not what I meant. I just wanted to make sure we were on the same page."

Aella huffed a short laugh. Now her sister wanted to keep her in the loop, but instead of vocalizing her bitterness, she swallowed it. "Thank you. If you want, I could go scout for the Oracle–"

"No," Cyra said too quickly and then explained, "I can't have you gone again. We need to all be here."

"We need a plan to deal with the Oracle. She's a problem and a threat to this kingdom and this family."

Her older sister sighed as she stood up from her seat by the window. "I know. I just don't know what the best course of action is. At least we have Natalie, Laney, and Cora working on the Cleansers situation."

Aella tensed at Natalie's name, unable to trust the woman who had ripped her heart out. Even the mere thought of her sent her blood pulsing.

"I'll try to think of something."

Cyra was quiet for a moment before she said, "I'm getting married tomorrow." Then she began to pace restlessly in front of where Aella was sprawled out on the floor.

"I know," Aella said, her voice softer now.

"I want one night," Cyra continued. "Just one where nothing is expected of us. No councils. No politics. No watching every word we say."

Aella snorted. "You're a queen. That doesn't turn off."

"I know," Cyra said. "But I want to try."

She paused, staring at Aella with large molten eyes. "Come out with us," Cyra said. "Rheanna already said yes."

Of course Rheanna had already said yes. Aella stared at the floor, tracing a crack in the stone. She didn't want to say no to her sister. The idea of noise and bodies pressed too close made her skin itch, but she could see plainly on her sister's face how badly she needed this. How badly she craved one moment of normalcy. Where she could be just Cyra. Not the Queen of Linnosa. Not the figure everyone bowed to and feared disappointing.

"I don't belong in places like that," Aella said flatly.

Cyra tilted her head. "You have gone to places like that many times, and anyway, I no longer belong in an alehouse even more so than you."

Aella exhaled slowly, a long, defeated sound. "I'm not wearing a dress."

Cyra grinned, relief flashing across her face. "I wasn't expecting you to."

"And if it's awful," Aella added, pointing a finger at the door for emphasis, "I'm leaving."

"Of course," Cyra said easily. "I won't even try to stop you."

"You're impossible." Aella stood.

Cyra stepped closer and bumped her shoulder lightly. "You love me," she said with a playful smirk.

Chapter 24

Cyra had been smiling all afternoon. Not the polite, practiced smile she wore in council chambers or hallways lined with bowed heads, but something looser. As though she had already decided that tonight would belong to her and that nothing else, not even the looming weight of the kingdom, would be allowed to intrude.

"We're going out," she had said, breezing into Rheanna's rooms without ceremony. "All of us."

Rheanna looked up from her lunch, a plain carrot soup, startled by her sister's sudden presence. "Out?"

"Yes," Cyra said, already pacing, her movements energized. "Drinks. Music. Somewhere loud. Loud enough to drown our worries."

"Where everyone will have their eyes on you? You hate that," Rheanna said.

"I hate *meetings*," Cyra replied, tossing a mischievous look over her shoulder. "This is different."

There was a pause then. Rheanna's gaze lingered on Cyra for a moment too long before she shrugged. "Fine, but Aella will not be easy to convince."

And that had been that. Somehow, her older sister had managed to convince Aella as she was walking with them, flanked by guards as they headed to an alehouse. She wore dark trousers and a fitted shirt, sleeves rolled to her forearms to reveal lean muscle, her boots scuffed and familiar. Her silver hair was pulled back behind her ears, rebellious strands already slipping free. She wore no jewelry, no unnecessary adornment.

Cyra, on the other hand, had gone all out. She wore a deep crimson dress that clung at the waist before falling loose around her legs, the fabric catching the moonlight with every step. The neckline dipped just enough to feel deliberate, the sleeves sheer and flowing, as if she'd dressed herself in molten coals. Her hair had been left mostly loose, wild curls tumbling down her back, only partially pinned away from her face with a thin gold clasp that glinted in the moonlight. She looked young and radiant, not like a queen, but a young woman determined to have fun.

Cyra had insisted that Rheanna wear a particular dress, so she wore a pale pink gown she never would have chosen on her own. It was simple in cut and elegant, the silk soft and light against her skin. Cyra had braided part of her hair back from her face, weaving in a thin ribbon that matched the dress, leaving the rest to fall in a smooth cascade down her back. Rheanna felt so unlike herself in it, but she presumed that tonight was about that, letting loose.

By the time they reached the alehouse, night had fully claimed the city. Lanterns glowed along the street, casting warm halos over stone and shadow. The stars poked out against the night sky like scattered diamonds. Music spilled from the building before they even reached the door, fast, reckless, and heart-thumping, the kind of sound that settled deeply into your bones.

The moment Cyra pushed the door open, heat rushed out to meet them. It wrapped around Rheanna, thick with smoke, spice, and the sharp bite of ale. Candlelight flickered everywhere, reflected in tankards and polished wood, catching on the worn beams overhead. The floor vibrated beneath her boots with the rhythm of the music, bodies moving together in a loose, joyful chaos.

And then the room noticed them. Not all at once. Conversation dipped. A laugh stuttered. A man straightened instinctively, then flushed when he noticed Rheanna's scrutiny. She heard the murmurs before she fully understood them.

Princess. Queen.

The words were not reverent nor resentful, but a hushed acknowledgment passing from mouth to mouth like a shared truth.

The guards lingered just inside the threshold, cloaked plainly, blending as much as men trained for violence ever could. Familiar faces such as Ryder and Malik, whom Rheanna knew Aella trusted and had handpicked to accompany them tonight, stood in the shadows. Rheanna felt their presence like a steady pressure on her back, subtle but constant.

Cyra didn't pause. She stepped forward as though the space had been waiting for her, her smile widening, her shoulders loosening as if she were shedding something heavy with every step.

"Well," she said lightly, glancing back at them, "We are here. Might as well enjoy ourselves."

Rheanna hesitated for a fraction of a second. The noise pressed in on her as it began again, laughter and shouting and music colliding until it all blurred into a dizzying hum. She had not realized how long it had been since she had been somewhere like this. Somewhere uncontrolled.

Cyra reached back and took Rheanna's wrist, her touch warm and grounding. "Stick with me," she murmured, her voice carrying only to Rheanna. "You'll be fine."

Aella snorted, her eyes scanning the place. "Debatable."

Cyra laughed, loud and unrestrained, and the sound loosened something tight in Rheanna's chest.

They moved deeper into the alehouse, drawing eyes as they went. Rheanna felt each glance like a brush of heat across her skin. Curiosity. Awe. Speculation. Cyra absorbed it all effortlessly, her presence a bright, steady flame, while Aella ignored it entirely, her focus fixed on the room itself rather than the people in it.

They claimed a table near the center, close enough to the music that conversation required leaning in. Cyra naturally felt comfortable as the center of attention, while Rheanna and Aella floundered a bit, both moving with a bit of a tight, uncomfortable manner.

Tankards arrived quickly, set down with wide grins and murmured gratitudes that Cyra accepted with easy grace. Rheanna lifted hers hesitantly, inhaling the sharp, spiced scent.

Cyra raised her cup first. "To tonight," she said, her eyes sparkling. "And to whatever comes after, as long as we are all together."

Aella clinked her ale against Cyra's. "I can drink to that."

Rheanna smiled and followed suit.

The ale burned pleasantly as it went down, a steady warmth blooming in her chest. She coughed once, embarrassed, then laughed when Aella shot her an amused look.

"Careful," Aella said, a rare smirk tugging at her lips. "That'll sneak up on you."

Rheanna wiped her mouth, cheeks warming. "I'll manage." She had only really indulged in ale one other time, back when she and Maude had snuck some when Mr. and Mrs. Bushnell weren't looking. You would think with Rheanna being older that she would be the one to influence Maude, but it was the other way around. The memory turned sour as thoughts of Maude quickly turned to Ivan. She managed another sip to help push it away.

Cyra leaned back in her chair, already looser, her laughter coming more easily now. The music swelled then, the tempo quickening, drums beating faster. Cyra's gaze drifted toward the dancers near the hearth, her foot tapping unconsciously.

"Oh no," Aella said, following her look.

"Oh yes," Cyra replied, already standing. "I am absolutely dancing."

Rheanna barely had time to protest before Cyra grabbed her hand and tugged her up, laughing as Rheanna stumbled after her. The way her older sister acted made her wonder what she was like before all of this. When she was a simple barmaid. When the weight of the crown didn't weigh so heavily upon her brow.

The space near the hearth was packed, bodies moving together in a wild, joyful rhythm. Cyra danced, fearless, unrestrained, hair slipping loose from its pin as she spun.

Rheanna laughed despite herself, letting the music carry her, the beat vibrating through her bones. Aella joined them after a moment, her movements sharper, more controlled, but there was an ease to her tonight that Rheanna hadn't seen before. Aella actually grinned when Cyra bumped into her, rolling her eyes when Rheanna nearly tripped over her own feet.

For a while, they were just sisters. No crown. No prophecy. No weight pressing down on them. Just laughter and music and the warmth of shared space.

Rheanna noticed Laney and Cora standing near the bar, drinks in hand. Laney's red hair was loose, her smile wide and unrestrained. Cora leaned comfortably against the counter, boots braced. They spoke enthusiastically, throwing their hands in the air, ale sloshing over.

Something shifted in Rheanna's chest as she watched them. This version of them, not maids or informants, but teenage girls, was endearing. But seeing them like this also brought a wave of guilt. She knew they needed their eyes and ears, but it did not make it any easier.

Laney caught her eye and lifted her tankard in greeting, surprise clearly flashing on her face. Rheanna smiled and waved them over. Laney caught Cora's shoulder, pointing to the royals, and then they began to make their way over to them through the throng.

Cyra noticed immediately. "They are so young," she murmured, her voice holding a sort of sadness.

Before Rheanna could respond, the girls were standing in front of them.

"Do you need something of us?" asked Cora, running her free hand through her brunette waves and attempting to look unaffected by the ale in her hand, although her eyes betrayed her.

Cyra shook her head vehemently. "Tonight is all about fun! No working!"

The girls raised their eyebrows at the carefree version of their queen as Rheanna said, "Join us!" She grabbed the two girls by their wrists, pulling them deeper into the fray.

Laney and Cora joined them easily, laughter flowing, conversation unforced. Aella even began to unwind, her hips swaying a bit more freely as the fiddle fastened its pace. Here, they were all just women and girls having fun. No titles.

Surprise lit Rheanna's face as Bianca Solo stood, pausing just inside the doorway as she took in the scene before her. Her white blonde hair lay in a straight curtain, framing her petite, rounded face. Her grey eyes scanned the area when she finally spotted them. She seemed to hesitate a moment before Cyra spotted her instantly and waved, beckoning her closer. Rheanna's eyes widened, but she quickly recovered, not wanting to make the girl feel unwelcome even if she had been unkind to them in the past.

Bianca threaded through the crowd with surprising ease, her cheeks slightly flushed from the heat of the room. She stopped just short of them, her gaze flicking briefly over Rheanna, Aella, Laney, and Cora before settling on Cyra. Aella noticed her, but turned away, her attention fully on Laney and Cora now, any irritation hidden in the moment.

"You didn't say it would be this loud," Bianca said, raising her voice over the music.

Cyra laughed. "I absolutely did not promise you comfort."

Bianca smiled at that, then glanced around, taking in the place. "I almost didn't come," she admitted.

Rheanna stepped closer. "You dance?" she asked, wanting to make Bianca more comfortable.

Bianca blinked and then shrugged. "Poorly."

Cyra grinned. "Perfect. Then you'll fit right in."

She caught Bianca's wrist and tugged her into the circle, the music surging around them as Bianca giggled in protest. Rheanna watched the way Bianca loosened as she moved, the way her caution softened into something freer, something curious.

"You look different," Bianca said to Cyra, breathless. "I have never seen you be anything but the Queen of Linnosa."

"That's the point," Cyra replied simply.

Rheanna nodded, the music pulsing through her chest, and let herself believe that this was how alliances began. Not in council chambers, but here, in the quiet invitation of a once-perceived foe, of young girls who had been taught to hate without even knowing why.

Bianca stayed for a while, and Aella kept her distance, returning to her alertness or at least as much as two tankards of ale would allow her. When Bianca left, she kissed each sister gently on the cheek. Cyra and Rheanna returned it while Aella stiffened but offered a sharp, respectful nod.

Not long after, Aella leaned close to Rheanna. "I'm heading out."

Rheanna nodded. She didn't ask questions, but she wondered if her younger sister was possibly headed toward the beautiful woman who now shared her room. She didn't believe anything had happened yet, but Rheanna's intuitive nature caught the way they leaned toward each other whenever they were in proximity, like two magnets fighting the pull.

After Aella left, Laney and Cora drifted farther into the mayhem of the alehouse, each swept away by a man, spinning and twirling, until they were just flashes of color in the crowd.

Rheanna stayed with Cyra, who was still clinging to the night like it might slip away if she loosened her grip. Rheanna did not mind being the one to hold everything steady; she had actually been growing quite used to it.

Chapter 25

Aella and Rheanna buzzed around Cyra frantically, smoothing loose hairs and making small adjustments to her dress that did not have to be made. A pin was slid into place only to be removed seconds later. A wrinkle that existed only in imagination was brushed away. Even Aella, usually a pillar of icy detachment, brimmed with barely contained anxiety, her fingers twitching as if she were the one about to be wed. Her sharp eyes scanned every inch of Cyra, hunting for flaws that refused to materialize. Rheanna fussed with the train, her movements jerky, betraying the emotions she fought to keep at bay.

The sisters had promised to stay with Cyra until the last possible moment, but she knew the moment was coming when they would have to leave her to face the aisle alone.

"You look beautiful," Rheanna crooned, her voice thick with a mixture of pride and unshed tears.

Cyra took the moment to admire her sisters, committing them to memory. Rheanna stood near the flickering torchlight, the glow catching on the pale gold fabric of her gown, making it appear almost liquid against her skin. The dress skimmed her frame like a slip, simple at first glance, but unmistakably intentional in its construction. A high slit traced up one leg, revealing smooth movement with every step, while off-the-shoulder sleeves rested loosely along her arms, delicate and unguarded. Darker gold detailing edged the seams and neckline. Her hair, freed from its usual braid, fell in gentle waves down her back, crowned by a braided circlet woven close to her scalp. Gold shimmer dusted her eyes and cheekbones, making her skin glow.

Aella's dress was the same pale gold, yet entirely different in its spirit. Where Rheanna's whispered of romance, hers sang of power. Long sleeves clung to her arms, the fabric molded to muscle and curve without apology, tracing the lethal strength carved into her by years of survival and violence. The darker gold detailing followed the lines of her body like armor made elegant, emphasizing her shoulders and waist. Her hair was pulled back from her face, drawn away on either side, and secured tightly. Gold shimmer framed her eyes as well, sharper and bolder than Rheanna's.

"You two look incredible," Cyra finally breathed, overwhelmed by a sudden swell of love for her sisters. They had been through so much together, loss and fear and the kind of darkness that should have broken them. Yet here they stood, beautiful and strong, whole in ways that seemed impossible given all they had endured.

Aella rolled her eyes, though her cheeks flushed pink with pleasure at the compliment. "Oh, come on. We all know you are the star of the show tonight. The rest of us are merely..." She waved her hand vaguely, searching for the word. "Decoration."

"What Aella meant to say was 'thank you'," Rheanna interjected with a knowing smile, shooting a pointed look at their younger sister. "But I think it is time we leave you."

For a second, Cyra felt a sharp spike of panic, a primal urge to run as far away as she could, but then she took a deep breath before nodding. "I love you," she said softly, the words carrying more weight than they ever had before.

Aella chuckled. "We will be just inside, but we love you too. Even when you're being insufferably sentimental."

"You got this!" Rheanna said, squeezing Cyra's hand one last time, her grip firm and warm.

The three sisters shared a quick hug, arms wrapping around each other in a tangle of silk and emotion. And then they pulled away, leaving the queen alone in the silence of the corridor.

The sound of the small band floated into the hall beyond the closed door of the grand ballroom. The tickling of the harp and flute soothed Cyra's nerves while also heightening them. The music swelled and faded like breathing, and she recognized the melody. It was an old Linnosan wedding tune, one that brides had walked to for generations. That was her cue to walk in.

The gilded doors, decorated with a carving of the goddesses descending from the heavens, heaved open, two guards on either side pulled them wide, their movements synchronized from years of practice. The room beyond overwhelmed Cyra. The ballroom had been transformed. Garlands of beautiful flowers draped from every surface, their scent heavy in the air. Candles flickered in crystal holders, casting dancing shadows across the marble floors.

Cyra froze for a fraction of a second before forcing her feet to march forward. There were not many guests due to the current political climate. In attendance were just the few Hefguard dignitaries who had made the journey, Atlas's mother and brother, the council members and their families, and her sisters with Hollin now at their side. The little girl wore a white beaded dress to match her mother, a white lace headband wrapped around her ears that made her look like an angel. When she spotted Cyra, she bounced on her heels, barely containing her excitement. Rheanna placed a gentle hand on her shoulder to keep her from running down the aisle.

Cyra, herself, wore a white dress with a beaded bodice, thousands of tiny pearls and crystals sewn in intricate patterns that caught every flicker of light. Tulle sleeves dripped off her shoulders. The gown accentuated her hips, then fell around her in fine layers of silk and tulle. It trailed behind her, a smooth river of fabric. Her fiery waves had been tamed into an elegant cascade, woven with threads of gold that caught the light like living flame, her crown resting just above the braids at her temples. In her hands, she held a bouquet of white roses and lilies, their petals soft against her fingers, their scent rising to mingle with the perfumed air.

Every step felt both too fast and agonizingly slow. She could feel the weight of every gaze upon her, the curious stares of the Hefguard dignitaries assessing their new queen, the warm approval of the council members who had watched her grow, the fierce pride radiating from her sisters. But all of that faded when her gaze finally fell upon her betrothed, her consort at the dais. Atlas wore a doublet of white silk, embroidered subtly with patterns similar to crystal fissures. A sash of hammered gold thread wrapped at his waist with gold embroidery climbing the sleeves, cuffs, and collar in curling patterns. His handsome face left Cyra breathless. His usually untamed black waves were styled back, fully exposing his forest green eyes, which burned with an intensity that made the rest of the room fade. His expression was soft and loving, full of awe as he took her in.

Cyra had never imagined she would be so lucky to find a man of his likeness to marry her and potentially be a father figure to her daughter. She had once believed she would be alone forever, just her and Hollin. Even when she was brought back to the castle, she knew if she married, it would not be for love, but for politics and alliance. But now she looked at Atlas and thought that perhaps this was love. They had never said the words, yet she felt it there, in the space between heartbeats, in the way her soul seemed to recognize his.

As she approached the dais, a guard walked forward, about to help her up the steps, but before he could reach her, Atlas stepped forward, intercepting him. The guard retreated respectfully. Atlas placed her hand in his, leading her up and in front of the altar. A nervous smile graced Cyra's lips, and he responded with his own without releasing her hand. In his other hand, he clenched a rose quartz, necessary to bond the two in the way of the witches. He now switched it to the hand holding hers so that they were both grasping the cool, pulsating stone. She could feel its energy thrumming against her palm, a heartbeat not her own.

Elsepth stepped forward, beautiful as ever in a robe of deep green, the color of moss after rain. The fabric was heavy and handwoven, trimmed with panels of raw gold thread that caught the torchlight like veins of ore. When she moved, the cords at her waist jingled softly with small charms of stone and silver.

Her voice rose low and steady as she wound a cord of hemp and woven gold around their joined hands. The rough texture of the hemp contrasted with the smooth warmth of the gold, representing the balance of hardship and prosperity that marriage would bring. Atlas's crystal pulsed faintly in their grip, light spilling into the braid until it glowed as if alive. When Elsepth's chant reached its peak, the cord unraveled, splitting cleanly into two perfect halves that fell away. Yet the shimmer remained, etched faintly across their palms where skin pressed to skin. Cyra felt the warmth hum through her veins, a bond that no council decree or oath could sever.

"Arathine blesses this union." Elsepth proclaimed, her voice carrying through the hall with unnatural resonance.

Elspeth stepped back, her words settling into a silence that seemed to breathe through the hall itself. The glow across their palms lingered, soft and steady, a private reminder even as the watching crowd shifted in awe. In years past, the Oracle herself would have spoken next as she did during Cyra's coronation, but with her missing, and at the top of the list for being the one behind all the monster attacks, she would not be doing so. In her absence, the duty fell to the Keeper, the high priest of the Goddess.

The Keeper stepped forward now, his navy robes a dark contrast against the pale marble, his staff carved with runes that no longer hummed with the power it once carried. He unrolled the scroll of vows, his voice sharp and deliberate, echoing through the vaulted chamber.

"Cyra Noelle Voelbel, Queen of Linnosa. Atlas Reign Nicola, Prince of Hefguard. Before crown and council, you will swear yourselves to Linnosa and each other."

His gaze shifted first to Atlas, assessing the foreign prince who would become consort to their queen. "Do you swear your loyalty to Linnosa? To stand beside our Queen in war and in peace, in counsel and in silence, to place the kingdom's best interest above your own?"

Atlas's green eyes flicked to Cyra's for the briefest heartbeat, and in that look passed a lifetime of promises. Then, steady and resonant, his voice rang out. "I swear it."

The Keeper turned to her, his eyes softening slightly. "And do you, Cyra Noelle, Queen of Linnosa, swear to honor this union and kingdom, binding his house to your throne and his oath to your reign?"

Cyra raised her chin, her fire thrumming steady in her veins, her bound hand still warm with the binding shimmer. "I swear it."

The Keeper lifted his staff, striking it once against the marble floor with a thunderous crack. "So it shall be. Linnosa accepts this union as law and as legacy."

Applause rose like a wave. Cyra looked out to the crowd to see Rheanna and Aella, both smiling, but of course, the older of the two had tears streaming down her face. Hollin, pink-cheeked and freckled, ran up to the dais and into Atlas's waiting arms. He spun her around, her legs and dress fanning out in a circle. Cyra laughed, glad to see her daughter so happy. Ron joined them next, shaking Atlas's hand awkwardly and giving Cyra a kiss on the cheek.

"I'm proud of yer, my girl," he muttered into her ear before walking away.

Each of the guests came up and gave their congratulations before heading back to a table for the feast. Council members offered formal blessings, Hefguard dignitaries expressed diplomatic well-wishes, and distant relatives shared familial warmth. When it was Bianca's turn, she hugged Cyra with more warmth than she had ever given before.

"Maybe you could set me up with the brother?" she giggled nervously, casting a shy glance over her shoulder at Malcolm.

Despite the rocky start with Bianca, she had tried to make amends in the weeks leading up to the wedding. While Aella thought she might be the informant, Cyra disagreed. It would be too obvious, too easy. Aella saw threats everywhere now, her warrior's instincts honed to a razor's edge by years of survival, but Cyra believed in giving people the chance to prove themselves changed. Bianca still had some growing up to do at her young age, and she was much too serious all the time, carrying herself with a rigidity that spoke of someone trying too hard to prove their worth. Perhaps Malcolm would prove to be a good influence. He had a quiet steadiness about him, a gentle humor that might help her relax, she thought.

"I'll see what I can do," she said with a wink, delighted when the gesture coaxed a genuine laugh from the younger woman, her usual reserve cracking just enough to show the girl beneath.

When everyone finished coming up to the newlyweds, they sat down at a table with Rheanna, Aella, Hollin, Malcolm, and

Elspeth. The joy in the room was palpable, a living thing that seemed to push back against the shadows that had plagued the kingdom for so long. The first platters of food arrived steaming, carried by servants who weaved in and out of the tables with practiced ease. Roasted pheasant, its skin lacquered gold with honey and herbs, gave off a sweet and smoky perfume that made Cyra's mouth water the moment it reached her. Bowls of spiced root vegetables followed, carrots and parsnips glistening with butter. A thick venison stew bubbled in wide clay pots, the broth dark and rich, peppered with wild mushrooms that still carried the damp scent of the forest floor and chunks of meat so tender they fell apart at the touch of a spoon.

Fresh bread was piled high in woven baskets, crusts dusted white with flour and the loaves still warm enough to steam when torn open. Hollin reached for a small roll, cheeks round as she bit into it with crumbs tumbling onto her lap. She made a sound of pure contentment, her eyes closing as she chewed. Cyra watched as Laney slipped a slice of cured boar into her mouth, smirking when Cora swatted her hand. Everyone ate as small talk was passed around the table. Rheanna and Malcolm found themselves in an animated discussion about the differences between Hefguard and Linnosan wedding traditions.

The musicians struck up a lilting tune, strings bright against the low hum of the pipes. Couples were coaxed onto the polished floor, but it was Cyra who caught Atlas's hand first, tugging him forward and out of his seat with a grin that glimmered like flame.

"You're not escaping this," she teased, her golden eyes alight with mischief.

Atlas, tall and broad in his white and gold, bent his head closer. "Anything for you, my queen."

The hall blurred as she pulled him onto the marbled dance floor.. The warmth of her laugh melted the tension from his frame. He stumbled once, and she threw her head back, laughing so loudly, so unapologetically, that several people stopped to look their way. Their movement slowed, steps dissolving into sways until it was no longer about rhythm, but their closeness. Atlas leaned in, his forehead brushing hers. As his lips skimmed her temple, the world seemed to disappear around them until only the two of them remained, breathing the same air, hearts beating in tandem.

After a while, when goblets were still full and laughter echoed across the hall, Cyra slipped her fingers through his and tugged him from the crowd. They slipped down a quiet corridor, the noise of celebration fading to muffled shadows. The castle was cool and dark compared to the bright warmth of the hall. Before they even had the door to his chamber closed behind them, Atlas had her face cupped in his hands, kissing her with the fervor of their vows. Cyra gripped the lapels of his coat, tugging him down to her. The weight of his body pressed her into the soft bedding, the silk sheets cool against her skin, while the decorative flower petals that had been scattered by the servants earlier were crushed beneath her back, instantly filling the air with their scent.

Her gown slipped from her shoulders under his hands and she kicked it off quickly, wanting nothing between them. Atlas drew in a sharp breath as he took her in like he always did.

"Beautiful," he murmured.

Cyra's hands found the nape of his neck, her fingers tangling in the dark hair she had been dying to touch all evening. She pulled him back down, her lips catching his with a desperate hunger that mirrored his own. Heat flared between them, raw and consuming. His hands roamed the curves of her waist and hips, slow at first, before growing bolder as her soft, jagged sighs urged him on. She raked her hands down the planes of his chest.

When he finally moved to enter, he stopped at her entrance, his muscles trembling with the effort of restraint. Their foreheads remained pressed together, their breaths uneven and mingling in the narrow space between them. Atlas's eyes searched hers, clouded with desire but also protective devotion.

"Tell me if–"

She silenced him with a kiss, whispering against his mouth, "Don't stop."

Their bodies found a rhythm, urgent and tender all at once, a joining that was more vow than lust. Cyra's nails dragged into his back, leaving small moon crests. Each movement drew her higher, until every nerve burned with him, every thought dissolved into the heat of his touch. She gasped his name and he held her closer. They came undone together, the world falling away until there was only the sound of their mingled breaths and the thrum of their hearts.

Afterward, Atlas gathered her against his chest, his lips brushing the crown of her head. Cyra's breathing slowed, soothed by the steady rhythm of his heart beneath her cheek.

Chapter 26

T HE CITY HAD WOKEN early for its queen. Streets that reeked of horse piss yesterday now glittered with garlands strung from balcony to balcony, their colors too bright against the soot-stained stone. Vendors tossed handfuls of petals into the gutters as though that could hide the jagged cracks in the stone. Bells clanged above in a discordant pattern that could not decide if it was music or a frantic alarm, and the streets shook with the sheer weight of bodies pressing forward to see their queen and her new king.

Aella rode near the front with the guard, her eyes flicking incessantly to the roofs and alleys. It was a habit more than a choice, a soldier's instinct. Her gaze moved the way a blade moves through flesh, in and out. Every shift of shadow, every flutter of curtain, every glint of metal caught her attention. She could feel the humming vibration of the air, a side effect of her heightened senses, as though the city itself was alive and restless beneath its finery.

Cyra and Atlas rode side by side, not touching, but the space between them felt stitched together by an invisible, unbreakable bond. The city saw it and roared their approval. Aella kept her mouth in a line. She let the cheers wash over her and then off of her, the way rain slides off an oiled cloak. Petals drifted down from balconies, snagging in her hair and on the black leather of her pauldrons. She didn't brush them away. A pretty assassin dusted by flowers. Let them pretend they did not know what her hands could do.

The column turned into the wide square that gave the capital its spine. Fountains sprang up at each corner, water catching sunlight and throwing it in restless shards over the crowd. Vendors had abandoned their stalls to get a look, bread left open to the air and pastries cooling on wooden planks. Children sat on the carved tails of the fountain lions, legs swinging dangerously close to the spray. Even the lions, worn by decades of touch, seemed to be watching the procession.

Aella scanned the rooftops once more, lingering on windowsills and the shadows under the statue where pigeons sulked. She felt the wind sliding along the buildings. It carried a thousand smells at once, not all pleasant: the sweetness of the petals, the salt of sweat from the gathering crowds, and the bitter charcoal of a baker's ovens.

Her jaw tightened. She shifted in her saddle and let her hand drop to the hilt at her hip, the leather grip warm and familiar against her palm. She was not here to bask in adoration; she was here to guard against the moment when the celebration turned to chaos.

"Relax," one of the younger guards breathed on her right without moving his lips. Jaro. Too new to know better and not new enough to be brave about it.

"I am relaxed," she said. "You will know when I'm not."

He swallowed and she smiled, though there was no warmth in the expression.

They took the square in a long loop so the people on every side could have their fill of the newlyweds. Cyra lifted a hand once, twice, the movement easy, natural. She had a way of showing her power without actually showing it. It simply radiated off of her.

Something rattled under the stones. One beat. Two. Subtle enough that it could have been nothing. Perhaps two cart wheels crossing cobbles in an alley. Aella felt it in the wind first, a ripple where the air should have been smooth. She turned her head a fraction and pretended to smile at a child who leaned so far out over a balcony that his mother clamped a hand at the back of his shirt.

A second ripple. Then, a sound like the last thud of a nail being hammered into rotten wood. Aella's skin prickled. Her pulse quickened, the hairs on her arms rising as if her body recognized the threat before her mind could name it. The square's celebration faded into the back of her mind, replaced by the heavy silence of anticipation.

"Cyra," she said, low.

Cyra didn't turn. "I feel it."

Atlas, on Cyra's other side, had already shifted his weight. The earth underfoot did a small, almost imperceptible shrug.

A nearby grate shivered. Just a quiver at first, the way something sleeping twitches as it turns toward waking. Someone tossed more petals.

"Form," Aella said, already swinging off her horse. Her boots hit stone with a heavy *thud*. The guards around them moved as one sheath of metal. "Shields up and backs in." The horses shoved, startled.

"Back!" Jaro shouted to the crowd before Aella could. "To the edges!" His voice was urgent, scattering families toward the walls of the square.

The heavy iron grate bowed under a pressure that should not have existed in the sewers below. The ring tore free of the stone with a sharp, metallic pop, then pinged across the cobbled square like a tossed coin. Black water bulged through the holes, thick and viscous, bubbling like tar. It carried a stench that could not be mistaken for the Black Lake. This was oil laced with rot. The odor was suffocating, a rancid fog that irritated throats and burned eyes until they watered. The fountains hiccuped in answer; the farthest sputtered brown at its lip before clearing again.

The first arm to emerge wasn't truly an arm, but a rope of muscle slicked with shadow, bending as if it had too many elbows. Then claws, wrong-sized and wrong-numbered, scraped at the lip of the grate until stone gave. The grate flipped, slammed down with a deafening crack, and the thing forced itself through, shoulders grinding. People screamed. Bodies moved in every bad direction all at once.

Aella did not waste breath naming it. She kicked a toppled crate into a makeshift step, launched herself upward, and landed on the statue base to buy herself a vantage. Wind gathered in the hollow of her chest on instinct, cold and sharp, screaming to be released.

"Get back!" she snapped and sent a blade of air along the ground. It hit a line of people and slid them back three paces as if a giant had reached out and nudged them out of harm's way. A man stumbled, eyes wide with terror, and then scooped his child up, running without looking back.

Cyra's fire rose in a smooth, sudden wall, a curtain of orange brilliance that hissed against the damp air. Heat strobed against Aella's cheek. The fire curved between the monster and the densest throng of people, a shield instead of a weapon. Rheanna's fingers lifted in a fluid motion. The fountain to the left of the well stopped being a fountain at all. Its water pulled itself thin and wide, defying gravity as it became a sheet, then an arm that reached across the square to wrap around a group too slow to move.

Atlas did what he did best. Using his crystals, he coaxed the world to remember it could be solid. Stone heaved up in a low barrier, turning the square into layered rings. If the crowd could not be quick, the ground would be cautious for them.

The monster unfolded the rest of the way onto the stones. It looked like something drowned and kept too long. Its skin was gray and bloated, translucent in places where a sickly pink shone underneath. But it also looked like something newly made, slick with an oil that never belonged to any river. Its face held eyes clouded white with no pupils, staring at everything and nothing all at once, and its mouth was a seam that didn't match its bones. Ragged gills sawed along its neck, opening and closing.

Aella brought her arm down and a violent gust hit the creature broadside. It skidded, and the shriek that came out of it was like a pipe torn from a wall. She gritted her teeth and hit it again from the other side, trying to keep it in the center.

"Careful," Cyra warned, her eyes tracking the creature's unpredictable movements.

"I am careful," Aella snapped, but she loosened some of the edge from her wind.

Rheanna's water curled like a hook and hauled two boys out of the way of a lashing limb. Atlas's stone ridge thickened, then parted like lips to swallow a stream of the oil runoff, dumping it into a crack that hadn't existed a breath ago.

"Draw it to the center," Atlas said, low. "Away from the edges."

"On it," Aella said, and drove the air hard against the creature's shoulder, sending it a staggering spin. It skated and planted its claws and left a gouge four handspans deep. She tasted the grit of stone in her mouth. It lunged for the nearest carved drain along the square's edge, the wide mouth cut with wave patterns. It was going to the water. Not for safety. Purpose. It wanted to get to the places the water moved.

"Block that!" Aella snapped, and Atlas was already raising a lip of rock in front of the drain.

Rheanna took a deep breath, whipping her water and striking the creature's forelimbs.

Cyra didn't throw her flame. She had it so close she could have. Aella felt that choice like a heat against her own bones. They both knew the oil would light. Fire would catch if they were not careful and a city square was a tinderbox disguised as stone.

"Keep it in the center," Cyra said.

"I will," Aella responded.

She jumped from the statue to the ground as the monster reared, landing in a roll that put her just inside striking range. She slid under the whip-crack of its limb as it slammed at her shadow.

She cut it then. A slice along the nearest joint. The blade took meat and something that felt like cartilage and wet rope. But the monster did not bleed. Instead, the cut filled with a slick clear gel that steamed when it hit air. Her knife hissed where a drop landed near the hilt. She swore and kicked, heel to the side of the limb she had opened, sending it bucking.

Wind slammed its other side at the same time. The thing crashed onto the stone and the ground shook. Aella rolled back and sprang to her feet.

It lunged again, this time dragging itself deliberately across the stones. The claws didn't strike at bodies; they dug into the ground and scored. It was writing. The patterns weren't legible, not at first. Lines. Curves. Aella's stomach turned. It wasn't carving for itself; it was carving for whoever would watch.

"Finish it," Cyra commanded.

Aella moved, a clean slice where she thought something like a spine might hide and the monster shuddered, shivered, and went limp. Its skin began to bleach in places as if the sun had burned a pattern through clouds. Steam rose in low curls. The gel hissed and smoked and then evaporated.

The creature did not rise again. It fell inward instead, the way a fire in a hearth collapses into itself when it is nothing but coal. In seconds, there was less of it. In a handful more, there was almost nothing. Where it had been, the stones showed what the monster had been writing in its final moments.

The Oracle does not forget.

Aella tasted iron and realized she had bitten the inside of her cheek hard enough to bleed.

"Clear the square," Atlas said quietly to the guard captain, who passed the order with two motions of his hand. No shouting. No panic. The crowd was shocked and horrified at what they had witnessed.

Rheanna stood with her shoulders straight and her hands still at her sides. She looked at the words and did not look away. Her jaw tightened but her lips trembled faintly, betraying the effort it took to remain still. Cyra's face did not change, but the air near her grew a degree warmer. She burned, but not in a way the people could see. Aella knew that kind of fire, contained and waiting. She had been that kind of fire herself more times than she could count.

The words on the stones hissed faintly, still smoking, as if the creature's last breath had not finished leaving this world. Aella crouched beside them, the stink of scorched oil burning her nose. She dragged her knife across one line. The blackened stone flaked but did not crumble. The words had been carved too deep. It had branded the city with something that would not wash away.

She spat on the ground, the taste of iron still in her mouth.

"Back away from it," Atlas said.

Aella stood slowly. "It's dead."

"It left more than a corpse," Atlas said. His green eyes flicked to the words, then to Cyra. "This is meant to stay."

Rheanna shivered, her arms wrapping tight around herself. "The Oracle does not forget," she whispered, repeating the words like tasting poison.

The square, bright with banners and laughter not long ago now looked like a battlefield. Petals had been ground into mud under fleeing feet. Bread from the shattered carts lay in the muck, soaked in black ichor that was already fading to steam. The air reeked of salt and rot. No music. No bells. Only the echo of chaos where there was once celebration.

Aella knew this feeling too well. How joy could be gutted in a single breath. How the world didn't ask before it took. Rage was too easy a trap. On top of it all, the unsteady thrum of her heart and ragged breaths threatened to spill over. While away with Karif, she had learned how to use her magic without a full-blown panic attack, but she had never used this much all at once. Not even as a child. She shoved her shaky hands into her pockets, determined to keep it all at bay.

She lifted her eyes to the sky. The people who hadn't fled entirely still hovered at the edges of the square. Men clutching children. Women with baskets clutched to their chests. A boy no older than Hollin staring openly at the steaming letters. His lips moved, whispering them to himself.

Aella's stomach turned. That's how fear spreads. Words.

Fear cut deeper than hope.

Atlas touched Cyra's shoulder, steadying her. Rheanna drifted closer, her lips pressed white. Aella stood a step apart, staring down at the letters one last time. *The Oracle does not forget.*

Neither do I, she thought.

She sheathed her blade and turned her back on the square, but the words followed her anyway, stitched into her thoughts like another scar that would not heal.

CHAPTER 27

R HEANNA SLIPPED INTO HER chair in the council chamber, which was scented with oil and grime. Not from itself, but from the memory of it, clinging to the clothes of those who had run through the capital square only an hour before. Wax dripped thick from a dozen candles, their light harsh and uneven. The members were already speaking in low, urgent voices.

Norton Hansfield slammed a fist on the table, rattling the inkwells. "Double the guard at every city well. If the monsters can crawl up through our water, we may as well be bathing in death."

"I agree," Bianca said quickly. Her violet cloak was draped neatly across her shoulders. Her voice didn't waver, though her knuckles were white where she gripped the table's edge. "The people are shaken. They'll need to see protection and reassurance. If we treat every drain like a battlefield, they'll believe the battle is already lost."

Cyra inclined her head slightly. "Wise words." Her tone carried quiet authority, enough to still the overlapping murmurs around the table.

Rheanna smoothed the fabric of her skirts, her heart thrumming against her ribs. She always felt a little out of place in these meetings, caught between the edges of power and politics. Cyra commanded. Aella glared holes through the table. And Rheanna listened and measured.

Her chance came when Talmadge huffed. "The people are frightened. Their fear will spread like a contagion."

Rheanna found herself leaning forward before she could stop herself. "Then we must give them reason to hope as well as reason to feel safe," she said softly. She felt the weight of every eye in the chamber turn toward her. Her pulse thundered in her ears. "They need to see guards in the streets," Rheanna continued, her voice steadying as she went. "But they also need to see markets open. Songs sung. If we only answer fear with steel, we'll teach them to live in fear forever. That's not survival. That's surrender."

Silence lingered, heavier this time. Then Bianca nodded, her braid swaying with the motion. "I think she's right. Hope and protection must walk together, or the people will break."

Relief loosened Rheanna's shoulders, and when she glanced across the table, she found Cyra watching her with quiet pride. For the rest of the time, though, she sat back and listened, having her fill of attention for this day.

The council broke at last, parchment gathered, chairs scraping, voices still buzzing. Rheanna lingered only long enough to dip her head toward Cyra, then slipped out before anyone could press her for more. The air in the chamber had been too close, thick with talk of soldiers and drains and strategies she had little gift for.

The corridor was cooler and quieter. She let her fingers trail the stone walls as she walked, grounding herself in their solidity as she so often did. Her sisters carried themselves like they were made for command, Cyra radiant and firm, Aella sharp as tempered steel. Rheanna always felt more like water, moving around things, not through them. She reminded herself that water wore stone down eventually.

She found Ripley in the training yard. The clang of steel echoed off the walls as the squires sparred, their laughter bright despite the shadow yesterday had cast. Ripley leaned against the rail, his tunic damp with sweat, hair sticking to his brow. He was watching the spar, arms folded, but his head turned the moment Rheanna stepped onto the stones.

"Well," he said, that half-smile tugging at his mouth, "you look like someone who has been chewing stones for breakfast."

Rheanna huffed a laugh despite the heaviness in her chest. "Close. Council."

"Ah." He gave a mock wince. "That explains it."

"They argued about soldiers and drains and defenses, but..." She hesitated, the words tight in her throat. "I said something. About hope. About how people need it just as much as they need protection."

Ripley tilted his head, watching her closely. "And?"

"And they listened." She exhaled, half-disbelieving even as she said it. "I don't know if it mattered, but Cyra..." Rheanna shook her head, a small smile tugging at her lips. "She looked proud."

For a heartbeat, she feared she sounded foolish, like a child boasting of a teacher's praise. Ripley's grin was slow and genuine. "Of course she was."

Rheanna let the silence hang for a moment, and she struggled with how to phrase her fears, but she decided she just needed to let it out. She was safe with Ripley.

"I keep seeing it," she confessed quietly. "The monster, the words it left. *The Oracle does not forget.* I wonder if I'm strong enough to face what's coming."

Ripley's gaze held hers. "You're stronger than you think. Strong enough to keep your sisters steady. Strong enough to calm a council full of squabbling fools. Strong enough to stand here and still laugh after all of it."

Her throat tightened, and she laughed softly, shaking her head. "You make it sound so simple."

"It is simple," he said. "You're Rheanna. You don't have to be Cyra's fire or Aella's steel. You're water. You shape yourself around what's needed, and that's why you'll last longer than any of us."

The words sank into her like physical warmth, chasing out the chill from the monster attack.

"Here," Ripley said suddenly, plucking something from the rail behind him. It was only a sprig of wild mint, probably meant for the kitchens, but he tucked it gently into her hand as if it were the rarest bloom in the garden. "Better than council flowers. Doesn't wilt when the air grows heavy."

Rheanna laughed again, a real laugh this time, the kind that lightened her chest. She closed her fingers around the sprig, holding it as though it might anchor her.

"Thank you, Ripley," she whispered.

His smile widened, and for a moment, the weight of monsters and prophecy slipped away, replaced by something quiet and solid and good.

The water was endless.

Rheanna floated in it at first, her hair fanning around her like a dark halo, the current soft as a lullaby. Then the lullaby broke. The water darkened, thickened, pulling her down with a sudden, violent weight. She kicked, but her limbs felt heavy, tangled in weeds that hadn't been there a moment before.

Through the murk, shapes appeared. Her sisters.

Cyra first, her hair burning even beneath the black water, fire that could not go out. She reached toward Rheanna, lips moving, but no sound carried. Behind her, Aella's violet eyes flashed like shards of glass, her hand on the hilt of a blade that dissolved into bubbles when she tried to raise it.

Petra floated just beyond them, still and pale, her golden-brown curls drifting like seaweed. Freckles stood stark against her skin. Her emerald eyes were open, fixed on Rheanna, but she did not blink.

Rheanna tried to speak, but the water pressed the words back into her throat.

Something tugged at her ankle. She looked down, and Hollin's small hand was there, gripping tight. The child's eyes were wide, emerald burning too brightly in the dark, her pointed ears catching the last shred of light. When Rheanna tried to reach her, the weeds pulled tighter, winding around her wrists and ribs, squeezing until her breath tore loose in a stream of bubbles. The water shuddered, splitting with a crack that was not natural. Out of the tear stepped a figure. The Oracle.

"Four shall emerge," she roared.

Rheanna's chest burned, her body aching for air.

The Oracle's hand extended, skeletal and pale. "But only one will rise."

The weeds pulled tighter. Cyra and Aella vanished into the gloom, their light snuffed out. Petra's eyes glowed green now, brighter than Hollin's, her lips curving into something that looked too much like a smile. Hollin clung to Rheanna's ankle, dragging her deeper until the water pressed against her skull.

The Oracle's voice thundered in her bones. "The Oracle does not forget."

Rheanna screamed, bubbles bursting from her lips, and in that moment, Petra's still face cracked wide like glass shattering. Hollin's hand slipped from her ankle and vanished into the dark.

Rheanna woke up gasping, tangled in her sheets. Her body was slick with sweat even though the room was cold. Her chest heaved as if she had truly drowned. The echo of the Oracle's words clung to her ears, fading slowly into the hush of the castle night, leaving behind only the pounding of her heart.

CHAPTER 28

E XHAUSTION HIT CYRA HARD and fast after the attack. Her rooms were a welcome reprieve from the stress of the day. Hollin already lay in their bed, tucked into the blankets with her ears uncovered. One poked out from underneath her curtain of strawberry blonde hair. Cyra carefully took off her slippers, then slid her dress off with practiced ease so as not to wake the sleeping child. She climbed into the bed, softly shifting Hollin so her body was comfortably nestled beside her mother's. Cyra took solace in the even rise and fall of her daughter's chest, wishing she could take the girl and run back to the Eye of the Storm Inn, where their lives were simple. To a time where there were no crowns or monsters or prophecies, only work and love. The only fear then was that Hollin's heritage might be found out. Now, the weight of the kingdom weighed heavily on its queen.

The next few days came and went without incident. The council had been so wound up about the drains and water, but it seemed that the monster was a one-off offense. It had served its purpose: to deliver a chilling message for the Oracle.

This is what urged Aella and Cyra to look through the Oracle's rooms once again. To perhaps learn about the creature that attacked them in the book full of monsters they had found in there before. Rheanna was charged with playing with Hollin, keeping her busy in the gardens and kitchen.

The black metal door, with its serpent doorknobs that almost looked alive, seemed to be even heavier than Cyra remembered. She struggled, pulling at the door, digging her heels into the stone flooring before the door gave way with a reluctant groan. A thin layer of dust now covered every surface, the shelves lined with tonics, organs, and trinkets, the desk at the center of the room, and even the comforter that sat upon the clawed wooden bed frame.

Cyra headed straight toward the desk where they had left the book, while Aella leisurely walked around the room, examining with a keen eye. The older sister picked up the old tome gently. It felt as if it would fall apart after the simplest mishandle. It was still open and bookmarked on the Jaquil, who had attacked during the coronation. It was the first time they had all seen a monster in person and definitely not the last. She flipped through the pages of giant spiders and creatures half animal/half human. She turned to a page and paused. *Conka*, it read. An image of a bird-like creature with a forked tongue stared out at her. It brought forth the vivid memory of slurping sounds and Nahlil's open, unseeing eyes. She shook her head, forcing herself to continue, refusing to let grief take hold.

Finally, she found what she was looking for. "Look at this," Cyra called to Aella, who appeared, looking over her shoulder at the open book in her hands.

Weaper. Only one of its kind could be summoned every hundred years. The power it took to control greatly depleted the summoner. Aella and Cyra looked at each other, both opening their mouths at the same time, but Cyra conceded to let her sister speak.

"She is weak right now," Aella stated. "If we knew where she was, perhaps we could end this once and for all."

Cyra sighed. "I won't lie, I had the same thought, but we truly don't know where she is. We only have hushed whispers and passed rumors."

Aella began to pace the room, deep in thought. "I could set out and chase these rumors."

"But you would be doing just that, chasing rumors. No." Cyra shook her head firmly. "What if she wants to separate us? Weaken us? We are stronger together."

"I guess, it just infuriates me to know she is out there, taunting us."

Cyra ran her hand through her hair, tangling in her red curls. "I know, but all we can do is prepare right now. Maybe, once we walk with Elspeth, we will have more answers."

"I'm tired of sitting and waiting. That is weeks away still," Aella huffed, sitting on the edge of the dusty desk.

"I know, I am just as frustrated as you are." Cyra sighed, placing the book down. "If only there were more entries in that journal Rheanna found."

"I won't lie, Cyra," Aella hesitated, then took a deep breath. "I am scared."

For Aella to admit she was scared was not something to take lightly. Cyra wanted to crush her into a hug and let her know that she would always be there for her, but she also knew how that would probably frighten her away. Instead, she sighed and admitted, "I am scared too, but we will get through this all together."

"That's what I thought before…" Her younger sister paused, her gaze falling to the floor. "Before Petra."

"I know losing Petra might have also felt like losing hope, but we cannot give up yet, Aella. We still have each other and this kingdom to fight for."

Aella nodded. "All I know is that I can trust you guys, but after Natalie, it is hard to put my faith in anyone else."

Cyra was silent for a long moment, then said, "That brings me to something I wanted to talk to you about."

Aella's violet gaze snapped up. "Go on."

Cyra exhaled, wringing her fingers before answering. "Natalie."

Aella's expression hardened in an instant. "What about her?"

"We know she didn't kill Petra," Cyra said, keeping her voice level. "She gave us the information about the informant."

Aella gave a curt nod, but her jaw tightened. "That doesn't make her innocent."

"No," Cyra admitted. "But it does make her useful." She hesitated, choosing her words carefully. "If we moved her out of the dungeon and into guarded chambers, the true traitor might show their hand. Letting her be seen might be our chance to catch them."

Aella shook her head. "You want to let her out? To free her? After everything?"

"Not really free," Cyra corrected quickly. "Just moved. A guard at her door night and day. She can only move through approved parts of the castle as long as she has a guard."

Aella pushed off the desk and paced once again, boots striking against stone. "You want to parade her around like bait."

"Yes," Cyra said firmly.

Aella stopped, her shoulders taut. Her silence was louder than her words, and Cyra could read the fury in the tense lines of her sister's body.

Cyra's own guilt twisted like a knife. She remembered Natalie's cries when fire licked against her skin and the smell of scorched flesh when her temper had flared. She had wanted to hurt Natalie, make her feel the pain they felt when losing Petra. And now she would have to live with seeing the scars of her magic on Natalie, scars that would never fade no matter how much time passed.

Finally, Aella spoke, her voice low and sharp. "If you want me to agree to this, we talk to her first. I want to see her eyes when she speaks."

Cyra nodded, relief loosening her chest. "I planned to."

"If she even looks like she's scheming," Aella added, "I'll put a blade through her before she draws her next breath."

"I trust you," Cyra said softly.

Aella's lip twitched in something between a grimace and a smile. "That's your first mistake."

They moved from the Oracle's rooms in silence. The corridor down to the dungeons smelled older than the rest of the castle, thick with dust and damp. Cyra kept her shoulders squared, but inside her chest, the knot of memory tightened; the scars she had left on Natalie's body were forever branded in her thoughts.

The guards bowed them through, iron keys groaning in the locks until the cell door swung open. Natalie was sitting cross-legged on the narrow cot, her dark hair loose around her shoulders, her hands folded in her lap. She looked up when they entered, her eyes landing on Aella first.

Aella stayed back, arms crossed. Cyra moved forward. "We have a proposal," she said. " I want to move you to the chambers above, but still under guard. You will have food, warmth, and a door with eyes on it at all times."

Natalie tilted her head, watching Cyra with an unreadable expression. "And what do you need from me?"

"Nothing," Cyra said simply. "Except that you understand what it means. Your presence in the upper halls will draw attention. If the informant is bold enough, they might seek you out."

Aella finally stepped forward, her voice sharp. "We need to know that you will not betray us again."

Natalie's gaze didn't waver. "I told you before, I love you." Her eyes softened, if only slightly, as they flicked to Aella. "If you still think I would betray you after all that, then you never knew me at all."

The words cut sharper than any blade. Aella's jaw worked, but she said nothing, her face a mask.

"This isn't about forgiving or forgetting. You did, in fact, betray us once, which means that you are more than capable of doing it again. We want to use you as bait." Cyra's golden gaze bore into their prisoner. She knew the scars that lay beneath her clothes.

Natalie rose from the cot, slow and deliberate, her bare feet whispering against the stone. "If it will help you trust me again, then I'll do it," she said softly. "Parade me through your halls."

Aella's lips parted, but whatever words had gathered there died unspoken. For a long moment, the past lovers only stared at each other. Cyra saw the storm that lived in her sister, the pull between fury and something gentler that she would never admit.

Cyra inclined her head. "Then it's settled. I'll arrange your transfer by nightfall."

Natalie nodded, though her eyes lingered on Aella until the sisters turned to leave.

When the dungeon door closed behind them, Aella finally muttered, "If this goes wrong, it's on your head."

"I know," Cyra said quietly.

She could tell by the looks between Aella and Natalie that their love story was not quite over. Cyra couldn't decide who she was more worried for.

CHAPTER 29

Aella had perfected the art of leaving since what had happened between her and Kaelith. She left rooms at the first hint of salt on the air. Left conversations that bent toward laughter. Left the training yard when a shadow crossed the tiles in the shape of long hair and too-blue eyes. She kept her exits clean. Efficient. A chair pushed back. A blade she suddenly remembered needed oil. A message she had to deliver, urgent, obviously, her face blank as stone while her pulse did something ragged and embarrassing under her leathers.

At night, Aella slept like someone braced for an ambush. That is, if she slept at all. She closed her eyes and there it was again. The choked, surprised little sound that had slipped free from Kaelith's mouth and made Aella's bones feel hollowed out. She could almost feel the way Kaelith's fingers had tightened against her shoulders, the way her body had arched.

Aella needed to forget. So she didn't stop. She sharpened daggers, ran the stairs two at a time until the edges of the castle blurred, and threw knives until her wrists burned. She told herself it was because she was head of the guard now, not because the memory of Kaelith's smile kept scraping over her, leaving an unbearable hunger in its wake.

Days became a week. Then two. It might have stretched longer if Kaelith had played along, but she did not.

Aella rounded a corner into the narrow east corridor and found the woman already there, lounging with her shoulder against the wall like she had been poured there on purpose. Sun slanted through a high window. Her hair fell down her back, the silver flinting in the afternoon light. She adorned a blue dress, close to the color of her eyes, that appeared as if it had been painted onto her body. The body that Aella struggled not to look at, though her flickering gaze betrayed her.

"Aella," Kaelith said, a small smile on her full lips. "Are you going to keep running away from me?"

Aella's jaw set. "Move."

"No."

Aella took another step. It was a mistake because the second she did, she took a deep breath of saltwater, of Kaelith. It was a reminder of the night she had tried to bury. She kept her eyes trained over Kaelith's shoulder, refusing to look at her face.

"Whatever you want," Aella said, "I can't help you."

Kaelith let out a smooth giggle. "Oh? That's funny. Because I distinctly remember you helping me a few nights ago, and I do recall you enjoyed yourself."

Heat crept in. Not across her skin. Inside her. It flared, sharp and humiliating. "It was a mistake."

"Sure," Kaelith said easily. "A very enjoyable mistake."

Aella felt the ground tip a fraction. She finally looked straight at Kaelith. "I don't want complications."

"Wonderful. Neither do I."

Aella blinked. "What?"

Kaelith pushed off the wall. Her eyes, that bright cerulean blue, slid over Aella's face, her posture, the coiled fists she hadn't noticed she had made. "Relax, stormcloud. We aren't in love. We had fun. You were drowning in your own head, and I threw you a rope. That's all."

The rope of it caught and pulled tight in Aella's chest. She wanted to drag Kaelith back into the dark, press her into stone, and get those little noises out of her again.

"I'm not good at this." The words felt like gravel.

"Which part?" Kaelith's tone stayed light, but her gaze steadied. "The part where you feel something and don't know where to put it? Or the part where you panic because you think feeling anything will ruin you?"

Aella's hands flexed. "Don't pretend you know me."

"I don't have to pretend." Kaelith leaned in, but not close enough to touch. "You carry rage like it's armor. You think if you set it down, everything will find you again and hurt you. You are probably right. That doesn't mean you have to sleep with your knives every night."

Aella reached out before she could stop herself and shoved Kaelith's shoulder into the wall. Not hard, but with just enough force to hear the satisfying thud of muscle and stone. Kaelith's breath came out in a laugh that lit Aella's nerves. She was too happy about being manhandled. It was infuriating.

"Careful," Kaelith said. "I bruise easy."

"Liar."

Kaelith grinned. "You would know, I guess."

Aella's mouth did a small, unwilling tug, then flattened. The silence stretched between them. Outside, a bell rang in the distant courtyard.

"You really don't care?" Aella asked, and she hated that it sounded like a test.

Kaelith tipped her head. "I don't care about labels. I don't care about a promise I can't keep. And I don't need you to be gentle with me unless you want to be, but I'd prefer if you weren't."

The last words landed hard in Aella's stomach. She stared at Kaelith's mouth and remembered the way it had parted. Remembered the sound in her throat. The memory hit clean and bright, cutting through her defenses. Aella's breath caught. She hated that her body answered, a pulsing in her core that dared to be stoked.

Kaelith's voice came quieter. "You're allowed to want something just for the fun of it."

Aella dragged a hand down her face and looked up at the ceiling. The stone above felt heavier than usual, as if the castle itself pressed down, demanding she choose. "If we do this," she said at last, "we do it my way."

Kaelith lifted two fingers. "May the goddesses bear witness."

"No telling anyone."

"Obviously."

"No lingering in bed together."

Kaelith's mouth twitched. "I do not linger. I lounge."

"No lounging either."

"Harsh."

"If I say stop, you stop."

Kaelith sobered instantly. "Of course."

"And if you start acting like a lovesick fool, I'll gut you."

"There she is," Kaelith said, delighted. "I was wondering when she'd come back."

Aella stared at her. The first tremor of something like relief slid through her bones. "I mean it."

"I know you do." Kaelith stepped aside, finally letting Aella go. "Go sharpen a dagger or glower from a tower. Later, if you want... you know where to find me."

Aella didn't move. Her body had its own ideas. She looked at Kaelith and let herself remember one more thing she had been trying not to. Not the sound, this time, but the way Kaelith's fingers had slid into her, pumping and swirling.

"Stop looking at me like that," Aella muttered, not sure which of them she meant.

"Like what?"

"Like you know I'm already thinking about later."

"I know because your murderous eyebrows soften when you are plotting pleasure," Kaelith said solemnly.

"That is not a thing."

"It is very much a thing."

"Go away."

"Gladly. But Aella?"

She didn't want to answer. "What?"

"Don't run from me, run to me," Kaelith said. "It's more fun."

The answer leapt out of Aella before she could dress it in armor. "I know."

Kaelith's smile hit her like sunlight off water. It dazzled, dangerously bright, and Aella hated how much she wanted to bask in it. Kaelith tapped two fingers lightly against Aella's wrist, not quite a touch, just a promise it could be one, then drifted down the corridor with that loose-hipped sway that made Aella want to chase after her.

Aella stood there a long moment and let her breath go slow before moving. She went to the practice hall and threw knives until the panic left her bones. It took fewer throws than the night before. When she finished, she washed her hands in a brass basin and watched the water run pink over her knuckles. Not blood. Oil and dust. The sight still tripped something old in her chest. She swallowed hard and shut it away again.

Evening slid over the castle in bands of amber and indigo. Voices rose in the great hall. Aella did not go there. She walked the east wing instead, slow and silent, checking windows, corners, the places a threat would hide. She told herself it was duty. It was also stalling.

At the end of the corridor, a door stood open on a small room with maps pinned to every wall. Kaelith was inside, perched on the table, boots braced on a chair, hair spilled forward as she flicked a dagger in and out of her fingers with lazy skill. She didn't look up when Aella leaned in the doorway, though a smirk began to play on her lips.

"You got lost on your way to avoiding me," Kaelith said. "Easy mistake."

Aella shut the door. She crossed the room. She stopped with the table between them and repeated her words from earlier. "We are not telling anyone."

"You really love that rule."

"We are not falling in love."

Kaelith's smile went slow. "Wasn't planning on it."

"And if I say stop, you stop."

"Yes."

"Come here," Aella said, and heard the roughness in it, heard the way it gave them both permission to be exactly what they were.

Kaelith slid off the table and came, her movements fluid.

Aella gripped her jaw to keep her still, fingers digging in harder than she should, but Kaelith only moaned into her mouth as if the pressure spurred her on. The sound broke Aella. That damned sound, low, raw, and utterly unguarded. She'd been hearing it in her head for nights, and now it was vibrating against her lips.

Her hand slid down without permission, beneath Kaelith's cloak, under the hem of her tunic. Hot skin. The twitch of muscle. And lower, where Kaelith was already wet and waiting. Aella swallowed a curse. She pushed two fingers inside and Kaelith's head fell back against the wall with a gasp that echoed sharply in the quiet room.

"Goddess, stormcloud." Kaelith's voice was ragged, her nails digging into Aella's arm. Aella set a pace rough and merciless, just shy of cruel. Each thrust dragged another noise from her, each noise seared itself into Aella's mind like a brand.

Kaelith tried to hold herself up, tried to meet Aella stroke for stroke, but Aella kept her pinned with one hand on her hip, forcing her to take it. She wanted control, but watching Kaelith unravel under her hand felt less like victory and more like a slow surrender of her own defenses.

Kaelith's body arched hard, hair spilling wild over the maps behind her, lips parted around a moan that broke into a cry when Aella's thumb found her clit. She pulled her fingers free and Kaelith slumped against the table, sweat shining along her throat.

Before Aella could catch her breath, Kaelith slid down to her knees. The shift was so sudden that Aella's stomach lurched. Kaelith's hands were already dragging at her belt, nimble and hungry.

"Don't," Aella started, voice sharp with warning.

Kaelith's mouth was already on her, hot and wet and devastating. The warning dissolved into a broken curse. Aella's legs buckled, her hand shooting instinctively to the back of Kaelith's neck, fingers tangling in her hair.

Kaelith hummed against her, the vibration tearing a gasp straight out of Aella's throat. Her tongue was relentless, her fingers pressing into Aella's thighs to hold her open when instinct made her want to snap shut. She tried not to give Kaelith the satisfaction of a sound, but when Kaelith curled her tongue just right, the moan tore free anyway.

Kaelith pulled back only to glance up, lips slick, eyes blazing cerulean. "There it is," she murmured, voice wrecked. "Knew I could get it out of you."

Aella scowled, but Kaelith only laughed breathlessly and buried herself back between her thighs. The rhythm built until Aella's vision blurred at the edges, her nails biting crescents into

Kaelith's throat. Her body gave way before her mind would, pleasure crashing through her in a violent wave she couldn't stop.

Her knees nearly gave out. Kaelith held her there, riding out every twitch and tremor until Aella shoved her away, panting hard.

Kaelith rose slowly, wiping her mouth with the back of her hand, lips swollen, cheeks flushed. She looked entirely too satisfied.

"Better?" she teased, her voice hoarse.

"Functional," Aella rasped.

Kaelith grinned, unbothered. "Good enough for me."

CHAPTER 30

T HE WEST WING WAS empty, sunlight spilling through tall arched windows, turning the dust motes to gold as they danced in the quiet air. The light was deceptively warm, contrasting the perpetual chill of the castle walls. Rheanna came here to walk off the heaviness that clung to her like a second skin after long hours in council chambers, the echoes of debate still ringing in her ears.

Bianca Solo stood at the end of the corridor, back pressed to the cold stone, violet silk trailing down her sleeves, the vibrant color stark against the gray monotony of the walls. Her arms were crossed like she meant to look impervious, but her eyes betrayed her, wide and rimmed with exhaustion.

"Rheanna," she said, her voice softer than usual. It wasn't the arrogant drawl she typically used to cut down opponents in council meetings; it was fragile.

Rheanna slowed her steps, wariness prickling along her spine like a sudden draft. "Bianca."

Bianca shifted her weight, as though unsure how to begin. For once, her pride seemed to waver. "I owe you, all of you, an apology."

Rheanna said nothing, but nodded slowly, her expression unreadable, allowing her to continue.

Bianca's throat bobbed with a hard, visible swallow. "I was rude when you three came back. I told anyone who would listen that you weren't fit to rule, that you had no right to wear crowns you hadn't earned." Her eyes flicked up, meeting Rheanna's gaze with something like shame. "I was bitter. My family had been slaughtered, one by one, while yours suddenly returned. I thought the world had handed you a kingdom while it left me with nothing but ash."

Rheanna's chest tightened. She remembered Bianca's sneering remarks in the war room, the way she had belittled Petra's youth, the way she spoke over Cyra and Aella with cutting arrogance. She had worn her grief like armor and wielded her tongue like a blade.

"We lost too. Before we lost Petra, we had lost our parents," Rheanna responded, her voice low and thrumming with old pain.

"I know, but you had each other, and that made me bitter," Bianca continued, her voice cracking. "And Petra, I was cruelest to her. Even when we were children, I mocked her. She seemed to have everything. I wanted to tear it from her. And when you returned, I carried that same envy with me."

Her hand twisted in the fabric of her sleeve, knuckles turning white against the violet silk. "But I was wrong. And now Petra is gone and I can't undo the things I said."

Rheanna's voice came quiet but firm, her words threaded with grief. "You're right. You can't take them back. Petra is gone, and no matter how sorry you are, she will not know."

Bianca flinched as if physically struck, but Rheanna didn't stop. She thought of Petra's laugh, bright and clear, how it had filled the castle's coldest corners with warmth, how she would never hear it echo off these stones again.

"All you can do now," Rheanna said, stepping closer, "is try to be better. Honor her memory and, most importantly, honor yourself."

Bianca's eyes brimmed, tears trembling but unshed. "Do you think that matters?"

"Yes." Rheanna didn't waver. Her gaze was steady, even in the face of such raw emotion. "All we can do is try to be better."

Bianca drew in a sharp breath, a faint, defiant huff that quickly softened into resignation. "Then I'll try."

Rheanna studied her: nineteen, arrogant, grieving, and alone. Perhaps there was more to her than bitterness and sharp words. This, at least, was a beginning.

Rheanna's voice softened. "That's all anyone can ask."

Bianca turned to leave, her silk hem brushing the stone. Sunlight caught the faint streak of dampness on her cheek, and for the first time, Rheanna saw not the haughty girl who had spat venom in the war room, but a lonely young woman, burdened with the same loss as all of them.

She lingered a moment in the corridor, watching the sunlight fade against the stone where Bianca had stood. The sound of hurried footsteps broke through the stillness, growing louder with each beat.

Laney and Cora rounded the corner, skirts gathered in their fists, faces pale and urgent. Laney's red hair had come loose from its braid, freckles standing stark against her flushed skin.

Cora's sharp eyes darted around the hall, scanning for unwanted watchers before she rushed to Rheanna's side.

"Princess," Laney gasped, clutching at Rheanna's sleeve with trembling fingers. The fabric of Rheanna's sleeve crinkled under the desperate grip. "We heard something down in the servants' hall." Her voice shook with urgency. "The Cleansers. They're whispering about the little princess Hollin."

Cora nodded, catching her breath. "They said her name, Rheanna. They spoke of taking her."

Rheanna's stomach knotted, but her face remained steady. Her heart hammered against her ribs, a frantic drumbeat of fear she refused to show. She reached out, laying a calm hand over Laney's trembling one. "Calm down. It's okay."

The girls stilled under her voice, lifting wide, frightened eyes to hers.

"You are brave," Rheanna said softly. "Aella already discovered their plans. We are not unprepared. Thank you for coming to me so quickly with this. Every word you carry makes all of us safer. Do you understand?"

Cora nodded fiercely. "Then we'll keep listening. We'll bring you everything."

Rheanna's hand brushed briefly over her arm, reassuring. "Yes. But promise me you will not linger where you might be seen and do not chase shadows. Poke for information, if you can, but choose safety above all else."

Laney and Cora exchanged a look, then nodded almost in unison. Their eyes, though still wide, held a new spark of determination.

Rheanna allowed herself the faintest smile. "One day, when this kingdom is healed, people will know how much they owe to quiet bravery. To the girls who carried whispers through these halls when others were too afraid to speak. That will be your legacy."

Laney's eyes widened, her freckles bright against the flush of her cheeks. "Do you mean that?"

Rheanna's golden gaze softened, her voice almost a whisper. "With all my heart."

They dipped clumsy curtsies, their skirts brushing the stone floor, before turning and darting back the way they had come. Their steps no longer rang with panic but with purpose.

Left in the empty corridor once more, Rheanna leaned against the cool wall, her chest rising and falling in a slow, heavy rhythm.

CHAPTER 31

THE GOLDEN DOORS SWUNG wide with a soft groan, the sound echoing faintly against the high ceiling, and light spilled across the receiving room in a sudden, brilliant wash. Crystal strands of the great teal chandelier glittered overhead, casting fractured reflections that danced across the plush white rug like scattered jewels. A grand piano, its surface gleaming like a dark mirror, waited silent beneath it. Yellow couches embroidered with curling flower patterns framed the room, their cushions inviting. The scent of polished wood and fresh blossoms lingered in the air, a gentler perfume than the earthy smoke of herbs Elspeth often carried with her.

The sisters gathered there, a silent semi-circle of expectant faces, waiting to hear the story Elpseth had promised of goddesses. Cyra eased down on the nearest couch, Hollin climbing into her lap and folding herself against her mother's chest. Atlas settled beside them, careful not to intrude, but close enough that his arm brushed hers when he leaned back. Rheanna sat more gracefully, smoothing her skirts, while Aella perched on the armrest, restless even in comfort. Malcolm took a chair near the corner.

Elspeth stood before them all, her presence steady as stone, though her gaze softened at the sight of them together. She moved toward the small table in the center, where a clay bowl smoldered faintly with herbs, the embers pulsing with a dull, red heat. She stirred the smoke with a twist of her fingers, and it rose in fine threads that seemed to tangle with the light of the chandelier.

She began, her voice soft and full of authority, cutting through the silence. "You must know whose hands first wove the world. Without knowing them, you cannot know what has been unraveled."

The room stilled, the air growing heavy with anticipation, eyes drawn to Elspeth as if the chandelier's fractured light now bent only toward her.

"There are countless goddesses," she continued, her eyes tracking the rising smoke, "but one name begins every story: Seradelle, the Weaver of Worlds."

"Seradelle gathered the wild strands of our world," she said, her hands moving to mimic the act of gathering. "She wove fire to air, water to earth, and bound them into a tapestry strong enough for life to cling to. Without her weaving, there would be no balance."

Malcolm inclined his head slightly, finishing the cadence for her, his voice a low rumble. "She is the loom upon which all else hangs."

A flicker of pride passed across Elspeth's eyes. "Yes. The first truth we teach our children in Hefguard."

Hollin lifted her head from Cyra's chest, her small fingers twisting in her mother's gown. "So she made everything?"

"Not all, child. Her sisters carried their own gifts, but Seradelle alone wove them into something whole. Where they gave fragments, she made a world."

"Even in our keeps, we name her first. Balance before vow. It is how all oaths begin," Atlas said, pride in his kingdom's ways resonating in his voice.

"Where Seradelle wove with balance," Elspeth said, her tone dropping into something steadier, heavier, "her twin did not."

The shift in the room was subtle, but Cyra felt it. The chandelier's teal light seemed colder, the plush rug under her feet not so soft. Hollin burrowed closer against her, her little body sensing what her words could not yet grasp.

"Her name is Arathine," Elspeth continued, the name hanging in the air like a warning. "She believed threads must never be left loose. They had to be pulled tight and knotted until they could not move. She thought strength came from control."

The smoke thickened, winding into itself until it looked more rope than thread. Cyra's jaw tensed at the sight.

Aella gave a sharp laugh from her perch on the armrest. "And let me guess, we're supposed to hate her for it? Every story makes these goddesses sound flawless, but I haven't met a flawless soul yet. Not even close."

Cyra turned her head toward her sister. Her voice was biting, but her posture wasn't. Her knees were drawn up, fingers digging into the couch's embroidered fabric. Aella's suspicion was not just rebellion. It was fear, sharpened into something she could wield.

Elspeth's eyes didn't waver. "Not flawless. Dangerous." She lifted a hand, and the smoke knot drew tighter, almost vanishing under its own weight. "A knot can guard. It can keep faith strong. It can also become a noose. Arathine's bindings are sworn in blood, and some still bind that way."

Atlas's voice cut in, firm and defensive. "We still do. In Hefguard, her name seals oaths between crown and soldier and even between kin. The ceremony we did during our wedding was bound by Arathine. Without her, loyalty would break at the first storm."

Cyra looked down at her right palm, where the shimmering coil still etched in her skin. She rubbed it now, a whole new meaning and importance.

"Or choke the first breath," Malcolm muttered from his post by the wall. He didn't bother to move, but his arms crossed tighter over his chest. "I've heard the old stories. Villages that bound themselves to every vow and law until no one could breathe. Their obsession with control killed them."

Elspeth inclined her head. "Both truths are hers. Gift and curse. Arathine was not wicked, but she never knew when to stop pulling the thread. That is her flaw."

Cyra stroked Hollin's hair, absently untangling a strand of strawberry-blond curl. Her mind drifted, not to oaths sealed in Hefguard halls, but to her own crown. Invisible, unrelenting, tightening around her throat day after day. Binding. Knotting. She wondered if that was what Arathine's worship truly felt like.

Aella leaned closer, eyes holding a childlike curiosity Cyra had never seen before. "So Seradelle gave us balance and Arathine gave us chains."

"Balance cannot exist without both."

The smoke knot gave one last twitch before snapping apart. Wisps scattered like cut threads.

Hollin peeked up, her voice almost lost in the silence. "I don't like her."

Cyra pressed a kiss against her daughter's temple. Neither did she, but she respected her.

The smoke thinned, only wisps left hanging like the trailing ends of a thread. Elspeth let her hand drop to her side, her gaze steady at the embers glowing in the clay bowl.

"From Seradelle's loom came four daughters," she said. "Each born of a single strand. Each carrying an element in its purest form. Fire, water, wind, and stone."

Her words seemed to hum in the room, tugging at something in Cyra's chest. She felt the familiar heat coil in her palms, waiting for her to summon it. She flexed her fingers in her lap, the power restless beneath her skin.

"And which one," Cyra asked, her voice breaking through the hush, "gave me fire?"

Elspeth's gaze moved to her. "Ilyra," she answered. "Goddess of flame. She was the boldest of the four. She reveled in passion, love, and rage both. Where she walked, rebellion followed."

A curl of smoke flared into a small blaze, no bigger than a candle flame, then vanished. Cyra stared at the space it left behind. She thought of how easily her fire obeyed her, how sweetly it could warm or how quickly it could destroy.

Beside her, Rheanna shifted, her voice soft. "And Petra?"

Cyra glanced at her sister. Rheanna's eyes were glass bright in the chandelier's glow, shimmering with unshed emotion.

Elspeth's expression turned gentle. "Terranelle. Patient, stubborn, rooted as stone. She does not abandon her children, even when they are laid in the ground."

The words pressed against Cyra's ribs, sharp and unrelenting. She swallowed, blinking away the heat that threatened her eyes. Hollin wriggled closer in her lap, and Cyra smoothed her daughter's hair, grateful for the weight of her, an anchor against the grief.

Elspeth's voice carried on. "Marethe was water. Calm, reflective, but also given to sorrow. And Sylithis was air. Bright, free, fickle as a song."

Aella tilted her head, violet eyes narrowing in thought. "So each of us ties to one of them."

"Each of you carries a gift from their line, yes. But remember this, no goddess gave without flaw. Fire can kindle joy or consume it. Water can heal or drown. Air can free or choke. Earth can grow or crush. Each gift demands choice."

Cyra leaned back slightly, pressing her cheek to the top of Hollin's hair. She could feel her daughter's small heartbeat through her shoulder.

The last curl of stone-smoke faded, leaving only a faint sting of ash in the air. The room seemed to breathe with it.

Aella broke the silence first. "And those are the good ones?" she asked, arms braced over her knees. "Because they don't sound much better than the rest of us. Rage, drowning, suffocating, what's so holy about that?"

Cyra almost told her to hush, but Elspeth didn't flinch. Instead, she added more flame to her bowl, smoke caressing the air once again.

"Not all were daughters," she said. "Some were born of frays at the loom's edge. Lesser threads, some call them. But power still clung to them."

Her words hushed the room once again.

The smoke bent low, thinning into something like a curtain. "Nytheris. Secrets were her worship."

Aella's mouth twisted, but she said nothing this time. Cyra caught it anyway, the flicker of recognition.

"Callenne," Elspeth murmured. "Renewal, after ruin. The fae still honor her with blossoms and a festival at the start of spring."

Atlas leaned forward, the lamplight catching the sharp line of his jaw. "In Hefguard, we light bonfires at the end of winter in her name. We wait for her spark in the dark."

"Veyra," Elspeth said, her voice low. "She carries those we have lost to the otherside. She is not death, but a guide to it."

Malcolm spoke then, not looking at anyone, his gaze fixed on the floor. "Healers learn her rites for when there is nothing more to be done."

His words made Cyra's throat tighten. She felt Hollin's small heartbeat against her chest, steady and alive, and thought of Petra. Thought of her parents. She wondered if Veyra had met them with open hands or, since Linnosa had been cut from the tapestry, if they had slipped away alone.

"None of them are flawless. Not Seradelle, not her daughters, not the frayed ones. They give and they take. Every gift can become a curse. Every curse can be turned to gift. You must decide how to wield them."

Cyra let her hand drift over Hollin's hair, smoothing it flat. Her daughter's eyes were wide, catching every flicker of smoke and light as if she could see more than the rest of them. Elspeth's words wound tight in Cyra's chest. She felt them there already, invisible and heavy.

CHAPTER 32

T HE CLASH OF STEEL echoed through the training yard, the sharp ring of metal against metal carrying into the open space. Rheanna pivoted, her boots scuffing against the dry earth as she raised her blade to meet Ripley's, but her timing faltered. He knocked her off balance with a practiced sweep, the tip of his sword grazing past her side before she could recover.

"You're somewhere else tonight," Ripley said, stepping back and lowering his blade. His grin was sharp, but his eyes searched her face with a quiet intensity. "I know when you're holding back."

She blew out a slow breath, lowering her sword and rolling her shoulders to ease the tension. "I was thinking."

He barked a laugh, the sound rough and genuine. "You should be thinking about how to not get your ass handed to you."

Rheanna only smiled faintly, walking to the edge of the ring. She rested the sword against her thigh, gaze distant as she looked past the flickering torches. "Elspeth told me of Marethe today. The goddess of water. " Her fingers trailed along the hilt of her sword as she spoke. "I wonder if magic were still with us, what it might feel like to have a connection with her."

Ripley tilted his head, his smirk fading into something softer. "I know nothing of the goddesses, but it would probably be pretty amazing."

Her laugh came quiet but warm. "Perhaps."

He moved closer, sword resting loose in his hand. The nearness prickled at her skin like static, making the fine hairs on her arms stand up.

"You think too much," he said softly, reaching out to brush a damp strand of hair from her cheek with the back of his hand, his calloused skin a stark contrast to her own. "And it's going to get you killed in here."

Their eyes locked. The torchlight flickered between them, shadows swaying with their breaths. The clang of her sword against the dirt rang in the silence when his mouth claimed hers. Heat poured through Rheanna like a rush of tide breaking against a shore, sudden and overwhelming.

Her hands gripped his shoulders, fingers curling into the damp linen of his shirt until the fabric bunched under her nails. His lips trailed down the column of her throat, tasting the salt of her skin, lingering at the hollow where her pulse raced frantically. The scent of sweat and steel surrounded them. He lifted her effortlessly, pressing her against the wall, her legs instinctively wrapping around his waist. The hard stone at her back was nothing compared to the heat of him pressed flush against her, every shift of his hips drawing a breathless sound from her lips.

Clothes fell between them in pieces, torn free in fumbling pulls and desperate hands that couldn't move fast enough. Ripley's shirt was the first to hit the dirt, then Rheanna's tunic, his fingers slipping beneath the fabric to slide it from her shoulders. When her skin was bared to him, his breath caught, his gaze tracing her with silent reverence before his hands followed, mapping the curve of her waist.

His mouth found her collarbone, her shoulder, her breast, kissing hungrily down the curve of her body. Rheanna gasped, her fingers tightening in his red hair, pulling him closer as heat bloomed low in her belly. The scrape of his stubble across her skin made her shiver, but his lips soothed every tremor.

When she pressed against him, she felt him hard against her thigh, the urgency of his body answering her own with a demand she was eager to meet. She tilted her hips, a soft moan escaping as the friction sparked through her like lightning. Ripley groaned against her chest, the sound low and rough, his hands grasping at her waist to drag her tighter against him.

He lifted her again, her legs wrapping around him, their bare skin sliding together as he pressed her to the wall. His hand slipped lower, fingers exploring with bold certainty, until Rheanna's breath hitched sharply, her nails digging into his shoulders. The flood of sensation nearly buckled her, her head tipping back against the stone as she gasped his name.

"Tell me," he murmured, his lips hot against her ear. "Tell me what you want."

Her reply was a whisper, broken and breathless. "You."

That undid him. He kissed her hard, devouring, as he pressed fully against her, the last barrier of cloth shoved aside. The contact was dizzying, overwhelming. Skin to skin, heat to heat. When he finally entered her, she clung to him with a sharp cry that echoed off the walls.

The world dissolved into the rhythm of their bodies. Every thrust, every gasp, every soft cry was a wave crashing, relentless and consuming. His forehead pressed to hers, their breaths tangled, their whispers raw and unsteady, promises, pleas, her name on his lips like a prayer. Rheanna's moans rose, her body arching against him as the tide built higher, faster, until it broke, a shudder tearing through her as she clutched him tight, lost in the storm. Ripley followed her with a groan, his body seizing, his arms locking around her as though he would never let go.

For a long while, only the sound of their ragged breathing filled the torchlit arena. Sweat-damp skin, tangled limbs, trembling hearts. He pressed a final kiss to her hair, holding her close against his chest.

"You undo me," he whispered.

While her conversation with Ripley turned heated and she would trade it for nothing, his warmth still lingering on her skin, Rheanna still craved more knowledge. Her mind continued to wander late into the night; unable to sleep, she tossed and turned restlessly until she decided to untangle herself from her silk sheets and take a walk to help clear her mind. She slipped on a pair of slippers and pulled on a cotton robe, wrapping it tightly around her against the midnight chill. Her arms slipped beneath her armpits as she walked into the gilded hallway. She absentmindedly strolled, her feet carrying her on a path they knew by heart, until she stopped, standing in front of a portrait of two people, two ancestors gone. The man, the King, did not matter; Rheanna knew she had come here for the woman.

Lewellyn Hormanick. Young, beautiful, a slight curve of her lips, barely there as if she held a secret. Her skin pale, silver eyes stark against her long, flowing black hair. She found herself getting lost in the young woman's image, how she could have been barely older than Rheanna herself, if that. She thought back to the journal entry where Selmana, the Oracle, talked about her twin's death. For the first time, Rheanna felt a spark of empathy for the Oracle. Having lost Petra, she could imagine the devastation Selmana must have felt, the hollow ache that threatened to consume everything in its path, but she let it drive her to who she was now, the Oracle. Hell-bent on getting vengeance and torturing girls similar to her sister. Rheanna would never bestow the pain of losing a sister on someone else.

"She is quite beautiful."

The sound of a melodic voice caused Rheanna to jump. She turned, pulling the robe tighter around her, to see Kaelith standing in a loose, flowing nightgown, one of the ones Rheanna had given her.

She recovered quickly, for some reason at ease around the strange woman. "She is. Her life was taken much too soon."

Kaelith stepped up, closer to the painting and now right next to Rheanna. "What is her story?"

"Her story is part of my sisters and I, the reason for us, in truth," Rheanna said, and she continued to explain it all, trusting her with no reason to. She told her of Selmana and Lewellyn, the Oracle, the Cleansers, the monsters, even of Petra. At the end of it all, Rheanna expected to be in tears, but instead she just stood there, breathing heavily and deeply into the night, the weight of the words hanging in the cold air. Kaelith placed her palm lightly on the middle of Rheanna's back in silent support.

"I'm sorry," she breathed out. "I don't mean to dump this all on you."

Kaelith smiled, a gentle expression on her face. "Never apologize, sister. We all must have those who help us carry the weight of our hardships."

Rheanna's head tilted, strands of black hair coming loose from the knot on top of her head. Sister? She had never been called sister by anyone other than her blood sisters. As if hearing her thoughts aloud, Kaelith laughed, a sound like windchimes caught on a breeze.

"Marethe is our mother, to you in a bit of a different way than me, but still true."

"Can I ask – what are you?" Rheanna knew from the moment she saw Kaelith that she was different. There was no other way to describe her but ethereal and entirely otherworldly.

"I will tell you, but I ask that you do not share it with anyone else right now." Kaelith's dark blue eyes bore into Rheanna's, holding a depth that seemed bottomless, and she could not help but nod, desperate for more information about the goddess who gave her power.

"I am a siren, born of Marethe and the ocean. We were created from the goddess' tears of sorrow."

Rheanna's jaw dropped open in awe. Like many creatures, she had heard rumors of sirens, beautiful women who lured men to their deaths with their voices. Similarly with the fae, it seemed that not everything was as it seemed. How many times had history been rewritten to fit a certain narrative? Rheanna decided then that she would one day find out the truth.

"How are you even in Linnosa? I thought it would make you sick? Like it did the fae," Rheanna questioned, curiosity overriding her shock.

Kaelith sighed, a sound heavy with longing. "I am like the little princess, half human. My siren side is dominant, but the human in me makes it possible to be here. I am disconnected from Marethe, from my magic in Linnosa, but never from the sea. I can hear it whispering to me even now."

The old Rheanna would be frightened by what Kaelith revealed to her, but after meeting her niece, she had learned that not everything was as it seemed. The revelation of this secret made Rheanna trust this strange woman even more. She closed her eyes, trying to imagine what the connection to Marethe might feel like, but instead, she felt the soft thump of her heart and the steady flow of magic that pulsed along with it. She tried to focus harder, trying to connect to the goddess, even if just for a moment.

"You will not feel her here, sister. No matter how hard you try," Kaelith said gently, her palm gently brushing Rheanna's back.

Opening her eyes, she sighed, frustration bubbling in her chest, "I want that connection. It was so hard for me to wield my magic; it came more easily to my sisters. Even Aella, who denied her magic for so long, can call it with such ease when she decides to."

"Everyone's journey is different. Marethe will be there for you when the time comes, believe in that."

She nodded, taking comfort in her words. Once they broke the curse and all magic was freed, Rheanna would feel that connection she craved so deeply. "Thank you."

Kaelith simply smiled and turned, her silhouette fading into the shadows, leaving Rheanna alone in the hallway once more.

CHAPTER 33

*T*HE CORD BITES. LEATHER, *wet with someone else's sweat, pulls tight around her wrists, chafing the raw skin until it burns. Her knees slip on cold stone. Her breath ghosts in the chill cellar, a shallow, frantic sound that echoes back at her.*

"Again," Creaton says. The word is bored. He could be asking for more wine.

Aella swallows hard, tasting copper, and calls.

Wind answers, thin at first, a breath through a crack, then a draft that lifts the hair from her neck. She reaches for it the way a child reaches for a mother's hand, desperate and trusting. It jerks away. The current snaps. The room tilts.

"Again."

She tries. The air shudders and the lantern flame gutters sideways, stretching into a needle. The pressure changes. Her ears hurt. Creaton does not move. He watches as if she were a fly pinned to a card. The switch rests easy in his palm.

It strikes when the flame steadies. A line of heat lashes her shoulder. She doesn't make a sound until the second strike lands, lower, and the third finds the welt the second raised.

"Control," he says. "Or it controls you."

Her lungs won't fill. It feels like the room shrinks around her ribs. Wind surges, then knots. The lantern wobbles on its hook, casting dancing shadows. The switch kisses the same place again, again, until the pain smears into a single, ugly color.

"Again."

She calls. The air comes like a flood down a narrow throat. The lantern bursts, glass skittering. The flame goes out. Dark crashes over her, heavy and absolute.

She can't breathe. She can't breathe.

Aella jerked up in the dark of her chamber, blade already in her hand, the steel cold and familiar. She was in her rooms in the castle. No cellar or whip. No noise, but her own breath tearing out of her in ragged gasps.

She lowered the knife an inch at a time. Her fingers were stiff from clutching too hard, as though she expected the shadows to strike. Her palms were slick, sheets tangled around her ankles, rough against sweat-damp skin. The first breath was shallow. The second caught halfway. She counted the third in through her nose and let it out slowly until her hands stopped trembling enough to set the blade back on the table.

The old feeling stirred, tightness where her ribs met. She stood barefoot on the rug and crossed to the window, her footsteps silent on the plush carpet. The latch stuck and she forced it with a flat, angry twist until the casement opened and the night breathed on her face. Cool air brushed her cheeks, carrying the faint scent of stone and distant smoke.

The palace roofs crouched below, black against a darker sky. Flags on the western tower hung limp. No wind to meet her. Fine. She would make her own.

"Not yours," she said to the memory of the hands that used to hold her under. The air lifted at her call in the smallest of ways, but it was enough to stir the hair at her temple. Enough to remind her that the thing that once crushed her was a thing she could hold.

Her hands were quick with blades because her lungs were traitors. She learned to fight without calling wind at all because it sent her into a panicked state. But she learned how to control it with the memory of Petra's blood cooling on stone and Karif's steady hand at her elbow.

"Again," Karif would say, and the word was kind in his mouth. She put him in the dirt with the force of her panic, both of them coughing on dust as the air bucked. He laughed from the ground, spit grit, and said, "Good. Now do it on purpose."

So she did. They found a stretch of scrub where the gusts came down from the hills in mean little bursts and she learned not to flinch. He stood two paces off and never reached for her unless she reached first.

"Your body remembers what he taught it," he said once, when she crouched with her forehead to her knees, palms flat, riding a wave of roiling breath. "Teach it different."

"How?" She hated that it came out thin and weak.

"Remind yourself why you want to do this," he answered, his voice steady.

After Petra, there was no other choice. Grief made edges on everything and put steel in places that were soft before. She could not be the sister who wanted and waited. So she called the air every day until her throat burned and her body learned that wanting it did not kill her; it made her stronger.

In the ruins of a farmhouse where the Cleansers had painted slogans on the hearth with soot, she lifted a column of dust slow enough to write their names in it without coughing. In a narrow canyon, she let a gust run itself out along her arms instead of across her chest, felt it rush and not take her with it. On a ridge at dawn, Karif let a rope fall and told her to catch it before it hit the ground without using her hands.

It never became easy. She did not trust people who said mastery was easy. The unease was still there, coiled under her ribs, a shadow that went wherever she went. When she called, the old panic sometimes lifted its head to see if it could still bite.

Aella pressed her palms to the window ledge and called now, gentle. Air threaded between her fingers, a cool slip. She kept her breath steady and shortened the call, not enough to rattle the latch she just bullied. Enough to prove a point to herself that no one else needed to witness. The current curled against her forearms like a cat and moved on. She let it go.

Walking to the washroom, she wet a cloth and dragged it over her face and the back of her neck. The tremor under her skin was down to a thread now. She sat on the edge of the bed but did not lie back. Sleep would only come carrying Creaton with it, and she did not want to see his mouth shape "again" and feel her lungs turn to stone. There were footfalls in the corridor, soft and regular. She catalogued them without turning. Weight on the heel first, short stride, likely one of the younger guards.

The night began to thin toward morning. She moved through the chamber, back to the window she left upon. The draft pulled a little harder now, enough to flutter the corner of a paper on her desk. She raised her hand and the air gathered. Not to show off. To remind herself of the way it felt when it answered because she asked.

She held until her shoulders ached, then let the air go limp. In the quiet that followed, she heard the city. A wheel on stone far below, a dog, the faint, far-off call of someone who still thought the night was for singing. Petra would have liked that sound. The thought landed and sat next to the others like a stone on a cairn. She didn't move it.

Aella rested her forehead against the cool window frame and closed her eyes. Creaton made a weapon and thought that was the end of the story. He did not live long enough to learn that weapons choose.

CHAPTER 34

T HE SISTERS WERE SEATED around the small table in the solar, the fire low, daylight thinning through the tall windows until the room was bathed in hues of plum and gold. The air carried the faint scent of ash and lavender oil, a reminder of the queen's attempts to soften the seriousness of the room. Elspeth stood at the head of the room, hands folded as if she were about to deliver a sentence rather than information.

"You will need anchors."

Rheanna tilted her head, a frown creasing her brow. "Anchors?" she repeated.

"For the journey beyond the veil," Elspeth said, her voice grave and echoing silently in the room. "Your bodies will remain here. Your spirits will not. Without something tying you to the physical realm, you may not find your way back."

Rheanna folded her hands in her lap, forcing herself to stay still despite the sudden chill in the air. Not finding your way back felt deliberately vague, causing an uneasiness that crawled deep into her gut. Her stomach tightened, and she fought the urge to glance at her sisters for reassurance.

Aella leaned against the wall, arms crossed tight over her chest, her posture defensive. "And what exactly is supposed to tie us here?"

"Someone living," Elspeth replied. "Someone whose presence is familiar enough to keep you grounded when the veil pulls."

The room was silent, though Rheanna felt as though everyone could hear the hammer of her heart thundering against her ribs.

Elspeth's gaze slid to her, dark and knowing. "A lover is best."

Cyra straightened in her chair, her golden eyes flashing. "A lover?"

"They will keep you grounded in the physical," Elspeth said calmly. "Your body knows their touch, relishes in it, feels comfort in it." She paused, letting the weight of the words settle. "Love keeps you tethered."

Rheanna swallowed hard. Ripley's face surfaced in her mind unbidden. The way he listened before speaking. The warmth of his hand when he guided her through training. The steadiness of his lips against her body. The way he made her feel when the rest of the world was spiraling out of control. She pressed her fingers into her thigh, grounding herself the way he always did.

"You will each choose one," Elspeth continued. "They will be with you during the ritual. They will not see what you see, but their hands will keep you from crossing too far."

"Okay, sounds easy enough," Cyra said, nodding.

"Choose wisely," the older queen said before leaving. The silence that followed felt louder than her words. It lingered, thick and suffocating, as though the air itself had grown heavier in her absence.

"Well," Aella said after a moment, her voice cutting through the tension. "That's... deeply inconvenient."

Rheanna almost smiled, but the weight in her chest refused to lift. "I mean, you have choices."

"I hate it," Aella muttered, rubbing her hands over her face as if she could scrub the thought away. "We aren't all like you and Cyra; I know exactly who you both will pick."

Smiling softly, Cyra said, "Atlas, of course."

Rheanna nodded back. Atlas had always been Cyra's constant. Her gravity. She had seen the way they worked so well, a family unit with Hollin. She guessed they would be with child soon enough. An heir for Hefguard. A promise of the future. The thought was strangely comforting, a reminder that some bonds were already strong enough to withstand the veil's pull.

Rheanna hesitated before speaking, staring at her hands. Pretending this was difficult would be dishonest. "I don't think it's a surprise."

Cyra's mouth softened. "Ripley."

Hearing her older sister say his name out loud made something shift inside Rheanna. This was not a quiet thing anymore. It wasn't something she could keep tucked away and undefined. It was a choice. A risk.

"I still find that all a bit disgusting," joked Aella, pretending to gag.

Rheanna rolled her eyes, knowing her younger sister was just trying to avoid her own choice she had to make. They both turned to Aella.

Aella's jaw tightened. For a moment, Rheanna thought she might refuse out of pure stubbornness. Then she sighed, sharp and frustrated.

"Kaelith."

Cyra's golden eyes widened, disbelief written clearly on her face, "Kaelith?"

Rheanna had already known this and she was shocked Cyra had not. She had not seen love between the two, but she had noticed the tension, the attraction. It was as if they were two magnets, fighting their own nature. The air between them had always seemed charged, a silent storm waiting to break.

"I am not explaining any further," Aella stated, her voice final, shutting the door on any further inquiry.

Cyra's curiosity was tempered with the look on Aella's face, steel and cold. Instead, she locked eyes with Rheanna, a look that promised she would hound her for information later.

Rheanna leaned back in her chair, exhaling slowly. The sisters knew who they were choosing and they were just one step closer to obtaining the information they craved.

When they finally parted, Rheanna found herself wandering the castle halls without direction, her mind a whirlpool of thoughts, her feet carrying her instinctively toward the one person she needed. The corridors stretched endlessly, torchlight flickering against stone, each step echoing like a question she could not answer.

Ripley.

She found him in the training yard, dusk settling over the stone like a heavy blanket, turning the grey walls to violet. He was alone, moving through a practice form with quiet focus. She stopped at the edge of the yard, watching him for a moment longer than she meant to. The rhythm of his movements was precise, each strike and pivot carrying the weight of discipline.

He stood near the center, shirt loose at the throat and darkened with sweat that shimmered in the fading light. He looked up when she moved closer, and something in his expression shifted immediately, attention sharpening like a blade.

"You are a woman on a mission today."

"Yes," Rheanna replied simply.

She crossed the yard swiftly, boots echoing softly against stone. There was no hesitation in her step, no uncertainty.

"Elspeth says we need anchors when we go into the veil," she said, stopping directly in front of him, so close she could feel the heat radiating off him.

"Oh, really?" He ran a hand through his sweat-slicked hair, his eyes never leaving hers.

"She says it has to be physical." Rheanna lifted her hand and slid her fingers onto the curve of his shoulder, curling there, firm and possessive. "Something the body remembers."

Ripley's breath stuttered. His hand came up immediately, gripping her wrist, holding her there as if he was afraid she might vanish. His thumb pressed into her pulse, slow and deliberate, grounding her.

"And you are here to ask?" he teased, though his eyes were dark with anticipation.

"I'm not asking," she replied quietly, stepping closer until her body pressed fully into his. Heat bloomed instantly between them, familiar but sharper now, charged with purpose. "I'm choosing."

His grip tightened as his other hand slid to her waist, fingers digging in, anchoring her where she stood. Her palm flattened against his chest, feeling the steady thrum beneath her hand. She leaned in, mouth brushing his jaw, her lips tracing skin, lingering there long enough to make his breath hitch again.

"I need something that will pull me back," she murmured. "Even if everything else tries to take me."

Ripley swore softly under his breath and moved, guiding her back until her spine met a stone pillar. Not gentle or rough, but controlled. His body caged her in, heat and strength surrounding her completely.

"This," he said, voice low, close to her ear, his breath hot against her skin. "This will do it."

He kissed her then. Slow at first, deep and unrelenting, mouths fitting together with the ease of familiarity and the hunger of something newly claimed. His hand slid higher, firm and certain, while hers tightened in his shirt, pulling him closer. The kiss deepened, breath mingling, bodies pressing together until there was no mistaking what this was becoming. The world beyond them seemed to vanish, the yard, the stone, the fading light, all swallowed by the intensity of the moment.

He hiked up her skirts, his pants falling around his ankles as she used one hand to unbuckle them. His hazel eyes pierced her blue ones as he slid inside her. She let out a breathy moan as he pulled out and then thrust back in with even more power. This was not simply about want. It was a binding of sorts. Two souls melding together.

When they finally pulled back, breath uneven, eyes dark and steady, she kept her hand fisted in his shirt, holding him there.

"So," Rheanna said softly. "Will you be my anchor?"

Ripley didn't hesitate.

"Yes."

Chapter 35

A ELLA FOUND KAELITH STRETCHED across her bed, as if it were hers. Boots discarded on the floor, one knee bent, the other dangling, a dagger turning lazily between her fingers. The blade caught the dim candlelight, flashing silver with each rotation. She hummed under her breath, a sound that didn't quite belong to this world. Aella paused in the doorway.

"Careful," Aella said. "That's sharp."

Kaelith smiled without looking up. "So are you."

Aella shut the door behind her, harder than necessary, the slam echoing in the quiet room. She crossed the room and stopped just at the edge of the bed, jaw tight, fists clenching and unclenching at her sides.

Kaelith finally looked up. Her dark eyes flicked over Aella's posture, the tension coiled too tightly in her shoulders.

"You're wound up," Kaelith said lightly. "Should I be worried?"

Aella rolled her shoulders once, trying to dispel the knot of anxiety forming there. "I need to ask you something."

Kaelith's smile softened, curious rather than alarmed. She set the dagger aside and sat up, the mattress dipping with the shift in weight. "You have my attention."

Aella scowled. "Don't do that."

The trinkets in Kaelith's hair tinkled as she tilted her head. "Do what?"

"Tease me."

Kaelith giggled, a soft, melodic sound, but stayed silent, waiting for Aella to grow the courage to speak, her patience a balm to Aella's fraying nerves.

Aella exhaled through her nose. "We're going beyond the veil, between the world of the living and the dead to search for answers to the prophecy."

"That is no easy feat," she responded, her blue eyes scrutinizing, tracing the lines of stress on Aella's face.

"Elspeth says we need anchors," Aella continued, her words tumbling out a little too fast. "Someone who stays on this side and grounds us here so we might not slip away."

Kaelith hummed again. "Mm. A tether."

Aella met her gaze, unflinching violet meeting deep ocean blue. "I chose you."

Kaelith blinked once, then laughed softly. A sound of surprise escaped her lips.

"What?" Aella began to fidget in her spot, unable to look at Kaelith now, all resolve gone as she stared at a loose thread on the rug.

"You are quite dramatic. You don't need to be afraid to ask me such things."

"That's not it," Aella cut in, quick and defensive.

Kaelith studied her now, eyes sharp despite the softness in her posture. "Then tell me what it is."

Aella hesitated. Elspeth's voice echoed in her head. *Physical. Someone you trust.* Another face surfaced: soft skin, almond eyes, long brown hair. Betrayal. Pain. Aella crushed the thought instantly. No. Never.

"It has to be physical," she said instead. "It has to be someone I can trust to keep me here, tethered in this world."

Kaelith didn't interrupt, letting Aella work through her thoughts aloud in the quiet of the room.

"This is different from what we have been doing, more than just sex." Her voice grew rough, thick with unspoken fear. "I have to trust you."

"I can be that for you and it does not need to be more, if that is too much for you," Kaelith said softly. Aella froze as she stood, stopping close enough that she could feel her warmth. She reached out, fingers brushing Aella's wrist.

"You know," Kaelith murmured, "the ocean is meant to drag people under."

Aella's mouth twitched. "Is that supposed to comfort me?"

"It means I know how to keep you afloat."

Aella didn't pull away but leaned slightly into the touch.

"I'll do it," Kaelith said. "I'll be your anchor." She said it with such a resolve that Aella felt her chest lighten. She could do this.

Inclining her head, she said, "Good."

A smile graced Kaelith's lips once again. "You're terrible at asking for help, you know."

Aella snorted and was about to speak when rapid, frantic knocking interrupted them. She crossed to the door in less than a second and whipped it open to find Laney and Cora, both out of breath. The latter clutched a hand over her heart, brown hair fraying from the sides of her braid.

"We need to show you something."

The two girls were still heaving as they rounded the corner and led Aella to an alleyway just outside the castle walls. She pulled her cloak tighter around her face, not wanting to be seen, especially with Laney and Cora outside of the castle walls. She did not wish to put a target on their backs more than there already was.

Aella held back a gasp as she took in the words painted hastily along the side of the alleyway in white, stark against the old brick. The paint dripped like tears down the masonry.

The Cleanser Queen shall rule.

Her mind drifted back to the night a few weeks ago, when she and Karif were hidden in a cramped cellar, spying on the Cleansers, and when she first heard about Hollin. They had been musing about making her their queen. Were they finally putting that plan into motion? Or was this something new?

"Do you know who they speak about?" Cora asked cautiously, her voice trembling slightly, almost as if Aella would snap at her just for asking.

She looked between the two girls, and instead of answering her question, said, "Thank you for bringing me here. We need to call an emergency council meeting."

The girls nodded furiously as they all turned back toward the castle. They went their separate ways; the maids to round up the council and Aella to retrieve her sisters. She strode down to Cyra's rooms, knocking three times in rapid succession. Atlas opened the door, his hand steady on the iron latch, surprise flickering across his face at the sight of Aella standing there.

"Aella, what brings you here?" he said as he stepped aside, allowing her to enter.

Inside, Cyra sat on the bed with Hollin, gently combing her hair. Both their eyes shot instinctively to the door when they heard Atlas say her name. Cyra, noticing the worried expression on her sister's face, rose from the bed and walked up to Aella, while Atlas lingered near the doorway, his presence both watchful and reassuring. The atmosphere was heavy, charged with unspoken worry.

Aella leaned close, whispering what Cora and Laney had discovered in the alleyway to Cyra, low enough that her words didn't reach Hollin's ears. Cyra's breath caught in her throat, leaving her momentarily speechless.

She then turned to Atlas and said firmly, "The council is waiting in the war room. We need to go immediately."

Atlas opened his mouth to ask what had happened, but closed it again, deciding it was better to just find out in the war room with the others.

"Ryder and Mikah are already outside. They will guard Hollin until you both return," Aella informed them.

Cyra hesitated, reluctant to leave Hollin, but then she sighed and headed to Hollin, bending to kiss her forehead.

"Be good, Holli-bean," she said with a smile. "We'll be back before you know it."

With that, Cyra followed Aella and Atlas out the door, entrusting Hollin to Ryder and Mikah's care.

Rheanna had been with Ripley in the courtyard, their hushed conversation breaking off as the summons reached them. She touched Ripley's arm briefly, a silent promise to return, before striding toward the war room. Ripley watched her go, his expression shadowed with concern.

When everyone was adjourned within the war room, Aella remained standing, her back rigid against the heavy oak of her chair, refusing to sit. The air in the room was stifling, heavy with the scent of wax and parchment, the faint smoke from the torches curling upward like restless spirits.

Atlas stood near the edge of the chamber, his broad shoulders squared, a silent anchor against the rising unease. Rheanna slipped into place beside Aella, her expression taut, the shadow of her interrupted conversation with Ripley still etched across her features. Cyra sat opposite, her fingers drumming lightly against the table, each tap betraying the tension of leaving Hollin behind and the implication of the words painted in the alleyway.

The council members shifted uneasily in their seats, the scrape of wood against stone echoing louder than it should have, as though the room itself strained beneath the weight of what was to come. Aella looked at each member of the council, her violet eyes acting as twin blades searching for a crack in their armor.

Lola Donovan, whose husband had been killed in a monster attack and whose daughter awakened after Petra's death, bore the weight of her traumas clearly on her shoulders. She bit nervously at her nails, skin broken and raw. They had never replaced her husband, Nell's seat, so it was empty, a glaring reminder of the cost of this war. Sidney Tapia and Levine Alverz sat together, silent and observing. Sidney looked as impeccable as always, dark hair in a braid down her back, hands folded on the table. The latter's peppered hair stood in all different directions, his face sagging in exhaustion, eyes bleary from lack of sleep. Jasper Talmadge, face scrunched up and in a grimace that seemed permanent these days, sat next to Bianca, who sat straight, giving Aella a polite smile which she did not return.

They were the ones who would be suspects, if it weren't so easy. Her eyes drifted over them, quickly scanning for any sign of guilt. She landed on Norton, recalling the strong voice that always defended and backed Cyra. She studied his dark features, the lines etched deep into his face and his bushy eyebrows, before turning her attention to Marine. Her old age had become even more apparent since the first time she met her; her auburn hair was sprinkled with gray, even the roots more white than anything now. Her bright blue eyes met Aella's, an understanding in her gaze. She nodded softly and Aella returned it before turning away.

She took a steadying breath as her mind shuffled through the thoughts that raced like a river in flood. It was infuriating that what usually came so naturally to her seemed impossible when it mattered. Aella knew she was too close to the situation and she could not see it for what it truly was. She would be considered compromised if this were a mission.

All eyes were pointed at her expectantly, heavy gazes pressing against her skin like physical weights, waiting for her to speak. Aella gripped the table, her knuckles turning white against the dark grain of the wood. "Tonight, we discovered something in the alleyway beyond the castle walls." She paused, the words bitter on her tongue, "Graffiti. A message."

"What kind of message?" Jasper asked, leaning forward, his chair scraping harshly against the stone floor.

"The Cleanser Queen shall rule."

The declaration settled over the room like a shroud, thick and suffocating, choking the air from the chamber. Rheanna's breath caught in her throat with an audible hitch at the revelation. Several council members exchanged glances, some confused, others knowing. Sidney remained silent, her hands still folded, watching the sisters with a cool, unreadable gaze. Marine's expression also remained unchanged, her weathered face a map of patience. Norton, however, looked as though he might collapse from the sheer weight of the tension.

Bianca was the first to speak. "The Cleansers have a queen now?"

"Not yet," Aella said. "And we need to keep it that way."

She took a deep, long breath before continuing. "A few weeks ago, Karif and I were in a cellar under the Southern market. We were in the crawlspace, inches beneath the floorboards of a Cleanser meeting. We heard them."

A collective gasp shivered through the room. Lola pressed a hand to her heart, her eyes wide with horror.

"They spoke of the queen's daughter, of Hollin," Aella continued, her violet gaze pinning each member of the council in turn. "They didn't just talk about kidnapping her. They talked about using her as bait to 'get rid of us all.' And then," she paused, her lip curling in disgust, "they proposed an alternative. To raise her as their own. The Cleanser Queen. A 'Queen of the people' who would inspire others to join their rot."

The silence that followed was suffocating. Aella scanned the faces of the council, her violet eyes searching for even a flicker of guilt.

Jasper scoffed, though the sound was thinner than usual, lacking its typical bravado. "You heard this weeks ago and you kept this from the council?"

"I told only the Queen," Aella snapped, her gaze narrowing on him. "And perhaps I was right to do so. If the Cleansers know of Hollin's existence, it's probably because someone in this kingdom, perhaps even in this room, whispered it to them."

The room fell into uneasy silence, the accusation hanging heavy in the air, all council members looking at each other with sudden suspicious scrutiny.

"But now that they are painting their intentions on our walls, you all need to understand: Hollin is a symbol of innocence they intend to corrupt. She isn't a child to the Cleansers but merely a tool to further their agenda." Her eyes flicked from one member to another. "She is being targeted by the very monsters who killed Petra, and I will not let them turn my niece into their puppet."

Cyra stood then, the movement slow and deliberate. The candlelight seemed to bend toward her, her golden eyes burning with a feral, protective light. "The guard will be tripled," she commanded. "Every well, every gate, every corridor. If a single person in this city so much as looks at my daughter the wrong way, they will not live to see the sunset."

Norton nodded solemnly, his bushy eyebrows drawn together in a fierce scowl. "We will find whoever held the brush in that alleyway. And we will find the informant who told them the child was here."

Levine leaned forward. "If they are bold enough to paint the city walls, they have someone watching the gates. We should consider a curfew for all non-essential staff."

"Agreed," Cyra said. "Dismissed. All of you. I want reports on the city watch by dawn."

As the council filed out, the scrape of chairs against the stone floor echoed like a death knell. Aella remained where she was, her knuckles still white against the table.

Rheanna stepped closer to her sisters once the doors were shut. "They don't know the rest," she whispered, her voice barely audible. "They don't know she's Fae. If they find that out while the Cleansers are calling her their queen..."

"They won't," Aella promised, her voice flat and dangerous. "Because I'm going to find the person who painted that wall. And I'm going to make them regret that they ever learned how to hold a brush."

CHAPTER 36

THE KITCHENS HAD ALWAYS been Cyra's favorite part of the castle. Even as a child, before the world fractured, she had found comfort in the warmth of the ovens and the bustle of the bakers. The clang of copper pans, the hum of voices, and the sweet haze of rising bread had always felt like a sanctuary, a place untouched by politics or prophecy. Tonight, after the emergency council meeting the previous night and the constant whispers of monsters and the Oracle, she brought Hollin and Atlas here because it felt safe.

The hearthfire glowed steady, flames licking the iron pot where cream simmered with a soft, rhythmic bubble. The air smelled of sugar and cinnamon. Hollin sat perched on a stool far too tall for her, legs swinging back and forth, cheeks pink from the radiant heat.

Atlas stood opposite her, sleeves rolled to his elbows, trying very hard not to look entirely out of place among bowls of flour and trays of cooling cookies. His hands, so sure with earth and stone, were clumsy around a wooden spoon. The muscles in his forearms flexed with each awkward stir, betraying strength in a task that required finesse.

"You're stirring too slow," Hollin declared, pointing at the pot with all the authority of a queen herself. "It'll get lumpy if you don't do it faster."

Atlas's mouth curved in amusement. "Is that so?"

"Yes," Hollin said. She leaned forward as if to demonstrate. "You've got to whisk it like this." Her small hand mimed the motion furiously in the air.

Atlas chuckled but obliged, whisking with exaggerated speed. The spoon clattered against the pot. Chocolate splattered onto the counter. Hollin squealed in delight.

"Better?" he asked.

"Much better," she said, grinning, her strawberry-blonde hair bouncing as she nodded.

Cyra lingered near the doorway, her heart softening at the sight. The kitchen's warmth wrapped around her and she let herself breathe. Atlas, her husband now, and her daughter, sharing laughter as though they had been doing it forever.

Hollin reached for the tray of cookies, small fingers hovering. Atlas caught her hand gently. "Not yet. They're still hot."

"But I like them hot," Hollin argued.

"You'll burn your tongue," he countered.

"I won't," she said confidently. "I'm half fire." She glanced over her shoulder then, spotting Cyra in the doorway. "Mommy! Tell him!"

Cyra laughed, crossing the kitchen. "Half fire, hm?" She lifted Hollin from the stool and settled her onto her hip, the child's weight familiar and grounding. "That doesn't mean you can eat molten cookies, Holli-bean."

Hollin pouted. "You grownups always ruin my fun."

Atlas met Cyra's gaze over Hollin's head and she felt the promise and warmth of their union deep in her chest. It was not just love; it was the quiet certainty of belonging, of having built something worth protecting.

"Here," Atlas said, dipping a ladle into the pot and pouring steaming chocolate into three cups. He set one before Hollin carefully, blowing across the surface before sliding it into her hands. "Not too hot. Taste."

Hollin sipped, her nose scrunching, then her face lit with delight. "It's good!"

"Good?" Atlas echoed, eyebrows arched as if he'd just been handed the highest honor. "Then I've done it right."

Cyra sat beside them, her own cup warming her hands. The chocolate was rich, spiced faintly with cinnamon and sweetened with honey. The heat slid down her throat.

For a while, they sat in comfortable silence, Hollin dipping a cookie into her cup, chocolate smearing her lips, and Atlas pretending not to notice when she wiped her fingers on his sleeve. Cyra watched them both with a heart that felt too full.

"You're messy," Atlas told Hollin at last, flicking a crumb from her curls.

"So are you," Hollin shot back. She leaned forward suddenly, pressing a cookie against his mouth. "Eat!"

Atlas took a bite large enough to make her giggle. "Delicious," he declared, though crumbs scattered down his chest. "A fine feast, don't you think?"

Hollin nodded vigorously. "We're the best cooks in the castle."

Cyra reached out, brushing a smudge of chocolate from her daughter's cheek. "I don't think anyone would argue."

Hollin beamed, then wriggled free of Cyra's lap to climb into Atlas'. He looked startled for only a breath before his arms wrapped easily around her. She nestled against him as though it were the most natural thing in the world.

Cyra's throat tightened with a sudden, sharp ache. She had carried the fear for so long that bringing Hollin here, into this life of crowns and danger, would mean losing the small, simple joys that made her who she was. But watching her daughter curled against Atlas, crumbs in her curls, hot chocolate staining her smile, it felt like the opposite. It felt like she was finally home.

Atlas caught Cyra's gaze again, his hand resting lightly on Hollin's back. Cyra rose, stepped closer, and leaned against him, her arm curving around both of them. Hollin giggled, pressing the last bite of cookie into her mother's mouth before collapsing into laughter at the chocolate on Cyra's lips.

The three of them sat there on a kitchen bench, surrounded by the scent of sugar and spice, firelight flickering across stone walls. Monsters prowled in the world beyond. Prophecies whispered in the dark. But here, in this circle of warmth, there was only love. And for tonight, love was enough.

Chapter 37

Tonight was the night the sisters would walk between worlds and hopefully find the answers they sought. The maps, scrolls, and polished wood had been cleared away from the solar. The room felt stark, stripped of its usual comforts, leaving only a hollow space for the magic to fill in.

Elspeth had remade the chamber into something out of a folk tale, a witch's lair. Dried bundles of herbs hung from the rafters, their scents sharp in the close air: sage, rosemary, wormwood, and juniper. Smoke rose from clay bowls set at the corners, curling in pale tendrils that clung to skin and hair. The very air seemed thicker and Rheanna felt the weight of it press down on her.

At the center of the room, Elspeth crouched low, grinding leaves and roots with the pestle of a stone mortar. The sound rasped in the otherwise silent room. It was a harsh, rhythmic scrape, each grind echoing with ritualistic intent. She poured hot water over the mixture, steam clouding upward, carrying a bitter tang that stung Rheanna's eyes and made the back of her throat itch.

"You must drink," Elspeth said, her voice low but certain. "The tonic will open the veil."

The vessel Elspeth poured into was plain clay, unmarked, but the liquid within gleamed dark green, flecked with floating strands of crushed herbs. She passed it first to Cyra, who accepted without question, her golden eyes steady and unblinking as she lifted it to her lips. Her throat constricted as she forced the liquid down, but her gaze never wavered, her queenly composure steady even as the bitterness clawed at her throat.

Aella took hers next, sniffed it once, and scowled. "Tastes like mud, doesn't it?"

Elspeth only arched a dark brow. "Drink."

Aella rolled her eyes but tipped it back, grimacing as she swallowed. Her lips curled in distaste, but she forced it down with the stubborn defiance that had always defined her.

When the cup came to Rheanna at last, her hands trembled faintly. The scent was sharp and earthy. She hesitated. The clay felt heavier than it should, as if the vessel carried not just liquid but consequence.

Elspeth's gaze fixed on her, unblinking. "To journey to the veil you must drink. There is no other path across the divide."

Rheanna raised it, closing her eyes as the liquid burned her tongue. It was bitter enough to twist her stomach, but she forced it down. Heat spread through her chest. She gasped when it reached her heart, a strange warmth settling there.

Elspeth moved to place four bowls of smoldering herbs at the circle's edges. She scattered crushed petals into the flames, and the smoke thickened, fragrant and strange. Shadows seemed to bend oddly in the corners of the room.

"You will sit within the circle," Elspeth said. "Behind you, your anchors will help guide you. They will not see what you see, but their hands will keep you from losing yourselves in the land of the dead."

Rheanna's eyes flicked upward as Atlas stepped behind Cyra, his hand coming to rest firm and warm on her sister's shoulder. Cyra glanced back once, their gazes locking, something silent and strong passing between them. It was a look that needed no words, a vow that he would not let her be pulled away into the darkness.

Ripley moved behind Rheanna. His touch was careful as if afraid to hurt her. The warmth of his palm through her gown steadied the tremor in her chest. She breathed easier with him there, though she could feel his pulse beating fast, nearly as fast as hers.

Kaelith settled behind Aella, her dark skin catching the candlelight, her fingers brushing the assassin's shoulder. Aella gave no sign of comfort, but she did not shrug her off. That was enough.

Elspeth lit a final candle and stepped into the circle. "Close your eyes," she murmured. "Breathe deep and relax. The tonic will do its work. Do not fight it."

Rheanna obeyed. The smoke pressed against her eyelids, filling her head with strange shapes. Petra's laugh echoed faintly in her ears, so sharp it made her chest ache.

Ripley's fingers tightened gently on her shoulder. She focused on the pressure, the steadiness of his hand, and let her breath fall into rhythm. The room seemed to shift. The floor softened under her legs, not stone but something that moved faintly, as if water lapped against unseen shores.

Elspeth's voice rose, low and resonant, chanting in a tongue that felt older than air. The smoke curled tighter, forming shapes that writhed and shimmered.

"The way is open." Rheanna could hear Elspeth's voice through her dreamlike state, though it sounded distant, as if spoken through a long tunnel.

Rheanna's stomach twisted. She reached for her sisters, her hand brushing across chalk lines until Cyra's fingers closed around hers on one side and Aella's rougher grip caught her other. The three of them linked.

The room tilted. The smoke swelled and swallowed the walls. The familiar shapes of the solar melted away, replaced by a sweeping, dizzying darkness. Ripley's hand pressed firmly against her back, the only thing keeping her from slipping into the dark before she was ready.

Rheanna gasped, heart hammering, as the world unraveled.

Her hands were suddenly wrenched free and the tether to her sisters snapped. The separation was violent, a physical tearing that left her feeling exposed and adrift. Her cry dissolved into the heavy silence as darkness swallowed her whole. When the smoke cleared, only a field, wide and pale, stretched out in front of her.

"Cyra? Aella?" she called out.

The grass rippled, though no wind touched it. The silence was absolute, a heavy blanket that pressed against her ears until her heart seemed too loud. She wrapped her arms around herself, wishing Ripley's hand still steadied her shoulder.

Laughter rang clear across the field, bright and familiar, and Rheanna's knees nearly gave out. It was a sound she had memorized, a melody she never thought she would hear again in this lifetime. She turned so fast she almost stumbled. "Petra?"

A girl stood just beyond the rise, hair tumbling golden brown, her gown loose and white as linen caught in a breeze. Freckles spilled across her cheeks, her emerald eyes lit like candles. She looked exactly as she had the last time Rheanna saw her, small and brilliant and far too young to die.

"Rheanna!" Petra's face broke out in a smile and she ran forward, bare feet flying across the grass. She collided with her sister in a hug so fierce that Rheanna gasped.

Rheanna clutched her, burying her face in Petra's curls. They smelled of wildflowers, just as always. Her throat ached and tears burned in her eyes.

"You're here," Rheanna whispered.

Petra leaned back. "I missed you so much."

Rheanna laughed through her tears. "I missed you too. Goddess, Petra," Her voice broke. "I didn't get to say goodbye."

Petra shook her head fiercely, curls bouncing. "You're here, I'm here, and that's enough."

The ache in Rheanna's chest cracked wider. She cupped Petra's face, memorizing every freckle, every spark in her eyes. "I thought you'd be angry. That you might blame us."

Petra blinked, startled. "Blame you? Rheanna, no." Her expression softened into something older than her years, wise and gentle. "None of you could have stopped what happened."

The words burrowed deep, loosening knots Rheanna hadn't even realized she had tied around her ribs. She sagged into her sister's arms again, holding her like she would never let go.

"You always worried too much," Petra teased, her voice muffled against Rheanna's shoulder. "Taking care of everyone, but yourself."

Rheanna brushed her hair back from her face, her fingers trembling. "I don't feel like I'm taking care of anyone. Cyra's the queen, Aella's the fighter, and me—I'm just—"

"You," Petra said firmly. "And that's what we need. You kept us together, Rhe. You always did."

The tears spilled faster now. Rheanna pulled her close again, rocking her gently as if Petra were still a child. For the first time since Petra's death, the grief didn't feel sharp; it felt like a wound finally being tended.

Petra pulled back once more, her eyes glowing brighter now, almost too bright. The light around her began to flicker, the edges of her silhouette blurring. "I can't stay long."

Panic jolted Rheanna. "No, please—"

"It's all right." Petra reached up, pressing her hand over Rheanna's heart. "I'll always be here. I'm a part of you."

Rheanna covered her hand with her own, holding it there, as if that could keep her here longer.

"I need you to promise me something," Petra whispered.

"Anything."

"Don't stop being the light when everything else is dark. Do not let anything or anyone dim you."

Rheanna's throat tightened, but she nodded. "I promise."

Petra smiled. "I'm so proud of you."

The words hit harder than anything else could have. Rheanna bent her head, pressing her forehead to her sister's, breathing her in, desperate to keep a piece of her sister within her lungs. Petra's form grew translucent, the warmth that was just there moments ago slipping away.

"No," Rheanna whispered, clutching at her, but her arms closed on nothing. "Please."

The field trembled. A low hum rolled through the air, deeper than any voice she had ever heard. Rheanna staggered back, chest heaving, the echo of Petra's words still burning in her heart.

CHAPTER 38

ONE MOMENT, SHE HELD her sisters' hands; the physical tether of their intertwined fingers anchoring her to reality, the next Cyra staggered, the ground tilting beneath her feet, and then she was alone.

The smoke cleared to reveal stone walls. Familiar. The same halls she had once run through as a child and now, ruled in. But the perspective was warped, the ceiling stretching impossibly high, the corridors elongated like a reflection in a twisted mirror. Shadows flickered across the portraits, and when she looked closer, they were not paintings of long-gone ancestors, but instead distorted and smeared, as if the oil paint had not yet dried.

Cyra's breath caught when she heard the click of boots on stone. The sound was measured, echoing with a familiarity that sent a chill down her spine. She turned sharply and froze.

Her father, the late King Edgar Voelbel, stood at the far end of the corridor. No crown on his head and no weight of command in his posture. His shoulders were straighter than she remembered, his icy blue eyes piercing as they swept over her. The sight was so impossible, so piercingly real, that her knees threatened to give way.

Cyra's throat ached and burned with a sob that threatened to climb out. "Father."

He came closer. The last time she had seen him, he had snapped iron cuffs around her wrists and told her to be strong while tearing her world apart. The sight of him cracked something deep inside.

Her flames flared at her fingertips before she could stop them. "Why now?" she whispered. "Why did you just abandon us?"

Edgar stopped just before her, close enough she could see the lines at the corners of his eyes, the faint stubble on his jaw. He looked like he had when she was a child, not a cold king but a man. A father.

"It tore your mother and I apart to send you away, but the Oracle told us you would all die if we did not," he said softly. "And because I could not tell you then and you deserve to hear it."

Her fire flickered, uncertain.

"I was cruel that night," Edgar admitted. "I let fear of the Oracle bind my hands. And I hurt you worst of all, Cyra." His eyes glistened with unshed tears. "I never wanted your last memory of me to be iron on your wrists."

Cyra's chest burned. His last words to her echoed through her mind. *You have to be strong now. You are not weak, you are not broken, do not act like it.* Tears pricked, but she swallowed them back. "Then why did you? Why did you put that weight on me? Why make me the one who had to be strong?"

He stepped forward, his large hand cupping her face. "Because you were already strong. Stronger than I ever was. I knew you could carry it."

Cyra's lips trembled. "I didn't want to carry it."

"I know." His thumb brushed a tear free. "But you did. That night, when I shook you and told you not to act weak… It was my plea. My last desperate act of a father trying to protect his daughter."

"I have my own little girl now," Cyra said, thinking about Hollin and how she would do anything she could to protect her.

"And that is why you have to continue to be strong. For her. For your sisters. For Linnosa," Edgar said firmly. "I love you, Cy."

Cyra broke then, throwing her arms around him. His arms wrapped tight around her, solid and warm. For one impossible moment, she was a child again, held safe in her father's embrace. She buried her face in his chest, inhaling the familiar scent.

His lips pressed to her hair. "Listen to your sisters. Trust them. And trust yourself."

When she pulled back, his form was already beginning to fade, light unraveling him thread by thread.

"I will always be with you." His gaze met hers one last time, fierce and full of love. "Wield your fire, but don't let it consume you."

And then he was gone, leaving only the cold draft of the distorted hallway and the lingering warmth of his touch on her cheek.

Thrown into a whirl of smoke and silence, Aella's boots skidded on stone that hadn't been there a heartbeat ago.

When the air stilled, she found herself in a chamber with pale walls and high arched windows, but no light came through. The air smelled faintly of lavender, a scent she couldn't place but that sent a shiver down her spine.

Her hand twitched for a blade that wasn't there. "Well, isn't this just great," she muttered.

From the far side of the room, a figure emerged. Tall, graceful, and with hair like spun gold braided loosely down her back. Ocean eyes that matched Rheanna's glowed gentle and knowing. Her gown was simple white and flowing as though the air itself carried it. She moved without sound, a shadow of grace and elegance sweeping over the room.

Sienna Linwood Voelbel.

Aella's heart quickened as she recognized the woman in front of her. She had seen portraits, imagined faces, but nothing compared to the ache of this reality. Her mother was standing before her. It was a face she had searched for in crowds, a voice she had tried to recall in her darkest dreams.

Her instinct was to sneer, to armor herself in sarcasm. "Took you long enough." But her voice cracked, betraying her.

Sienna only smiled softly, stepping closer. "My little storm."

Aella felt as if her chest was wide open, as if her heart was bare and bleeding to the world. The walls she had built brick by brick over the years began to shake under the weight of those few simple words.

"I don't…" Aella's hands trembled at her sides. "I don't remember you. Not really."

"Of course," Sienna said gently. "You were only a child. You should have grown with me beside you, but that was stolen from us. Stolen by the curse of a woman who knew nothing of love, only loss."

Anger surged, sharp and reflexive. "Then why didn't you fight harder? You were queen."

Sienna reached her, close enough to place a hand on her forearm. Her touch was warm, impossibly so, and it stole the fight from Aella's throat. "I did fight. I would have burned the kingdom for you all, but fate tore us apart. I had no choice in the matter. I am so sorry."

The words sank into the cracks Aella had buried deep. Her vision blurred and she hated it. She hated that her wounds were so clearly visible to this woman. The walls she had built for years shattered. A sob ripped from her throat as she collapsed forward, and Sienna caught her, pulling her tight against her chest. Aella buried her face in her mother's gown, clutching her as if she would vanish. The fabric smelled faintly of lavender, a scent that felt impossibly familiar, as though it had lingered in her memory all along. And for the first time in her life, Aella did not feel like she had to hold herself together.

"I wanted to hate you," Aella gasped. "I told myself that I never needed you."

Sienna pressed a kiss into her hair. "But you did and that is nothing to be ashamed of."

Years of loneliness, pain, and fury poured out of her until her body ached. Sienna held her through it, murmuring soft words Aella barely heard, words meant only to soothe.

When the storm inside her calmed, Aella pulled back just enough to see her mother's face again. "I'm not like Rheanna. I'm not like Cyra. I don't know how to be gentle."

"You are exactly who you were meant to be," Sienna said firmly, brushing away a tear with her thumb. "You are fierce. You love with your whole soul, even when you pretend you don't."

Aella shook her head, but her chest felt lighter. "I'm so angry all the time."

"Then be angry," Sienna said simply. "Just don't let it consume you. Use it as courage to protect what is yours." Her form was starting to blur, light spilling from her edges. Aella's heart lurched. The edges of the room began to fray, signaling that time was slipping away.

"I will always be with you," Sienna whispered.

Aella's eyes burned as she reached for her, fingers closing on air as Sienna faded. "Don't leave me again."

But only her voice remained, soft as the lavender air. "Never."

The world around her shifted again, its endless dark thinning until the three sisters stood together once more. Their cheeks were wet and their eyes raw. They looked at each other, a silent exchange of grief passing between them, acknowledging the ghost they had each embraced. The smoke parted and a woman stepped forth.

Her raven black hair gleamed, her braid falling over one shoulder. Her features were sharp and beautiful, but lined with heavy sorrow. Her eyes were a sharp silver and when she looked at them, the weight of centuries pressed into their chests.

Rheanna's breath caught. "It's her," she whispered. "Lewellyn Hormanick. The Oracle's sister."

Lewellyn inclined her head. "Yes. You already know much of my story, more than anyone else, perhaps. I was lost to time."

Cyra's hands curled into fists at her sides. "So it's true. The Oracle is the reason this is all happening."

"Yes," Lewellyn said quietly. "She was my twin. We were born into a long line of Oracles, powered by the Unknown, and like all before us, we were meant only to see. But Selmana reached too deep. When I died, she lost herself to grief. She blamed your line. She let the Unknown devour her and gave it her vengeance. The curse you live with was her gift of hate."

Aella's lip curled. "We know this already. Why drag us here to repeat it?"

Lewellyn's eyes softened. "There are things the diary did not tell you. Things you must know if you wish to live."

She spread her hands when the sisters did not say anything. "Selmana twisted the prophecy. *Four shall emerge, but only one will rise.* She wanted you to believe you were doomed to devour one another, that unity was impossible. But the prophecy was not hers to give; it was mine."

The sisters stiffened. The words struck like a blade, cutting through years of fear and doubt, unraveling lies they had carried as truth.

Lewellyn's voice grew firmer. "I saw four powerful threads rising. Four becoming one. That was always the truth. She poisoned it because she feared what you could become together."

"Then what must we do?" Cyra asked.

"There is a ritual," Lewellyn explained. "An old one, woven into the blood of our line. It requires the binding of all four elements into one act. Fire, water, air, earth."

Rheanna swallowed. "What does it need? Tell us."

Lewellyn looked at each one of them, appraising, before continuing. "It must be done at the heart of Linnosa, where the curse first rooted. The royal garden. You must give yourself to each other fully."

Cyra shook her head, her voice a rasp. "But Petra is gone, if you say we need all four elements, we only have three."

"Then it cannot be done," Rheanna whispered, turning pale. "Not without her."

Lewellyn's expression shifted, sorrow shadowing her features. "Earth has not vanished from your bloodline."

The sisters froze. Aella glanced at Cyra, whose face was stark with horror.

"No," Aella warned. "Do not say it."

"The child. Hollin."

Rheanna staggered, tears welling in her eyes. "She's five years old..."

"Petra's thread runs in her. The ritual could be completed with her blood," Lewellyn pressed. Her voice was not unkind, but it carried the weight of inevitability.

Aella's violet eyes flashed. "She's a baby. She's not part of this."

"Selmana will come for her. She will come for all of you," Lewellyn said, voice both low and urgent.

"She is mine," Cyra hissed, finally finding her words. "My daughter. I swore I would protect her."

Lewellyn's face softened with sorrow. "I only give you the truth. The curse can only be broken when four threads bind again. If you cannot, then you must find another way, but your time is running out. My sister will come. And she will not show the mercy I have shown you in giving you this warning."

The ground began to tremble beneath their feet, cracks of light spilling through. The realm of the dead was rejecting them, pushing them back toward the land of the living.

"Four shall emerge and all will rise, if you succeed."

Chapter 39

Cyra woke with a start, breath ragged, her body heavy as if water pressed against her chest. Cold clung to her lungs, a phantom chill that no fire could chase away. For a moment, she thought that she was still trapped in that place of shifting shadows and voices, but the faint light of the chamber told her otherwise. Candles guttered low, wax spilling across the stone floor. The air was thick with the sour bite of burnt herbs and ash dusted her palms where they rested against the rug. The silence of the chamber was oppressive, broken only by the faint hiss of the dying embers.

Her sisters lay beside her. Rheanna's head lolled against Ripley's shoulder, her face pale, lips trembling with breath that came too shallow for Cyra's liking. Aella was rigid even in her collapse, jaw clenched, Kaelith's hands still firm on her shoulders as if she dared the girl to break free even while unconscious. The anchors looked as drained as the sisters themselves, their faces shadowed with worry, their bodies taut with the strain of holding them tethered.

"Easy," Elspeth's voice cut through, calm and grounding. The witch-queen stood behind them, the last wisps of smoke curling in her hair like threads. "The veil takes its toll, but it did not keep you all."

Cyra tried to sit up and nearly toppled, the room swaying too fast for her eyes to follow. Atlas caught her wrist, steadying her. His hand was warm, a stark contrast to the cold nothingness she had just returned from. She clung to that, drawing a breath that scraped her throat raw. Her gaze fell again to her sisters. Protective instinct burned through the weakness in her body. She reached, fingertips brushing Rheanna's arm, then Aella's. She needed to feel them breathing.

Rheanna's lashes fluttered, and the name left her lips in a whisper: "Petra..." Tears shone against her cheeks before she could brush them away.

Aella's eyes snapped open sharper, violet burning with a fierce, defensive light.

Cyra swallowed, the ache in her throat unbearable. She could still hear her father's voice echoing from the veil, words carved too deep to forget. But she couldn't say his name, not yet.

Silence fell between them, heavy with the shadows of the dead. It was a silence of revelation, each of them carrying ghosts that had spoken truths too sharp to ignore,

It was Rheanna who spoke next, her voice thin but certain. "Lewellyn said four must rise." Her hand trembled as she dragged it over her face. "But Petra is gone."

Cyra's chest tightened, and she knew Aella felt her fury too, the way her younger sister's whole body stiffened.

Cyra forced the truth into the air before it strangled her. "There is only one other of our blood who carries earth." Her stomach turned to iron as the words left her. She didn't want to give them a voice. It would be a betrayal of the innocence she had sworn to protect.

"No." Aella's answer came sharp and immediate, her voice like a blade across stone. "We will not drag her into this. I don't care what was said. She is a child, not a soldier for this war."

"I never said we would," Cyra snapped, though her chest ached with guilt for even speaking Hollin's existence into the room. The words tasted bitter, as if even naming her daughter had already placed her in danger.

Rheanna's eyes brimmed, her hands shaking in her lap. "Then what do we do?" Her voice cracked.

Elspeth had been silent until then, watching with her unblinking calm. Now she stepped forward, her voice low but steady. "Do not bind yourselves to despair so quickly. There may be another way."

All three sisters looked at her. Cyra's pulse hammered in her ears. The witch-queen's presence seemed to steady the air, her words cutting through the panic.

Elspeth's gaze did not waver. "I will not speak it until I am certain, but know this, your sister's child cannot be the only answer."

The words fell over them like cool water, not enough to wash the fear away, but enough to breathe again. The smoke had burned to nothing, yet it felt as though the darkness lingered still, pressing invisible fingers against their skin.

Rheanna bowed her head, strands of dark hair falling into her lap. She whispered again, softer this time, "Petra." Like the name itself was a tether, something she couldn't let go of.

Cyra wanted to gather her sister into her arms, but her body was too weak, her arms trembling from the effort of sitting upright. All she could do was watch Rheanna fold inward, Ripley's hand firm at her back, steadying her. Aella was different. She sat upright, shoulders taut, her violet eyes narrowed on the floor as if she could burn a hole through stone. She hadn't looked at Cyra once since Hollin had been named. Her silence was worse than her anger because it meant she was holding it inside, letting it cut her raw.

Atlas shifted beside Cyra, his hand brushing hers. A quiet offering. She didn't look at him, but she didn't pull away either. She needed the reminder that he was here.

Finally Aella spoke, her voice as thin and dangerous as a blade. "We finish this without Hollin. Whatever it takes."

Cyra's jaw tightened. "Of course we do."

Elspeth's gaze swept over them, unreadable. "Then rest," she said at last. "Rest is as sacred as any rite."

When they rose, their movements were sluggish, driven by wary bones and aching muscles. Elspeth watched in silence.

Cyra leaned into Atlas's arm for the first few steps, her legs stiff beneath her. She hated how it felt, remembering the last time she felt close to this was after her burnout avenging Petra's death, but she didn't shrug him off; he was there for her then too. She let herself be held until her stride steadied, accepting the support she usually felt compelled to give.

The doors opened and the corridor light nearly blinded her, a stark assault of gold and white after the dim gloom of the solar. Polished floors, bright sconces, and banners stirred by the draft. It all felt too clean, too ordinary after the shadows they had walked through. Her sisters walked at her sides. Rheanna was quiet, eyes still red, and Aella stiff and bristling, as if she dared the world to come at her now. They said nothing, but their steps fell into rhythm, three hearts tethered by silence.

Cyra pressed a hand to her chest, feeling the ghost of her father's voice echo there. She thought of Petra's laugh, of her mother's hands, of Hollin's small arms when she held her at night. Threads tangled and cut, and none of them knew how to weave them back.

But Elspeth's words clung to her. *Not the only answer.*

Sleep that night did not come easily. Cyra tossed and turned, disrupting little Hollin so much that she begrudgingly slid out of bed and into her Aunt Rheanna's. The empty bed made things worse and when darkness found her, it was not gentle.

Gold. Endless. A hall lined with crowns, each one chained to the floor.

She tried to move, but the air clung thick. Hollin stood ahead, small hands clutching at a crown far too large for her head, her face straining with effort and eyes wide with a terror she should never have known.

"No," Cyra whispered, but the space stretched, pulling them apart, the distance growing impossibly vast with every heartbeat.

Chains slithered down, glowing, wrapping the crown tighter. Hollin whimpered. "Mommy, it's too heavy."

Cyra ran, or thought she did, but her fire sparked only to turn into cuffs. Chains fused to her wrists and her throat.

A voice wove through the hall, soft and merciless. Balance before vow. But if one fails, the other binds.

A figure rose in smoke and knots. The Goddess, Arathine.

Cyra screamed, clawing at the chains, but every pull only dragged her down. Hollin's face blurred, reaching for her, and then she was gone. Swallowed by the gold and the dark.

The last sound was a whisper in her ear: A mother clings. A queen stands. Which will you choose?

Cyra shot out of her bed, already out the door and halfway down the hall before she was fully awake. She stumbled a moment, sleep still pulling at her, and she held onto the ornate wall to steady herself for a moment before pushing forward. She slowly creaked open the door to Rheanna's chambers. Her breathing steadied as she saw her daughter wrapped in the protection of her sister, safe, sound, and blissfully unaware of the prophecy threatening to claim her. She closed the door and slumped against the wall.

She did not want Hollin to feel this weight ever, but she knew it was inevitable.

Chapter 40

H EAT LAY ON THE laundry like a damp hand, oppressive and inescapable, turning the air into a thick, wet blanket that clung to every inch of exposed skin. Boilers hissed like angry cats. The mangle groaned as sheets slid between heavy rollers. Lye and lavender sharpened the air and steam made every voice sound softened, as if the room insisted on civility.

Aella moved through it like a blade through fog, her steps precise and measured. She didn't bark orders. A glance, a tilt of her head, and the nearest guard straightened as if a string had been pulled. Rheanna kept a half-step at her shoulder, letting Aella's hard edges cut the path while her own presence smoothed what needed smoothing with gentle nods and soft smiles that eased the tension her sister left in her wake. She followed after Aella as she conducted her daily sweep of the guards and their stations, in awe of the way her sister managed everything with such natural ease.

"Post?" Aella asked the young guard at the service stair, her voice flat and demanding.

"Service stair and yard hatch, Captain," he blurted too quickly, his Adam's apple bobbing nervously in his throat as he snapped to attention.

"Eyes on both or just your mouth?" Aella said, shifting a fraction to block his sightline to the far corridor door and forcing him to focus on her intense violet gaze. "Who covers that when you blink?"

"Torres—"

"Torres is fetching water." She hadn't looked at the dipper by the copper, but she'd already noted it was gone and the wet prints led out, her mind cataloging every detail of the room with military precision. "When he leaves, you call Renn to hold the hatch and you take the door. No gaps."

"Yes, Captain," he responded, his voice steadier now.

They moved on, leaving the young guard to his post with a new understanding of vigilance. At the laundry chute, Aella's gaze flicked to a nick on the iron lip, then to the tally slate where a washerwoman had marked neat columns. Steam rolled, thickening the room.

Two guards stepped from the kitchen corridor, making space. Between them walked Natalie, a stack of folded linen in her arms. Her chin was a fraction high, the careful stillness of someone who had learned to keep her face from telling on her. She saw Aella first, then Rheanna. Nothing in her expression shifted.

"State your purpose," Aella said, her voice a low vibration.

"Stocking the north corridor closets," Natalie answered. Then, to Rheanna, "No one has approached me. I remain under escort at all times," her voice measured and professional.

"Good," Rheanna said, keeping her tone neutral. "Did anything feel off?"

Natalie considered, her brow furrowing slightly as she thought of her day. "Two maids. A brown braid. A ginger with a gap in her tooth. They've kept to my shoulder for two days. They change baskets when I change floors."

"Laney and Cora," Rheanna said, meeting her eyes so the rest could go unsaid. *Ours.*

"Then the tail is friendly," Natalie replied, relief flickering in her eyes before it vanished.

"Not friendly," Aella said. "Competent." She turned to the escort. "Distance."

"Two paces," the taller guard answered.

"One in tight halls," Aella corrected. "If you can touch her shoulder, you can stop a hand. If you lose her for a heartbeat, you whistle. You do not chase alone. Say it back."

"One pace in tight halls. Whistle if separated," he repeated, his posture stiffening.

Natalie's knuckles tightened on the linen and then loosened. She didn't look at Aella when she said, evenly, "I know why I am here."

"Good," Aella returned, the word cold and final.

"Captain." Natalie dipped her head and moved forward.

Steam surged off a copper, blurring the room for a breath. When it thinned, the mangle sighed and a sheet slid out smooth as a lake. Rheanna watched a bead of water tick from the chute lip and darken the stone. Aella finished her last glance at the posts, service stair, hatch, door, and moved for the corridor.

"How are you with her moving around the castle?" Rheanna asked. She kept her voice even, though her heart ached with the memory of her sister's past heartbreak.

"I'm fine," Aella said, the words clipped, raising a shield against any further questions.

Rheanna's mouth tugged. "That isn't an answer."

Aella's jaw went tight, then slack, like she'd caught herself bracing. "She's watched. That's what matters."

"It also matters that she used you," Rheanna said instead, gentler, reaching out to touch her sister's arm. "I'm asking how you are."

"My feelings are irrelevant to the safety of the castle. But if you insist, I'm not letting it touch me."

Rheanna nodded once. "If that changes, tell me."

They took the next bend. A guard dipped his head. Aella checked the angle of his stance without breaking stride. Rheanna let the laundry heat slide off her shoulders and felt the hard pulse of the castle under her feet. So many corners for grief to stand in and pretend to be something else.

She glanced sideways, choosing to steer the conversation toward a different but equally important matter. "And don't think I don't see what's happening between you and Kaelith."

Aella's look was quick and sharp. "What do you think you see?"

"Late nights. You leaving your rooms with your hair a mess," Rheanna said. "I'm not blind."

Aella huffed, almost a laugh, almost a warning. "It's sex, Rheanna. That's all."

Rheanna weighed the words, the steadiness in them. *Just sex* sounded simple until it had a face and a mouth that made you forget your wits. "Does she know that?"

"Yes." No hesitation. "I was clear. That's how she wants it as well."

"Are you clear with yourself?" Rheanna asked.

They passed a narrow window, the light cutting across Aella's cheekbone like a blade. "I'm not starting anything I can't carry. Not now."

Rheanna believed her. She also knew Aella had a talent for starving herself of softness until the hunger made her sharp. "Good," she said. "Then be kind about it. Don't let it bleed into the rest."

"It won't." Aella's gaze slid over a pair of pages wrestling a crate and returned to the hall ahead. "And if it does, I'll end it."

Rheanna accepted that with a small nod. "And Natalie?"

"Distance," Aella said. "I'm not giving her another inch."

"That's the right call."

Rheanna's thoughts drifted to the laundry again: Natalie's chin a fraction high, the way her fingers tightened once on the stack and then went still. She knew that there was not just history between the two woman. Love was still there. Aella fought so hard to hide her emotions: love, betrayal, all of it. But Rheanna knew better and had learned to read her sister.

"You know," Rheanna said after a moment, breaking the silence that had settled between them, "I don't think you hurt less than the rest of us. I think you hide it better."

Aella's mouth curved, not quite a smile. "You think too much."

They reached the stairs. Aella paused at the top, eyes flicking down the treads, then back to Rheanna, finally looking at her rather than avoiding her gaze.

"I'm not what I was with her," Aella said. "I won't be again."

"I understand as long as it's enough for you."

Aella started down. "If it becomes that, you'll hear it."

"From you," Rheanna said.

"From me."

Chapter 41

The quiet intimacy of the moment was shattered in an instant. Aella's head snapped up from Kaelith's neck, her senses sharpening even before the sound fully registered. They both froze at the sound of explosions. The castle began to shake not even a moment later, ornaments rattling on the shelves, and the two women were on their feet instantly. Aella looked at Kaelith, her heart hammering against her ribs.

"I need to find them."

She didn't need to say any other words. Kaelith only nodded, her cerulean eyes darkening with a shared understanding of the looming danger. The door was thrown open and they were down the hall within seconds. The yells of commands and the sound of armor clanking filled Aella's ears, mingling with the thunder of her own heartbeat. She took a deep breath, using the steady clatter of Kaelith's braids as an anchor in the chaos.

They made it to Rheanna first, who was out in the hallway, already banging on Cyra and Hollin's chambers, her whole body shaking. She looked at Aella, tears streaking her cheeks.

"I tried to use my water, but I couldn't gather enough strength to break down the door."

Evidence of her desperation glistened across the stone floor, water pooled around their chambers.

Aella pulled her back sharply. "Move."

She summoned her air magic, blasting forward. The door splintered and ripped free, flying off its hinges and slamming into the far wall with a deafening crash that sent dust raining from the rafters.

"Cyra! Hollin!" Aella called out as the three of them spilled into the room.

"They are not here," stated Kaelith, already backing out of the room.

Rheanna's knees almost buckled, but Aella caught her arm and forced her forward. They stumbled into the hall again, where the noise of screaming and shouting outside swelled like a tide threatening to drown them.

Natalie appeared at the end of the hall, her face a ghostly white. For the briefest moment, Aella's chest seized; this panic was too close to memory, too much like the day they lost Petra.

Natalie gestured to them frantically, her hands trembling. "Cyra is losing it. Hollin is missing."

The words sent a spear of ice through Aella's lungs. For half a breath, she couldn't move, couldn't think. But she forced the panic down and clawed her way back into focus. She couldn't break. Not now. Kaelith and Rheanna were already running and Aella shoved herself forward to follow.

"The Cleansers?" Kaelith asked Natalie without breaking stride.

She nodded, her expression grim. "Yes. The leftover Hefguard soldiers who stayed behind are helping fortify the castle. So far, no one has made it into the castle."

Aella's throat loosened a bit. If the Cleansers hadn't made it in, Hollin could be safe. Rheanna and she exchanged a look, a silent prayer for the safety of the little girl who was close to their hearts before they continued on.

Natalie paused, looking both ways. "When I saw her, she was by the kitchens..."

"Follow me," Kaelith cut in, her tone leaving no room for protest. She sprinted and the others obeyed without question. She had that uncanny sense, a knowing no one could explain or deny.

They raced through the twisting halls until the air grew cooler, the scent of damp stone thickening, replacing the smell of smoke and fear. They had reached the stairwell leading down to the castle's underbelly. That was when they saw her.

A flash of fiery hair disappeared down the spiraling steps.

"Cyra!" called out Rheanna, her voice cracking on the name.

She did not pause and neither did they. The stairwell seemed to close in on them as they descended. Aella's boots struck hard against the stone, echoing with Kaelith's braids and Rheanna's uneven breaths. The walls sweated with moisture, every draft colder than the last until the air itself felt weighted.

Aella caught glimpses of Cyra's hair, her figure darting down the steps with reckless speed. The sight hollowed Aella's chest. She had only known this desperation once. Petra. The memory of her loss fueled her speed, pushing her past the burning in her lungs.

At the base of the stairs, Cyra stopped so abruptly that Aella nearly slammed into Rheanna's back. Her sister stood rigid, shoulders heaving, one hand braced against the wall. The metallic tang of blood filled the corridor.

Aella swallowed hard and forced her voice steady. "Cyra–"

But she was already moving, sprinting down the hall, a woman possessed by the urge to find her child. Aella followed, her lungs screaming, her body remembering every nightmare of chasing a sister she could not save. The iron dungeon doors loomed, already half-ajar. Cyra tore them open with a strength born of fury. The shriek of metal against the stone echoed down the passage, a sound too sharp, too final.

Aella froze. The dungeon was no longer orderly rows of cells and torches. Vines writhed along the ground like petrified snakes and twisted tight around the cell bars until they groaned in protest. Chunks of stone jutted from the floor at jagged angles as though the earth itself had tried to rise. Soil smeared every surface, mingled with blood. And at the center–

Laney.

She knelt on the filthy floor, freckles lost beneath streaks of blood and tears. Her arms cradled Cora against her chest, rocking back and forth in a rhythm of utter despair. The smaller girl's dark hair spilled over Laney's lap, her skin pale in the torchlight, mouth slack, her eyes open and staring at nothing.

"Cora," Cyra's voice broke, nothing of the Queen in it now, just a woman watching another body join the tally of the dead, the weight of the crown forgotten in the face of such raw loss.

She staggered forward, dropping to her knees in front of the bars where the two were locked. Her hands gripped the iron so hard that blood welled where the jagged vines had cut into her palms, but she did not flinch, the physical pain lost to the agony of her heart.

Laney's gaze lifted slowly. Her hazel eyes were raw, red-rimmed, almost vacant. When she finally spoke, her voice was shredded, barely above a whisper. "They wanted Hollin to obey. They–" Her throat closed. She buried her face against Cora's hair, her body trembling. "They killed her to make her listen."

Rheanna crumpled against the wall, one hand pressed over her mouth, her shoulders shaking violently. Kaelith caught her before she hit the ground, lowering her with gentleness. The siren's face was unreadable, save for the sharp shine of her eyes.

Aella couldn't move. Her hands clenched at her sides, nails cutting into her palms until she felt warm beads of blood. She focused on the pain, on the way her breath scalded her throat, because otherwise she would shatter, fracturing into a thousand pieces of rage and grief. Her eyes then traced the room, forcing herself to see what others might miss, forcing her mind to work where her heart wanted to stop.

Iron cuffs lay discarded at the far edge of the cell, chains rattling faintly in the draft. Child-sized footsteps marred the dirt floor, mingled with adults. Near the door, the stone was stained darker from where vines had erupted violently. Hollin's magic, wild and desperate. The bars bent inward, as though she had forced the earth itself to lock Laney and Cora inside, to protect them, a selfless act from a young child.

Aella's chest constricted. The little girl, barely older than a babe, had surrendered herself for others.

Cyra's knuckles were white where she gripped the bars. Her golden eyes burned, wild and feral. Her whole body began to shake as her breath came out in jagged sobs, the sound tearing from her throat like broken glass.

"This is my fault," she choked out, bowing her head against the cold iron. "I should have kept her closer. I shouldn't have ever left her." Her voice cracked again, drowning in guilt. "Goddess, Hollin..."

Laney sobbed harder, rocking Cora's body, clinging to the dead girl as if she could shield her from the world even now. "She made me swear to stop fighting. Said she would keep us safe if she went. I didn't–"

Cyra shook her head fiercely. "You tried. Both of you did. You fought for her." Her hands tightened, flames sparking along her skin. "This is on them. On the Cleansers. And I swear, they will burn for it."

Kaelith's voice cut through the dungeon. "I can feel her, but I won't be able to for long. We must create a plan."

Rheanna lifted her face from her hands, streaked with tears, shaking her head. "She's just a child. She's just–"

"She is more," Kaelith said softly, almost a whisper. "And we all know it."

Silence fell across the group, the air thick with grief and panic. Aella felt the grief claw at her insides, demanding to be unleashed, but she forced it down. Someone had to move. Someone had to think. She would not let her niece's fate be sealed by inaction.

"Enough." Her voice cracked the silence like a whip. She stepped forward, forcing her gaze away from Cora's lifeless form, away from Laney's shaking shoulders. She fixed her eyes on Cyra instead, commanding her sister's attention. "It's do or die."

"You're right," Cyra rasped. "We find Hollin and we kill everyone who stands in our way." Her fire flicked, licking along her arms. She turned, looking at each of them. A queen.

"Natalie. You will stay with Laney. Get Cora out of here. She does not deserve to rot in this hole."

Natalie swallowed hard, her throat bobbing. "Of course."

Laney clutched Cora tighter, shaking her head violently. "I won't leave her."

"You won't," Cyra said, softer now. "You'll carry her. She'll be laid to rest as she deserves. This is your duty now, Laney. You kept her safe as long as you could. Now keep her honored."

Laney's tears spilled faster, but she nodded, pressing her lips to her friend's hair.

Cyra turned sharply, her eyes blazing again. "Rheanna. Kaelith. Find the council. Find the Hefguard royals. They must know what's happening before panic swallows the castle. Send Atlas and Ron to us. Tell them to bring weapons, armor, and a few men they can spare. And Kaelith, return with them."

Kaelith inclined her head slowly, her eyes glimmering like the reflection of moonlight on dark waters. "I will."

Rheanna staggered to her feet, still pale and shaken, but her chin lifted. "We'll find them." Her voice trembled, but there was a current of determination beneath it. She grasped Kaelith's arm, and together, they turned toward the stairwell, footsteps already fading away. Laney and Natalie carefully lifted Cora's body, slowly lifting her up and out of the cold room, bearing the burden of a life ended too soon. Cyra's fire still shimmered faintly, but her hands were steady now, jaw set. She was no longer breaking, but readying herself for war.

Her gaze met Aella's. "She's my daughter." Her voice cracked. "If they hurt her–"

"They won't. We will get her back."

Cyra's throat bobbed. She gave one short nod, gripping the bars one last time before she straightened herself, throwing back her shoulders, assuming the posture of a warrior queen.

Moments later, footsteps thundered down the stairwell. Kaelith returned, hair swaying, and behind her came Atlas and Ron. Atlas's jaw was stone, his eyes blazing with fury. Ron's hand was already steady on the hilt of his blade.

"Tell me what happened," Atlas demanded, his voice low and cold.

"No. We go after Hollin," Aella ordered, cutting off explanation in favor of action. "Now."

CHAPTER 42

T HE CASTLE QUAKED AS though the earth itself meant to swallow it whole. Shouts echoed in the halls, urgent and terrified, metal clanged against metal outside the walls, and the scent of smoke threaded through every corridor, stinging the eyes. Rheanna's lungs stung with each breath, but she kept moving, her bare feet silent against the cold stone. Beside her, Ripley moved like a mountain in motion. He had intercepted her near the kitchens, his auburn hair wild and his hand already white-knuckled on the hilt of his blade. He didn't ask where they were going; he simply stepped into her shadow, his presence a sudden, heavy anchor against the gale of her panic. Servants rushed at their sides with lanterns raised, their shadows stretching across the walls as they beat on doors with frantic fists.

"Up, my lords, my ladies," one of the women cried. "To the war room, now!"

The guards were fighting, every sword in the castle pulled to the walls. Rheanna had only scraps of help left, servants with frightened eyes and trembling hands, and Ripley's grounding presence, but she clung to Cyra's orders like a lifeline. The thought of Hollin's face nearly buckled Rheanna's knees, but she did not stop, forcing her body forward, each step in defiance against the terror clawing at her.

Whenever the crowd of fleeing staff became too thick or a pocket of smoke obscured the way, Ripley was there, his hand firm on her shoulder or his voice cutting through the din to clear a path.

She forced her trembling hands to knock again, harder this time, until the oak door of Norton Hansfield's chamber creaked open. The northern man appeared, white hair loose around his shoulders, his robe hastily tied. His eyes widened at the sight of her, taking in her disheveled state and the panic etched into her features.

"Princess Rheanna–"

"There's no time," she said, breathless, cutting off his question before it could form. "To the war room. Now."

Norton's gaze flicked to Ripley, who stood behind Rheanna with his jaw set in a grim line. He gave a single, sharp nod of confirmation, and Norton didn't argue; he simply turned to grab his cloak.

One by one, they came. Marine stumbled barefoot into the hall, muttering prayers under her breath. Bianca appeared in a thin nightgown, hair unbound and eyes sharp despite the sleep that still clung to her, her posture rigid with forced composure. Talmadge shoved his way forward, relying heavily on his cane, snapping at a servant for not bringing his boots. Levine and Lola walked in still rubbing sleep from their eyes. Sidney was the only council member who could not be located.

They looked nothing like the council who had sat so straight-backed in daylight. They looked like frightened people, dragged from their beds into a nightmare they could not comprehend. Their dignity had been stripped away by urgency, their titles meaningless in the face of the chaos rattling the castle walls.

As they reached the war room, Ripley didn't join the table. Instead, he took up a position at the heavy doors, his eyes scanning the hallway.

The war room blazed with candlelight, hastily lit by servants who darted in and out, leaving trails of wax and ash behind. Shadows flickered over the maps stretched across the walls. Rheanna forced herself to the head of the room, though her knees wanted to give beneath her. She imagined Cyra's voice in her throat, steadier than her own, projecting a confidence she did not feel.

"The Cleansers are outside the walls," she announced, though the distant screams made that truth undeniable. "But the Hefguard and our guards are holding them. Cyra and Aella have gone below to find Hollin. She was kidnapped."

A sharp ripple moved through the council, fear and fury in equal measure.

"They should not have gone themselves," Bianca said, her tone gasping and worried.

"They are queens and soldiers both," Lola answered hoarsely, her eyes glistening, "Hollin is their blood."

Rheanna's throat tightened. She wanted to shout that she should have gone too, that she should be fighting instead of standing here in the glow of candles. She remembered Cyra's command and she clung to it.

Talmadge grunted, arms folded over his chest. "And if they don't recover the child?"

Rheanna's stomach churned. She saw the fear etched in their faces, their hair mussed, their nightclothes half-buttoned. They looked so human, so fragile. *Like me,* she thought bitterly. But she straightened her spine and met their eyes, one by one. "They will."

For a moment, silence. Then Marine nodded, her pale hands clasped as if in prayer.

The doors banged open. A young messenger staggered in, sweat streaking down his soot-marked face, his chest heaving. Ripley caught the boy by the tunic before he could collapse, steadying him. "The Cleansers have been pushed back," he panted. "The gates still hold."

The council exhaled as one, some weeping, some sagging into chairs. Everyone knew the greater battle was still being fought in the dark below, where no word had reached them until her sisters returned.

Rheanna dismissed the servants, telling them to see the council back to their chambers and fetch healers for the wounded guards. Ripley remained at the door until the last council member had filed out, his eyes never leaving the shadows of the corridor until he was sure the way was clear. When the room finally emptied, she was left in the candlelight alone. Or so she thought until she felt a presence behind her.

Ripley didn't say a word. He simply stepped closer, his warmth cutting through the chill of the stone room. He didn't try to offer empty promises. Instead, he reached out and squeezed her hand, his palm calloused and rough, but steady. It was the only thing keeping her from shattering.

Rheanna leaned into him for a fleeting second, drawing on his strength before she pulled away. Her hands shook as she braced them on the table. The maps blurred, lines of rivers and mountains smearing into nonsense through the haze of her tears.

Petra's wide eyes swam in her memory, her baby sister with her eyes wide open and unseeing. And now, Cora, broken in Laney's lap.

Hollin could not be added to that tally.

The weight of it hollowed her chest until she thought she might collapse.

Ripley retreated to the shadows of the doorway, giving her the space to mourn even as he continued to watch the hall, his hand never leaving his blade.

Rheanna stumbled to the window, pressing her forehead to the cool glass. Dawn was breaking, painting the sky in soft bands of gold and rose. It felt cruel, this light after so much darkness.

"Please," she called out to the goddess. "Please, Seradelle, Weaver of Worlds, protect her. Don't take her too."

Her tears fell hot and fast, splattering against the sill. She clenched her fists until her nails cut crescents into her palms.

CHAPTER 43

T HE SCENT OF BLOOD followed Cyra everywhere she went, seeping into her skin and thoughts. She could not wash it away, not while Cora's body still lay cooling above them and Hollin was missing. The thought alone was enough to burn a hole through her chest. Kaelith walked in front, leading the others, as if the ground whispered truths that only she could hear.

"We move quickly," Cyra reminded them. She cast her gaze around the group that came with her. The group that would save Hollin. Aella, with her knives glinting at her sides, and Atlas, crystals glowing faintly at his belt, his face a mask of grim determination. Ron, her father figure and the only person she truly trusted with her daughter's life, walked with his hand resting on the hilt of his sword. Ryder and Mikah, trusted guards who had proved themselves time and time again, flanked the rear, eyes scanning the shadows. Then, a few other men and women whose blades had kept Linnosa standing through all of this.

They pressed forward, past the last row of cells, into stone that looked unremarkable to any ordinary eyes, but Kaelith slowed, tilting her head, pressing her palm to the wall. The air seemed to hum. Atlas stepped beside her, slipping an emerald veined with black out of his pouch. He pressed it into the stone, whispering words in a cadence Cyra could not pinpoint. The crystal glowed brighter, light seeping into the cracks until the wall groaned. The stones unlatched themselves, revealing a narrow arch. A tunnel.

Cyra felt her fire surge. "Go."

Above ground, the castle was a hive of controlled chaos. The usually pristine halls were choked with the clatter of armored boots and the frantic shouts of runners relaying orders. While Cyra and Aella had vanished into the damp dark of the tunnels, Rheanna stood in the center of the war room, her hands flat against the oak table to keep them from shaking. Ripley stood directly behind her, his shadow long and steady in the flickering candlelight. The hilt of his sword was never more than an inch from his palm.

"The southern wall is secure," Ripley said, his voice a low rumble that cut through the frantic murmurs of the servants. "But the gates are under pressure. I've sent word to the Hefguard reinforcements to bottleneck the main courtyard. We won't let them breach the castle."

Rheanna turned to him, her eyes searching his for a certainty she didn't feel. "And if they come from beneath the castle?"

Ripley's expression softened, but his jaw remained set. "Then they'll have to go through me first. I've stationed three men at every gate. You focus on the council; I'll focus on the steel."

Talmadge, who had returned to the war room and was huddled in the corner, let out a derisive snort. "And what of the little girl? While you play soldier, she is in the hands of monsters."

Ripley didn't even look at the man, but the way his fingers tightened on his sword made Talmadge fall silent. "The Queen is bringing her back," Ripley stated with a finality that needed no argument. "Your only job is to pray they succeed."

He stepped closer to Rheanna then, lowering his voice so only she could hear. "You're doing well. Your sisters are the fire and the blade, but you're the spine. Don't let them see you bend."

Rheanna drew a jagged breath, drawing strength from his proximity. "I'm not bending, Ripley. I'm waiting."

"Good," he whispered, his hand briefly covering hers on the table, a quick, grounding heat before he pulled away to check the door again. "Because when they come out of those tunnels, they're going to need a castle that's still standing."

Down below, the space beyond was tight and oppressive, the air stale and thick, but Cyra's flames lit up the dark, exposing only more darkness beyond the damp, stone walls. Their boots splashed in trickles of stagnant water, the sound echoing like cracks of a whip in the confined space. Every drip and scrape of stone echoed too loudly. Cyra's eyes caught on the grooves in the silt, twin lines dragging as if small wrists bound in chains had been pulled alone. Her heart cracked open. She dropped to her knees, brushing her fingers over them.

"Hollin," she whispered.

Aella crouched beside her, sharp-eyed. "Dragged, but she resisted. See here?" She pointed to a particular scuff mark in the dirt. "She fought them."

Cyra's throat tightened. *My brave girl.* The sight of those marks was both agony and pride, proof that Hollin had not gone quietly, that even while bound, she had fought with every ounce of her small strength.

"They went this way," Kaelith said. She pointed to the trail of scuffs leading deeper into the earth. "And they didn't cover it. They weren't afraid of being followed."

"They should have been," Aella threatened.

Their footfalls turned into a sprint. The tunnel twisted, dipped, and widened into a chamber dripping with stalactites. They reached the end, an iron-banded door in place, and guarding it were nearly a dozen Cleansers.

Cyra's fire leapt higher on her skin, ready to turn flesh to ash. "Goddess help them," she growled.

Atlas pulled three crystals free and whispered low. The earth answered and the ground shivered under their boots.

"Now!" Cyra commanded, and chaos ensued.

Her fire erupted in ribbons, scorching two men before they could even try to raise their shields. Aella, a storm, moved with a lethal grace that was terrifying to behold, her air slamming men into walls while her blades finished the work. Ryder's shield splintered a strike. Mikah caught another blade, shoving it away. Atlas drove a crystal into the ground and jagged stone spears tore upward, splitting the fight into fragments.

"Enough!" A familiar voice rose above the chaos.

The Cleansers stilled and from behind the iron door stepped out Sidney Tapia.

Cyra froze, disbelief slamming into her chest. The older representative from the West walked into the torchlight with her mask pulled back, her dark braid coiled tight, her eyes cold, void of the warmth she had feigned in the council chambers.

"You," Cyra hissed.

Sidney smirked faintly. "Did you think your council whole, *Queen*? Did you think we would bleed for your throne?"

Betrayal tasted of ash and bile on Cyra's tongue. "You stood in my war room," she spat, remembering the maps Sidney had pored over, the secrets she had been privy to. "You swore oaths on Linnosa's soil."

"I swore to withhold Linnosa's values," Sidney replied, chin lifting. "The Cleansers offer purity. No more cursed bloodlines. No more false queens."

Aella lunged, a blur of motion and steel, but Sidney moved with startling grace, retreating into the shadows, disappearing into the labyrinth she knew better than any of them. The rest of the Cleansers converged, attacking and protecting their leader.

"After her!" Aella barked.

"No!" Cyra commanded. "Hollin!"

Cyra met their attacks head-on. Fire burst from her palms, a river of gold searing across the narrow corridor. One man screamed, his cloak catching, and another dropped his weapon as flame licked his wrist, the smell of charred flesh filling the tunnel. She didn't stop to see if they lived. She didn't care.

Aella darted past her, twin daggers singing. She ducked under a sword. One of her daggers drove up and into the gap of the attacker's armpit and twisted. The air bent around her, sudden gusts slamming the Cleansers into the walls hard enough to crack bone.

Cyra worked in tandem with Atlas, blasting them with her fire while he worked slowly, deliberately. He slammed a crystal into the floor, chanting. More stones jutted up in jagged spikes from the ground. One of them pierced a Cleanser, ripping through his thigh. Atlas's sword finished the job, ending the man's agony with a swift, clean stroke. Cyra pivoted, flames curling into a whip. She cracked it across another masked figure's face, skin blistering instantly. He clawed at his mask and she let Aella's blade end him.

A spear skimmed her shoulder, a hot, stinging pain. She turned with a snarl, flinging fire in a wide arc. The tunnel filled with the stench of burned flesh, iron, and sweat. Metal against metal clattered in her ears. Her heart hammered too fast.

Bodies slumped across the floor, twisted in blood and ash. Two were left alive, on their knees, one clutching a scorched arm and the other bleeding from a cut across his brow. Cyra stood amid the wreckage, chest heaving, fire still licking up her arms. She could barely feel her own wounds. Her eyes centered on the iron door.

Cyra was across the tunnel and at the door, shoving it in mere seconds. It appeared to be a home base of some kind, with maps and diagrams covering the various tables. The chairs were pushed out as if the people sitting in them left in a hurry. A plain cell in the far corner caught her eye. A cot in the corner and a chain bolted to the floor.

Her daughter sat with her knees drawn up, wrists raw where the iron shackles bit into her skin. Her strawberry-blonde hair hung in tangles, her emerald eyes wide and wet.

"Mommy!"

Cyra and Aella went to her, the latter ripping the lock from the cell with one cut of her magic. Cyra fell to her knees, gathering Hollin in her arms before the chain could pull taut. She kissed her cheeks, her hair, her little hands bound in iron. "I'm here. To the stars, Hollin. To the stars."

Hollin clung to her, sobbing, her small frame shaking with terror. "I tried, Mommy, I tried."

"I know," Cyra whispered soothingly, rocking her gently. "You're okay."

Atlas came up behind them, holding a key, his face pale but his eyes bright with relief. "I believe this is for the cuffs."

Cyra gingerly grasped the cuffs as Hollin whimpered and turned the key. They fell to the ground clattering and the little girl smiled brightly, but that smile suddenly fell into a frown as she looked over Cyra's shoulder, her mouth falling open in a shriek.

A Cleanser lunged from the tunnel, spear raised high, heading straight for Cyra. Time seemed to slow as Ron jumped into its path, moving with a speed that belied his years. The weapon sank into his chest with a loud thud. The sound that tore from Cyra's chest wasn't human. She got to her feet, catching him just before he hit the ground.

"Ron!" she gasped as she clutched his face, head in her lap. Blood soaked his tunic already, hot and slick.

His eyes found hers. "Little flame, don't cry."

She shook her head, tears blurring her vision. "I'll burn them all. Every last one of them. For you."

"Good girl," he murmured, his hand pressed against her cheek one last time. Then it fell and his chest stilled.

Cyra bowed her head and kissed his brow once. She lowered his head to the ground, turning to clutch Hollin to her chest and straightening. Her daughter's sobs broke against her shoulder.

"Wrap him," she ordered. "He will not be left with these traitors. They will rot here."

Ryder and Mikah obeyed, swathing Ron's body in their cloaks, lifting him with reverence.

Cyra turned to the two Cleansers still alive, bound and shivering. Her eyes burned with firelight, a promise of pain for the hurt they had caused. "They will be sent to the dungeons, a guard kept at their cells at all times. They will name every traitor they know. Sidney may have fled, but she can't run forever." She shifted Hollin on her hip, kissing her temple.

When their group emerged back into the castle, dawn was breaking.

CHAPTER 44

C ANDLES BURNED LOW ON the bedside table, their small flames bowing to the drafts that slipped under the heavy door. The fire in the hearth had shrunk to embers, glowing softly instead of crackling. The silence pressed against Aella's ears until she could hear the sound of her own pulse, heavy and constant.

She hadn't moved from her post against the far wall since they had carried Hollin back into the chambers. She couldn't. Her eyes refused to leave the bed, as if her gaze was the only thing tethering the little girl to the safety of the mattress.

Hollin lay curled against Cyra's side, swallowed by a heap of blankets, her small fists tucked beneath her chin. Damp curls clung to her temples, lashes stuck together from too many tears. Her breathing was uneven.

Aella counted them. One. Two. Three. She waited for the chest to rise. If it didn't, her own lungs seized until the next breath finally came. She didn't blink often, afraid that if she closed her eyes even for a heartbeat, Hollin might slip away again.

Cyra hadn't moved from the bed. She sat propped against the headboard, her spine rigid, one hand smoothing Hollin's hair in slow, rhythmic strokes. The gold in her eyes had dimmed to a dull glow. When Hollin whimpered in her sleep, Cyra bent her head and whispered something only her daughter could hear, voice low and comforting.

Atlas sat close beside her, his thigh against the blankets. His hand rested gently over Hollin's knees, broad and steady. He hadn't spoken much since they returned, and he didn't need to; his presence was enough. Aella had never trusted easily, but she had seen enough to believe he would stand between Hollin and anything that dared come near her again.

Rheanna moved like a tide on the far side of the room. She paced, straightened the pitcher of water, shifted the curtains, and tugged a blanket higher even though Hollin was already cocooned. She couldn't seem to stop moving, as though if she stayed still too long, she might come apart at the seams. Her robe slipped from her shoulder and she dragged it back up with shaking fingers.

Aella pressed her shoulders harder against the wall, grounding herself in the cold stone. Her knives still hung at her hips, her harness biting into her skin. She should have removed them, but she couldn't. The weight was necessary. It told her she could still do something if the world tilted again.

But even blades had no use against the thing that hollowed her chest. The girl's face wouldn't leave her. The sight of Cora, pale and still in Laney's lap, dark hair spread like spilled ink, mouth slack, eyes void of the light that had once danced there so freely.

Cora, who should have been laughing in the halls with Laney. Cora, whose sweetness was contagious. Cora, who had died because Aella had wanted another pair of eyes.

I brought her into this. The thought seared over and over. *Her blood is on my hands as surely as if I'd cut her throat myself.*

She clenched her fists, nails biting her palms, forcing the sting to ground her. She would not cry. Cora's death was hers to bear. She clenched her fists even harder. The sting grounded her, but it didn't erase the guilt. Nothing could.

The door opened with a soft knock.

Aella's hand twitched toward her dagger before she caught herself. Cyra's head lifted, eyes narrowing with fire until she saw who stepped inside.

Elspeth.

Her presence shifted the room at once. She closed the door behind her, her dark gown pooling around her feet, her hair braided back from her face. The weight of her gaze swept over the bed, softened at the sight of Hollin, then rose to Cyra.

"Elspeth," Cyra murmured, voice raw from whispering too many prayers into her daughter's hair.

"Cyra," Elspeth answered, her tone a low comfort. She moved to the foot of the bed and paused, hands folded before her. Her eyes flicked once to Rheanna, then to Aella at the wall, before settling on Cyra again. "She sleeps?"

"Barely," Cyra said. Her hand tightened protectively on Hollin's head.

Atlas shifted just slightly, his thumb stroking over the blankets. "None of us can bear to leave her," he said quietly.

Elspeth inclined her head, then she drew in a long breath. "Then you must hear what I have found."

The room stilled, even Rheanna pausing mid-step.

"I have walked in places thinner than breath," Elspeth continued. "Listened where the living do not go and someone has answered." Her gaze lingered on each of the sisters, then softened. "Petra."

Rheanna's hand flew to her mouth. Cyra's grip on Hollin tightened. Aella's chest hollowed out, a rush of cold tearing through her.

"She cannot give blood," Elspeth said, her tone firm, measured. "The dead have no such tether. But her line can. That is what the ritual requires: a living thread to bridge the way. Hollin carries that thread."

"No." Cyra's voice broke, sharp as flint. She pulled Hollin closer, fire glinting in her eyes. "She has suffered enough."

Elspeth raised a hand gently, calm as always. "It will not harm her. A drop of blood, no more. Malcolm will take it, so she feels safe."

Atlas's hand slid over Cyra's, steadying her. "Malcolm will be careful," he murmured. "Hollin trusts him, I trust him, and I would never let anyone hurt our daughter."

Our daughter.

The words struck her with unexpected force. With that simple declaration, Atlas had crossed an invisible threshold, binding himself not only to her sister but to the child she had raised on her own for so long.

Cyra's jaw worked, her throat tight. She looked down at her daughter's sleeping face, at the bruises circling her wrists, the physical marks of a trauma that would take years to heal. A tremor ran through her shoulders.

Aella stayed silent for a long moment, watching Hollin's uneven breaths, watching her small fists twitch in restless dreams. Guilt cut sharper. She thought of Cora again. She would never forgive herself for dragging that girl into a war that was not hers. She would not let Hollin pay the same price.

Finally, Cyra spoke, voice low but steady, "If Petra agrees, then so be it. But Hollin will not suffer."

"She won't," Elspeth promised. Her eyes softened, lines of weariness easing for a heartbeat. "Petra has already agreed. She is willing. She will help you."

The sisters fell quiet, the weight of it settling over them. Petra would stand beside them one last time to restore magic to Linnosa.

Hollin stirred in her sleep, a soft sound escaping her throat. Cyra bent to press her lips to her daughter's temple. Atlas's hand stayed over them both, a silent shield.

Aella moved closer too, unable to resist. She brushed a curl from Hollin's damp forehead, her knuckles grazing the child's skin. She closed her eyes for a moment, letting the promise root deep inside her.

No more children dying because of me. Not Cora. Not Hollin. Never again.

Elspeth's voice broke the hush once more, calm and certain. "When the moon is high, we will call her. Petra will answer."

Aella leaned against the bedframe, her hand resting protectively on the blankets near Hollin's leg. She did not look away from the girl. Not once.

Chapter 45

Moonlight curtained the marble paths, turning the fountains to bowls of mercury and laying a fine silver over every blade of grass. Lanterns along the cobblestones burned low, their wicks pinched to embers so the moon could do most of the work. Roses bowed with the weight of the hour and night-blooming jasmine woke and spilled sweetness into the cool. Even the old willow stood with its veils stirred by a slow breeze, the leaves whispering against one another as if gossiping about what had begun here a century ago. Every rustle sounded like a secret carried forward.

Elspeth waited in the clearing where the paths crossed, a dark figure amidst quiet light. No crown. No jewels. Ash-black robes brushed her ankles and gathered soot at the hem. On the stones, she had chalked a circle, white sigils laid with a care that read as reverence, the old curves of goddess-writing that made Cyra's pulse slow just to look at. Four vessels stood in the circle's compass points: a shallow brazier full of coal, a marble basin of still water, a low earthen bowl, and a flat dish strewn with pale feathers that shivered before the breeze even touched them. Around all this, little clay cups smoldered, herb smoke roping upward, twisting and unspooling into the night.

Rheanna came to Cyra's left, silent and pale, her blue-black hair gathered at the nape. Aella took her right, chin high and jaw locked. She didn't fidget, but her fingers flexed once, twice, as if reaching for an invisible blade. The three of them drew into the circle together, skirts brushing chalk. No one else would follow them tonight. No guards with stiff faces, no Hefguard princes, no anchors to tether their souls. The garden breathed with them and that was all.

Elspeth lifted her head. Moonlight netted in her eyes. "This place remembers," she said, and her voice didn't need to be loud to carry. "Selmana cut your kingdom here. Her knot still gnaws. Tonight, you undo it."

Cyra's throat worked. She did not look at the spot where she had once stood with her sisters as children, making crowns out of flowers and grass. Memory was a luxury she could not afford tonight. She looked only at Elspeth because forward was the only direction worth a queen's time.

"Blood binds what words cannot," Elspeth continued. "You will each give your own. Fire to fire. Water to water. Air to air." She set a small glass vial on her palm and the moon snared on a red liquid with a glint of gold inside it. "For earth, a drop from your line."

Hollin's blood. The gold tint was just another marker of her fae heritage. Cyra kept her face still and her hands unclenched. They had agreed. Hollin would not be in the circle, but the blood of the earth needed to be represented.

Elspeth did not ask if they were ready. She extended a small knife with a narrow, bridal edge toward Cyra. Steel bit the pad of her palm cleanly and she held her hand over the brazier, her blood falling like beads of garnet on coal.

The coals woke in gold and red, sizzling with heat. It seemed to climb up her forearm as if in thanks and she welcomed it. The warmth settled across her chest, a steadying hand. She passed the knife.

Rheanna's fingers trembled, but she cut without hesitation, her eyes squeezing shut as the blade did its work. Crimson broke open and pattered into the marble basin. The water rippled once, twice, then took her offering as if it had been waiting.

Aella pressed the blade into her palm harder than either of them had, her face twisting into a grimace of defiance rather than pain. When her blood fell, the air caught it and made it a cloud of faint light. It didn't drop, but drifted and then simply wasn't, as if the night itself had swallowed it whole.

Elspeth stepped forward last. She uncorked the vial with Hollin's blood with her teeth, humming something under her breath that set the hair along Cyra's arms to attention. She tipped the gold-tinted red drop into the earthen bowl. The soil shivered, a tremor that passed through the ground and up through the soles of their boots. Vines along the border stones stirred as if a wind had passed, though Cyra felt none.

"Stand as you are," Elspeth said. "Do not break the circle. " She moved to the perimeter and touched her fingers to chalk. When she spoke next, her voice carried the weight of someone repeating a thing said a hundred times before and expecting to say it a hundred times again. "Seradelle, Weaver. Loom before knot. Arathine, Knotmaker. Hold only what must be held. Ilyra, Marethe, Sylithis, Terranelle. Open your hands."

Cyra's skin prickled. The herbs that burned thickened into a sweeter note that made her mouth water, then soured until her eyes burned. The fountain's trickle sharpened. The world felt too tight as if the air held it's breath, waiting for what might happen.

"Petra Eden Voelbel, I call to you to complete this circle. Help your sisters and release your kingdom," Elspeth called.

The garden darkened at the edges and brightened at the center. The fountain's mirror-black face gathered light in a thin veil that didn't belong to the water. Smoke began to braid itself, the braid turning into hair, a tumble of curls catching the moonlight as if it had been spun for the night alone. Freckles rose like stars. Emerald eyes lifted and found the three of them at once.

Petra.

No one gasped. They had known she would come. It didn't prevent Cyra's heart from beating faster. Rheanna's lips parted and trembled, tears slipped down without sound, releasing the grief she would always hold. Aella swallowed and blinked fast, refusing to look away to the girl who managed to worm her way into her cold heart. Every part of her wanted to fold, to press her forehead to Petra's and beg the night not to take her again. That would do no good. She held her ground, anchoring her sisters with the sheer force of her will. The ghost of their sister had been haunting them long before this night.

Petra did not speak. She did not need to. She looked at each of them as if she loved them as fiercely as she ever had and then more. Then she held out her hands, pale and translucent, yet solid enough to save them.

Cyra's fingers closed around one small, cool hand; Rheanna's around the other. Aella reached and found Cyra's free hand with hers, her grip tight. The four of them closed the circle without a sound and the world around them seemed to hold its breath. The singing of insects and whisper of foliage in the breeze silenced.

The air tightened immediately.

Suddenly, the brazier's flame rose. Water domed up from the basin, defying the laws of nature in the way only magic can. The feather dish sank and then lifted as if an invisible breath had drawn them in. Earth crumbled from the bowl and then grew, a thin seam of green climbing and twining until a vine laced around their ankles.

Heat ran up Cyra's arm from Petra's fingers. Cool rose from Rheanna's grip and met the heat, and they did not cancel, but instead they intertwined. Air lapped at the back of Cyra's neck and along her scalp like laughter in high summer. Goosebumps pebbled along her flesh, her hand standing on end. Something deeper pulsed beneath their skin, in their blood.

Cyra's breath hitched. She felt Rheanna gasp at the same time, felt Aella's breath pull long and fierce, felt Petra's image falter, flickering like a candle in a strong draft. The circle did not widen and yet the garden felt too small to contain what they had called.

"Do not fight it," Elspeth's voice came from somewhere far and distance. "Let it pass through you."

The column of elements rose, light caught into a spiral that climbed from bowl to hand to bodies to sky. The full moon met it and seemed, impossibly, to burn brighter. Stone groaned, not in protest but in relief. The willow's branches lifted as if set free from a long-held, breathless posture.

Somewhere beyond, the chain that had wrapped Linnosa's throat snapped, the sound echoing not in ears but in the blood of every single magic wielder in the kingdom.

Cyra sensed it more than heard it: the sound of a great thing letting go. The garden answered first. Every closed bud on every stem opened at once, thousands of little mouths drinking air, painting the dark garden in a sudden bright color. The fountain leapt. The vines that had wrapped around their ankles slid their green toward the chalk and dared it. The feather dish whirled and released a small storm that tore through the smoke. Flame shuddered, then steadied into the shape of a tall candle, clean and bright, a beacon of hope in the restored light.

And the city, the kingdom, moved.

Cyra could not see it, but she could feel it as if they were moving through time and space with the magic as the curse lifted. A mystical well far from the castle's shadow clearing itself and offering a mirror for the first time in a generation. Someone's old grandmother in a dark one-room house closing her eyes and finding a thread in her blood she thought was a rumor. A boy up too late with a book, blinking because the words had lifted from the page and were hanging in the air around his head like moths, fluttering with a life of their own. Fields answering hands. Stone answering footsteps. Rivers shrugging off old insults and running truer.

The sisters' hands locked tighter without anyone telling them to do so. The power ran and ran and ran. She could feel it all lit inside her, the way her own flame had always lived, greeting this new company like family. Water curling around her ribs in a cool embrace, air singing in the hollows of her bones, earth standing up under her soles like a vow. The sound it made in her chest was not delicate. It was a roar.

She did not want to let it go. A queen knows when to hold. A woman with her hand in her dead sister's knows to hold on.

But the world cannot survive on one long exhale and it would force them to let go.

The spiral peaked, light burning clean. There was a long, level moment of balance. The Goddess' reintroducing themselves to the land. Then the column at the center of their circle thinned like a taper and snapped into a thousand stars. They arced out over the garden, over the wall, over the sleeping city, like the last embers of a fire kicked free of its own ashes and happy to go.

Petra's hand in Cyra's cooled. Petra smiled that soft, lopsided smile and then she let her hands fall. Her light thinned until the silver around her hair was only the moon playing tricks and the freckles were only a distant memory.

Rheanna's breath broke and turned to a wet hiccup. Aella's jaw trembled once, hard enough to hurt, and then steadied by sheer stubborn will. Cyra did not cry. The fire in her chest made a different choice. It stood and watched and said goodbye with fervor that did not scorch and did not consume.

Her knees found stone. She tasted iron in her mouth and jasmine high in the back of her nose. Rheanna folded beside her, shoulders shaking. Aella went down, catching herself on her palms, breath sawing in and out.

Every part of Cyra hummed, but it was not her fire alone. She could feel the strangeness of her sisters' powers. Water. Air. Earth. It was too much to hold. It wanted to be released.

Cyra closed her eyes. She breathed. The last threads of the power, hers and not hers, unwound. The garden exhaled with her.

"Enough," Elspeth said softly from just beyond the circle and the word arrived like a blanket rather than a command.

Cyra let her head tip forward until her brow touched the cool stone. The cement bit her skin. It felt good to be reminded she was still bound to a body.

None of them could speak. Words would come later and ruin it.

Above them, the moon rode on, as tired and relentless as any queen. The full weight of it made the fountain look deeper than it had before. Somewhere beyond the hedge, a toad sang once.

Cyra's pulse steadied. The roar inside subsided to a thrum that felt permanent. As if something had been knotted and then left there.

They hadn't meant to understand anything tonight. They still didn't. But Cyra knew this much: the kingdom would wake different in the morning. And so would they.

CHAPTER 46

R HEANNA WOKE WITH THE taste of riverwater in her mouth. It clung to her tongue, cool and metallic, like she had been drinking from a stream in her sleep. She pushed upright and slowly, her muscles aching as though she had run for days. Every joint protested, heavy and stiff, her body carrying the weight of unseen miles. The curtains were open just enough for the morning light to paint thin bars across the chamber floor, illuminating dust motes that lingered in the air.

Rheanna flexed her hand, meaning to call a thread of water to clear the taste from her mouth, but instead, a curl of flame leapt into her palm.

She gasped and jerked back, expecting pain, expecting the blistering sting that fire had always promised her unless Cyra wielded it, but the heat was gentle. It curled across her skin as though it belonged there, flickering and then steadying until it pulsed with the rhythm of her heartbeat.

Her other hand trembled as she lifted it, calling for the flame to vanish. Wind answered instead with an eddy that stirred her hair across her face and scattered parchment from the desk.

The floor shivered beneath her bare feet and she stood. A steady, earthy pressure rose through the stone, rooting her in place, as though the castle itself had decided she was its anchor.

Rheanna clutched her hands to her chest. "What is happening?" Part of her wondered if she was still dreaming, pinching her arm to test her theory and wincing at the sharp sting that proved she was awake.

The door to her room opened without a knock. Aella stood framed in the doorway, silver hair unbound, eyes sharp even through her exhaustion. "You feel it too." It wasn't a question.

Rheanna nodded slowly, the weight of the realization settling on her shoulders. "I have all four elements."

Aella stepped inside, shutting the door with her heel, the click of the latch loud in the quiet room. "Cyra tried to snuff out her lamp this morning and ended up flooding the corridor." Aella's tone was sharp, but the faint tremor in her voice betrayed her unease.

Rheanna could still feel the fire curled in her veins, the wind humming at her fingertips, and the ground reacting to her. "Then it's not just me."

"No," Aella said, folding her arms. "It's all of us."

"We need to call the council and hear how the kingdom has been affected."

Rheanna still felt the warmth of flame curled in her palm, the hum of earth steady beneath her feet as they walked the long stretch of corridor together. Every step seemed to echo louder than it should; her whole body seemed to answer things it had no right to command. She glanced at her sister, who moved like a blade unsheathed even in the quiet, wondering how she truly felt about all of this.

By the time they reached the doors of the council chamber, Cyra was already waiting, Atlas holding her hand and at her side. Their eldest sister looked visibly shaken, her red hair in a messy bun, strands of hair sticking out in every direction. She did not wear a crown today. Cyra never showed her stress; at least not like this, not so raw. Something more had to be happening. Rheanna looked at her with concern, but her older sister only shook her head once, as if to say: *not here.*

The noise of voices swelled, then quieted, the scrape of chairs and shuffle of papers falling into silence as the three sisters entered. Sidney's seat sat empty, polished wood glaring in the lamplight, a reminder of betrayal still too fresh to name.

Norton Hansfield rose at once. "Majesties," he said, an expression mixed with joy and hope written across his face. "Streams run clear again. Our people, even in the smallest villages in the North, will not have to worry come spring as the crops seem to have grown strong over night. "

Rheanna lowered into her seat, every eye turning toward them. She wanted to shrink from the weight of it, to disappear into the upholstery and escape the scrutiny. Instead, she wanted to grab her sisters' hands and drag them into a private room to discuss and explore their new found powers.

Lola Donovan dabbed at her eyes with a kerchief. "The air sings again," she said, voice breaking into a laugh. "As if the kingdom itself thanks you. For the first time since Nell's death, I feel like I can breathe."

Bianca leaned forward, silks whispering as she folded her hands. Her blonde hair, so light it was almost white, was loose today, cascading around her like a blanket. "You have done what no one believed possible. You restored Linnosa to its greatness."

A murmur of agreement ran around the table until Jasper Talmadge cleared his throat. He clenched his brittle hands tightly around his walking cane, his eyes shadowed beneath heavy brows and wrinkles. "We know that magic does not return without a price. What will we have to pay?"

The room quieted, all those hopeful looks wilting into unease. Rheanna's pulse raced. She thought of Petra's hand in hers. The weight of every element now thrumming in her veins. She wanted to tell them the price had already been paid in Petra's death, but her voice caught. She knew that it was not that simple. The fight with the Oracle was long from over and with Sidney on the run, the Cleansers would surely not give up.

Cyra answered for them. Her tone was calm and unwavering. "The price has already been paid in the dead of our fallen. We will not let it take more."

The authority in her tone settled the council more than anything else could have. Even so, Rheanna noticed the way Bianca studied them and how Talmadge's frown did not ease, fingers tapping on his wooden cane. Everyone knew the lie that laid beneath those words.

The rest of the reports rolled forward. Whispers of the Cleansers had completely vanished since Hollin's kidnapping and the exposure of Sidney. The council exhaled with relief, but the tightness in Rheanna's chest stayed taut. Her fingers restlessly pulled against the edge of her dress.

Bianca lifted her cup to her lips, but before it touched them, a current of wind brushed across the table, scattering her violet silk sleeves against her cheek. She froze. Her eyes went wide and her hand trembled mid-air. "That was me," she said, half shocked and half in awe.

A silence fell, heavier than before. The council stared at one another. This served as a reminder that releasing magic meant giving power back to anyone who had it in their lineage. One of Lola's daughters had already been identified with earth magic after Petra's death and now Bianca clearly had the affinity of air. She wondered if any of the other council members had powers that they were not showing signs of yet, or perhaps that they were hiding.

Jasper Talmadge slammed his hand on the table. "You see? Already it spreads, uncontrolled. Magic is an infection." His voice was sharp with fear, but Rheanna caught something else beneath it. Resentment. Sour and ugly because he alone sat unchanged while others had been touched.

"Magic is not something to be afraid of," Atlas corrected. "In Hefguard, we have lived in harmony with it. It will simply take an adjustment period for Linnosa."

When the meeting finally adjourned, the scrape of chairs echoing across marble, Rheanna rose on unsteady legs. Talmadge was right about one thing, with magic comes consequence.

CHAPTER 47

A ELLA HAD SEEN HER sister bruised, furious, and pressed to the edge of her temper, but never like this. Cyra's hair was a mop on top of her head, knotted and frayed, as if she had been pulling at it in the dark hours of the night, eyes sunken in from lack of sleep. Her eyes did not hold their usual steady confidence, but instead wildness and fear. Atlas kissed her on the forehead before departing, shooting her a worried glance over his shoulder. Something was wrong.

"Follow me," Cyra said after the council meeting, not bothering to explain. She didn't look back, only moved, skirts swaying fast against her legs. Rheanna's gaze flicked to Aella in confusion, but they both followed, wordless, through corridors that just began to buzz with early morning traffic. The murmur of servants, the clatter of boots, the faint scent of bread baking, all of it felt strangely distant, muted beneath the urgency of Cyra's stride. The guards and servants stepped aside hastily at the sight of the queen's hurried pace.

When they reached Cyra's chambers, the guards stationed there looked uneasy, avoiding the queen's gaze. Cyra dismissed them with a sharp flick of her wrist, her authority enough to send them off without question. She shoved the doors open and stepped inside.

The hairs on Aella's arms rose as if lightning had struck nearby. The chambers smelled of Cyra's desert oils and incense, laced with something different like wild mint crushed beneath boots. Then she saw her niece.

Hollin stood barefoot in the middle of the rug, curls spilling in strawberry-gold waves down her back. They caught the light strangely, less like hair and more like spun glass, shimmering with an otherworldly light in the dimness of the room. Every strand was alive, shifting from honey to copper to faint rose gold when she moved. Her face was no longer the soft roundness of a child's alone. Her cheekbones had grown sharper, her jaw more defined, the beginnings of elegance etched where only innocence had been the day before. The freckles scattered across her nose and cheeks had deepened, vivid as constellations, and they seemed almost to glow against her skin.

But it was her eyes that rooted Aella in place. Emerald, sharper than the green of Linnosa's summer hills, clearer than cut gems. The irises glimmered faintly, light rippling through them as if alive, a distinct gold circle surrounded her irises now. They belonged to no human child Aella had ever seen.

And the ears, pointed sharper now, no longer something that could be tucked beneath a piece of fabric. They peeked through the fall of her hair, delicate and unmistakably fae.

Hollin's whole face lit up when she saw them. "Aunt Aella! Aunt Rhe!"

She darted forward, too fast for any human, let alone a child. Her small body blurred, and for a heartbeat, Aella's assassin instincts kicked in, hand going for a dagger that wasn't needed. Hollin skidded, about to tumble, but the air caught her, lifting her just enough to set her down safely. The girl only laughed.

"Look at my new powers! I am just like you!"

Aella's stomach dropped, a sense of dread settling in her gut.

Hollin clapped her hands and a spark of flame leapt between her fingers, fizzing like a captured star. A vase trembled on the table, water rising in a thin ribbon that danced to her laughter. Roots pressed up through the seams of the rug, curling like curious snakes. Every element answered her just as it did the sisters, but her control was even more absolute.

"Goddess above," Rheanna said quietly, hand pressed to her mouth.

Aella's gaze snapped to Cyra. "What the hell?"

Her sister looked wrecked, arms crossed tightly over her chest, gold eyes shining with exhaustion and barely restrained panic. "I climbed into bed with her last night after the ritual, same as usual, and when we woke this morning, all of these changes had manifested. She can no longer be hidden."

Aella's jaw clenched, her teeth grinding together. "Her fae blood is strong. Who is her father?"

Cyra sighed, sitting on the edge of the bed. Her hands covered her face as her shoulders slumped under the weight of the secrets she carried. Aella might not have ever seen another fae before, but she knew this child was not a typical halfbreed. She looked more fae than human, indicating a strong, perhaps royal bloodline.

"Cyra, we cannot help protect her if you do not tell us." Aella tried her best to sound gentle, though the urgency was evident in her voice.

She lifted her head, tears filling her eyes. "He is a king." She glanced helplessly toward her daughter, who was now spinning in slow circles, petals from a vase lifting and orbiting around her. She was so entranced by the magic that she was oblivious to her mother's revelation.

Aella's mouth dropped open. She had expected some distant cousin of royal blood or perhaps even a prince, but not a king. Hollin could be an heir to the Fae Realm, a princess of a world they didn't truly understand.

Rheanna took a shaky step forward. "She's beautiful," she whispered, almost in awe, trying to ease the tension.

"She's a target," Aella said, the harsh reality cutting through Rheanna's wonder. She didn't mean it to sound cruel, but the words landed heavy anyway.

Hollin looked up at that moment, grinning, tugging on Aella's sleeve. "Wanna see something?" she asked, her voice sweet, unbothered by the fear in the room. She spread her hands and the petals above her head shifted into a perfect crown of white blossoms, weaving themselves together with impossible speed. For a flash, Aella caught a glimpse of Petra, wild curls, freckled nose, flowers gleaming around her face.

The assassin crouched before Hollin without thinking, rough fingers brushing a curl behind the girl's pointed ear. The magic hummed off her skin, dangerous and raw, but Hollin's smile was only that of a child proud to have shown off a trick.

When Aella looked back up at Cyra, her voice was low, flat, dangerous. "You kept her secret because you were afraid. But now there is no more hiding. And if anyone so much as looks at her wrong, I'll cut them down before they even get the idea to do something to her."

Cyra didn't argue. She only nodded, something fierce and broken shining in her eyes, a silent pact between the sisters.

Hollin giggled and skipped back toward the table, sparks following her tiny feet, leaving scorch marks on the stone hearth that healed themselves instantly. Her speed startled Aella again, the kind of speed even trained assassins couldn't manage. The rug shifted beneath her as roots tried to catch her steps and Hollin only squealed with delight, treating the ancient magic like a new toy.

Aella rose slowly, her chest tight, caught between awe and dread. She knew one thing with certainty. Hollin was the most dangerous secret in Linnosa.

CHAPTER 48

R HEANNA FELT THE NIGHT most in the hush of the corridors, the way candlelight leaned toward shadow and danced along the portraits in an unsettling way. Every flicker seemed to warp the eyes in the portraits, turning them watchful, as if the ancestors themselves were watching and listening. The kingdom, especially Reddel, had been alight with celebrations all day, the sound of distant laughter and music drifting up to the castle walls. The people rejoiced at the return of magic because it not only brought power, but also made people whole again. Linnosa no longer sat under the oppressive weight of the curse; it now bustled and sang with life. The contrast was stark. Within the castle, the hush of duty and memory; beyond it, a kingdom reborn, breathing as though it had just awakened from a long, terrible sleep.

Cyra had hardly spoken since the council adjourned and she showed her sisters how Hollin's secrets could no longer be hidden. Rheanna shivered at the child's inhuman beauty, the way it seemed to demand attention, striking and terrifying at the same time. She had only seen one other person nearly as beautiful: Kaelith, whom she knew was a siren.

Elspeth was already sitting in the receiving room where the sisters had asked their most trusted friends to gather. Her posture was composed, hands folded neatly in her lap, but her eyes betrayed a restless energy, darting between the sisters as though she expected more revelations to arrive at any moment. Malcolm lingered at the far side of the rug, turning a small vial over in his hands, always restless when thoughts consumed him. His brow furrowed as he stared at the liquid inside, as if it held the answers to questions he hadn't voiced yet. Ripley leaned against the wall, arms crossed, expression watchful as he surveyed the others. His gaze moved from face to face, measuring, weighing. The faint scrape of his boot against the stone was the only sound he allowed himself, a reminder of his presence without words.

Kaelith slid easily into one of the couches, cerulean eyes flashing with some secret knowledge, as though she had been waiting for this very night. Her fingers drummed lightly against the armrest, the rhythm deliberate, and her smile curved in a way that suggested she knew more than she intended to share. Atlas stood near the grand piano, his hand resting against the polished wood, his expression unreadable but steady.

Rheanna chose the far corner of the couch, folding her hands in her lap to keep them from fidgeting. She kept her gaze lowered, studying the weave of the rug rather than the faces around her. Aella didn't sit at all. She hovered behind Cyra, arms crossed, violet eyes daring anyone to argue before words were even spoken.

Cyra cleared her throat and then broke the silence. "You all deserve to know the truth. Sooner than later, everyone will know whether I like it or not. I can't keep it hidden anymore."

The chandelier cast fractured teal light across her face, softening nothing and highlighting the dark circles under her eyes and the tense set of her jaw. She looked like caged fire tonight, burning but contained, desperate for release.

"Hollin," she said, the name breaking in her throat. "Her father was Fae. I thought I could keep her heritage hidden at least for a little white longer until we figured everything out, but since the ritual..." Cyra's voice faltered. "She is changed. Her blood and magic demand to be seen and heard. She cannot pass as human now. She, as my sisters and I, can now wield all the elements."

Malcolm's head jerked up. The vial stilled in his hand, forgotten by the shock of the revelation. "All the elements?" he asked.

"Yes." Cyra's gaze fixed on the floor as though she couldn't bear the weight of their eyes, staring at the patterns in the rug as if they might offer an escape. "Since last night, we can all summon fire, water, air, earth, but Hollin is something even greater. Her ears, her eyes, her beauty. They mark her for what she is. She is fae royalty."

The room released a collective gasp.

Elspeth tilted her head slightly, her gaze grave, heavy with the foresight of a queen who had seen empires rise and fall. "The people of your kingdom will whisper. Some will call her salvation. Others will call her a curse."

"She's a child," Malcolm said suddenly. "A little girl who wants to play and laugh. Whatever she can do, don't let that make you forget. Linnosa is too stuck in old ways, too quick to banish what it does not understand. In our country, she would be celebrated."

Aella gave a sharp laugh, bitter at the edges and devoid of humor. "Forget? We need to do whatever we can to protect her, which is why if anyone so much as breathes in her direction, I'll kill them before they draw their next."

"Goddess above," Malcolm muttered, looking up at the ceiling.

"I'm not joking," Aella snapped.

"Neither am I," Malcolm said back. "If she holds all the elements, her body is going to strain under it. She's young. She needs guidance."

Atlas stepped forward at last, his calm a sharp contrast to the room's crackling energy. "That is why it is our responsibility to teach her. We are her family. She is my daughter now." He looked at Cyra lovingly before continuing. "From now on, her safety is our main priority."

"This is not just Cyra's cross to bear," Rheanna agreed, shifting forward in her seat on the couch and staring straight at her older sister. "You are not alone."

Kaelith leaned back against the couch, her smile small but unreadable. "The girl hums with power," she said softly, her voice melodic. "I felt it when I first saw her. It's not something that can be smothered or silenced. Better that we carry it together than pretend it isn't there."

Elspeth's voice followed. "She is my granddaughter. Hefguard will do anything to safeguard her."

The room felt softer as though the tension had burned itself out, leaving behind a weary but determined quiet. Rheanna watched her sister and the ache in her chest deepened. She did not see the queen or her sister standing in front of her. She saw Cyra the mother, terrified of losing the one thing she cherished most in the world.

"I'll kill anyone who threatens her," Aella muttered again.

"We don't doubt it," Ripley said as he shifted closer to Rheanna, brushing her hand with his. She startled at the warmth of it, but he gave her that lopsided grin and the knot in her chest eased further.

"I'll charge some crystals to keep in her pockets and put around your bed and room," Atlas said. "They can work as extra protection." He reached for Cyra's hand. She let him take it, her fingers intertwining with his in a desperate grip.

"Good," Kaelith murmured, her eyes gleaming with approval. "She'll need more than blades."

Elspeth stood, her gown whispering against the rug, her presence commanding without effort, drawing every eye to her as she solidified the pact they were making. "Hollin belongs to all of us now. We will keep her safe, whatever it takes."

Rheanna let the words sink into her bones, settling alongside the strange new hum of her magic. For the first time since Petra's death, warmth spilled into the hollow space inside her. Not because the danger had lessened because it hadn't, but because the circle had widened, drawing in more hands to hold the weight. Hollin wasn't just Cyra's secret anymore; she was theirs. And family, Rheanna thought, had always been their strongest weapon.

CHAPTER 49

THE HALLS WERE LIGHTER, as though the very stones had soaked in the magic that had returned. Guards stood straighter at their posts, their chests swelling with a renewed vigor, and servants moved with a buoyancy they hadn't seen in years. Their footsteps no longer dragged but carried a rhythm, a cadence of purpose, as if the castle itself had awakened from slumber. Even the air smelled fresher, tinged with something green and alive, like the first breath of spring after a long, harsh winter. Yet none of that lifted the weight pressing on Cyra's chest. The brightness around her felt almost mocking, a celebration she could not join. Every smile she passed was a reminder of the secret she carried, the danger that still lurked beneath.

They had broken the curse. Linnosa hummed with magic again. But peace was not theirs yet. The backlash of Hollin's heritage, Sidney Tapia and the Cleanser, and the Oracle still loomed over them like a ticking bomb. Every heartbeat carried the echo of danger, every silence felt like the pause before a blade fell.

Cyra sat at the edge of her bed, elbows braced against her knees, head hanging low as she listened to the soft sound of her daughter's breath as it drifted from the nest of blankets near the hearth. Hollin had always slept like that, curled on her side, one hand clutching the corner of the quilt. Her hair shimmered strangely when the light touched it, gleaming like copper spun into rose gold. Even asleep, she radiated magic as if her small body could hardly contain all that churned inside it.

A soft knock broke her thoughts. She turned as Rheanna slipped through the door first. Aella followed, closing the door behind her.

"She's asleep?" Rheanna whispered.

Cyra nodded, exhaustion carving deep lines around her mouth. "Finally."

The sisters moved closer, their presence pulling at the quiet room. Aella crouched near the hearth, violet eyes flicking to Hollin's small form before resting on the flames. Rheanna lingered at Cyra's side, her hand brushing her older sister's shoulder once before folding into her lap, a touch of solidarity in the overwhelming quiet.

"I miss Petra so much," Rheanna said suddenly, the words tumbling out as if she could no longer hold them in.

"I know," Cyra murmured, her throat tightening. "I see her in Hollin, her laughter, her eyes."

Aella's gaze hardened, but when she spoke, her voice was rougher than her usual steel. "She should be here now. She should be standing with us, not just haunting our memories."

The quiet stretched again until Hollin shifted in her sleep, rolling onto her back. A faint glow sparked at her fingertips, tiny flames, flickering against her skin. She breathed in and the flames guttered out, replaced by a shiver of wind that rustled the curtains and stirred the loose strands of hair around her face. Even in her sleep, her power was great. The sisters watched in silence, awe and dread entwined, knowing the child's dreams alone could call her magic.

Aella straightened from the hearth, shadows carving her sharp features. "We will protect her."

Before anyone could speak, the air shifted, growing dense and cold.

The flames in the hearth guttered, sinking low as if cowering in fear. The teal light of the moon through the curtains dimmed. Hollin stirred, frowning in her sleep, but did not wake. Cyra's stomach turned to ice. A familiar feeling of dread and despair was building low in her gut.

The shadows at the edges of the room thickened, stretching longer, until they pulled together at the far corner. From them, a figure emerged.

The Oracle. Selmana Hormanick.

Her face was half-hidden beneath a hood, her eyes depthless pools of black that seemed to swallow the light around them. She looked older than she had before, if that was even possible. A walking ghoul. Her voice, when it came, was low and sharp, like wind slicing through a dark night.

"You think you have won."

Cyra rose to her feet instantly, placing herself between the intruder and her daughter, flames licking at her arms, though her body trembled beneath them. "Stay away from my daughter."

Selmana's gaze did not shift, remaining fixed on Cyra with a predatory stillness. "I would have her if I wanted her, but I think

I will play with you all a little longer." Her gaze slid to Hollin, still sleeping soundly, her freckles catching the faint firelight.

Aella's blade was in her hand before the thought had even finished forming. "Look at her again and I'll cut you apart."

Selmana's lips curved faintly, not into a smile but something colder. "I have come to give you a new prophecy, one you cannot stop." Her voice dropped to a whisper.

A sister waits in the shadows. Blood demands blood.

About the Author

Kayla Cosentino writes new adult and fantasy fiction while juggling college courses and spending her days as a high school Special Education and English teacher. She is currently working on the next installment of *The Sisters Who Were Promised* series. She received her Master of Fine Arts in Creative Writing and English from Southern New Hampshire University and is currently pursuing her Master of Education. She spends her free time reading, listening to heart-wrenching music, and binging Netflix. She resides in New Jersey with her two cats, Theo and Will, and mini dachshund, Tallulah.

www.kaylacosentino.com

author@kaylacosentino.com

Acknowledgements

This book was truly a labor of love. I wrote it in less than a year after the release of my first book, scared that my readers would forget me if I didn't publish something quickly. So before I thank anyone else, I want to thank you. My readers. For being here. For reading what I have to say. Without you and your support this book would not exist.

To Rose Dinsmore, for encouraging and understanding me. For not only being a reader and editor, but a friend. Thank you for being there at 2am when I needed to run ideas past someone. Thank you for stepping up when I needed it most. You are irreplaceable and truly invaluable.

To my family — Shanna, Dad, Mema, and everyone else — thank you for anchoring me.

To Dylan, thank you for being my light in the darkness.

And thank you to the Voelbel sisters. Writing Cyra, Rheanna, Aella, and Petra has helped me see myself in a different light. They are now a part of me, alive in both my mind and heart.

www.ingramcontent.com/pod-product-compliance
Lightning Source LLC
Chambersburg PA
CBHW031958150726
47990CB00005B/1769